STARTING
TOMORROW

NIKKI LAMPE NALCHAJIAN

sunshine
PUBLISHING

SUNSHINE PUBLISHING INC.
sunshinepublishinginc.com

First published in the United States of America
by Sunshine Publishing Inc. 2020

Cover design by Deni Lampe Mileski

ISBN: 978-1-953435-08-8 Paperback
ISBN: 978-1-953435-05-7 Hardback
ISBN: 978-1-953435-06-4 eBook

**DEDICATED TO
THE INFINITE WORTH
INSIDE EACH OF US.**

"You are your best thing."
Toni Morrison, *Beloved*

**MACK STEWART
OFFICIAL FOOD JOURNAL**

JANUARY 1· SUNDAY

New Year's Resolution: Stop doing things that are bad for me!

8:00 p.m.

I'm moving from my Moleskine journal to my computer. Typing is the only way my hand can keep up with my thoughts.

My goal is to be skinny, but I have to figure out a better way to do it.

Step One: RESOLUTION

Step Two: FOOD LOG

WEIGHT 110

in/out	description	calories
breakfast	smoothie	200
lunch	peanut butter toast	300
dinner	pasta, broccoli, chicken	400
exercise	run 3 miles	-300
	total	600

If anyone found out my secret, they would think—make that,

know—I'm totally disgusting. I look in the mirror and tell myself it's the last time. Sadly, it never is. UNTIL NOW.

Once I asked Mom if I looked fat, and she said I looked healthy. I know she considered it a compliment, but it's not the response I was hoping for. Healthy is a burly woman serving up a plate of goulash.

It doesn't help that my little sister, Maddie, is tall and skinny, and I'm just average all around.

If I looked more like Maddie, maybe Diego would like me. Aaah Diego...He's a senior and the hottest guy at school. Last year he didn't look at me once, but this year he actually talked to me. To be precise, he included me in a group text, but close enough. I wonder if it's because I'm skinnier. Nothing else about me is different.

My secret weight loss strategy began six months ago. I owe my success to my friend Shayla who has been a camp counselor with me for the past three summers.

One night when we were sitting by the fire, I asked her, "How do you eat so much and stay skinny?"

She turned her marshmallow in the flames. "Do you really want to know?"

"Yes!"

"Promise not to tell anyone?" She looked like she had the

answer to life.

"OMG, yes!" Edge of my seat.

"I don't really eat."

"What do you mean? I just saw you eat three s'mores."

She looked around to make sure no one was listening. "I throw up," she whispered.

"How?"

She pointed the end of her skewer into her mouth.

"I've tried before. I can't do it." It wasn't a new concept, just an impossible one.

"Ah, perseverance, my young Padawan. You have to keep sticking your finger down your throat, and eventually the food will come up."

In her best Yoda imitation: "And drink lots of water, you must."

Poof! In that moment everything changed. The key to the universe was mine! The Force was with me.

Regular Shayla voice: "One thing, though—it takes a lot of work. It's like a full-time job."

"Why?"

"You can't eat a ton and just throw up once or twice. You have to get it all out, every time. One binge is all it takes to move the scale."

3

I made a vow to look just like her. That was June, and I've lost ten pounds. #onmyway

As a sustainable diet plan, however, it has some major drawbacks...

1. Finding privacy to vomit
2. Trying to be quiet when I'm gagging
3. Massive panic when there's no opportunity to throw up
4. Lingering smell in my nose
5. Bad breath worries

Recent additions to the list...

6. Hair loss
7. Breakouts
8. Dark under-eye circles
9. Constant fights with Maddie. (But she's always in my business, which bugs me no matter what I'm doing in the bathroom.)

The pros of being skinny outweigh the cons, but it's exhausting.

I have confidence in my new plan:

RESOLUTION + FOOD LOG = SUCCESS

JANUARY 2 · MONDAY

WEIGHT 110

in/out	description	calories
breakfast	granola	300
lunch	nothing	0
dinner	pizza	600
other	oreo	45
exercise	none	0
	total	945

My bowl of granola almost sent me on a binge. Cereal is tricky. Milk left over, add a little cereal. Not quite enough milk to cover the added cereal, add a little milk. The cycle easily repeats itself.

I just entered the calories in my log, and I feel better. Back in control. If I don't eat much else today, I'll be fine. Hmmm... What should I eat? What shouldn't I eat? To eat, or not to eat, that is the question. I wish someone would tell me the answer. I feel pretty alone in this department. My friends are awesome, but I don't think they would understand. They're all skinny.

My three best friends are:

♥ London

♥ Rachel

♥ Skye

We've been friends since kindergarten.

Rachel's little sister, Alexis, and my sister, Maddie, are also best friends.

Rachel threw an awesome New Year's Eve party this year. Maddie and Alexis decorated for a week. They're freshmen, two years younger. We allowed them to attend the party to compensate them for all their hard work. Just kidding. We have to, they're our sisters. Just kidding again. If we didn't, our parents would think we were up to no good. That's the truth.

Since Maddie and Alexis attend Rachel's parties, my parents conclude we're Making. Good. Decisions.

If they only knew....

THE MACKENZIE TIMES
New Year's Eve Party Edition

DIEGO DOES MORE THAN LOOK AT MACK
SMACKDOWN
IT WAS THE LAST TIME

(Side note: This food record is an excellent way to work on my reporting skills. My journalism teacher would be proud.)

Back to the news...

I still can't believe Diego and I danced at the party! The only bummer is I'm not the only girl he danced with, but it's not like we're together—I don't even know if he likes me. One minute, I felt like the center of his world, the next, he was gone. Literally.

But while it lasted, it was heaven. We danced to a fast song and then a slow song came on. He pulled me close, and...

WHAM! Eden slammed into us. (Eden is a frenemy—we hang out when it's convenient, but we're usually not talking because of some recent drama.)

Me: Do you mind?

Eden: Sorry, Mack. It was Rachel's fault.

Rachel (hands on hips, glaring at Eden): Pretty sure you pushed me first.

Eden: Yeah, to get you off Tyler. Or are you unaware he's taken?

Rachel: If you go around shoving everyone Tyler dances with, you're gonna have serious problems.

Eden (looking around for Tyler, I assumed): Whatever. Just stay away from him, Rachel.

Rachel: ☹

Eden walked into the house.

Me: You okay?

Rachel: Yeah. I'm sorry I broke up your dance. I need a drink. See ya.

She walked away and I turned my attention back to Diego.

Or I would have, but he was nowhere to be found.

I walked around and found Skye and her boyfriend, James, hanging out by the snacks.

Skye put her hands out, then made a hang-loose sign under her chin. *What's wrong?*

I touched my fingers and thumb together to make a zero. *Nothing.*

Skye made a salute sign and pointed to me. *I know you.* She frowned.

Being able to sign at parties is a major advantage. The reason we can is because Alexis lost her hearing when she was five, and since our families spent a lot of time together back then, we learned sign language. You would never know Alexis can't hear if you just met her because she's pretty awesome at reading lips, but we usually sign with her because she says words get lost. And it's an excellent skill when we don't want anyone to know what we're saying.

I swiped my hand across my forehead. *Forget it.* I didn't want to go into my love life in front of James.

She made a circle with her index finger and thumb. Skye always understands.

The next few hours flew by—dancing, eating, talking. A few minutes before midnight, Rachel stumbled across the dance floor to the mic and we all counted down the last ten seconds to Happy New Year!!! Skye, London, Rachel, and I put our arms around each other. Friends Forever. Then Skye moved away to kiss James, and Dax pulled Rachel away to kiss her. (Dax is Rachel's on-and-off boyfriend. Lately off, but apparently on tonight.)

"Happy New Year, loser," London put her arm around my shoulder.

I laughed. I'd be lost without London.

Eventually the party mellowed, and the house was filled with couples making out, and the rest of us in the kitchen chowing down pizza.

I tried to stop at one piece, but my hunger took over and I ate four. I was in a total panic—I couldn't start the new year fatter! There was only one solution and it was easy to find a secluded bathroom in Rachel's enormous house.

I hate that technically I've already thrown up this year, but now I'm starting over. It's a relief to know that was REALLY the last time!

JANUARY 3 · TUESDAY

WEIGHT 112

in/out	description	calories
breakfast	nothing	0
lunch	coffee, chocolate graham cracker	150
dinner	nothing	0
exercise	run 3 miles	-300
	total	-150

11:00 a.m.

Nooooooo! Up two pounds.

I skipped breakfast and went for a run. Staaaaaarving.

Someone just posted a picture of Rachel and Tyler kissing at the NYE party. Guess Eden was right it was more than a dance. I don't know what Eden's doing with Tyler anyway. He's such a pig. That means Rachel kissed two guys on New Year's, while I kissed ZERO! I wonder if Dax saw the pic.

Text just in...

> London: Want to go to Cava?
>
> Me: Yes!
>
> London: 15?
>
> Me: Perfect!

I don't have a car which sucks. I do have three awesome friends who have cars, so that helps. And Mom lets me borrow hers sometimes too.

Coffee for lunch—starvation dilemma solved! Cava Java is our favorite hangout spot these days.

...

3:00 p.m.

We picked up Rachel on the way to Cava. Skye couldn't come because she had to clean her room (no surprise).

Guess who was there? No, not Diego.

Eden and Melissa. (Melissa is also a frenemy.)

We sat down at a table on the opposite side of the room. Eden waved her phone and smirked. I couldn't see clearly from that far away, but I assumed she was holding up the picture of Rachel and Tyler.

In response, Rachel put her hand to her chin. *Bitch.*

I shrugged my shoulders with my hands turned up, like, I don't want to be in the middle of it, but if you mess with my best friend I'll have to kill you. I wonder if she understood. Rachel's middle finger was probably easier for her to decipher.

London raised her eyebrows. "So Mack, dancing with Diego,

11

hmm?"

"Yeah, 'til we got slammed by Eden." Side eye at Rachel.

Rachel laughed. "Sorry again. I don't even remember kissing Tyler. Why does Eden put up with him?"

"Why do *you*?" I said.

"I don't. He's not *my* boyfriend. I'm just having fun."

Sometimes I wish I could be as carefree as Rachel.

London said, "You should stick with Dax. Tyler's a waste of time."

"Definitely." I agreed. I watched London sip her blended coffee and felt insanely jealous she never gets fat. I ate one chocolate graham cracker with my black coffee. How can that tiny thing have 150 calories?!

As if on cue, Tyler strolled in the door and sat down with Eden and Melissa. They whispered and looked over at us.

Battle of the Glares.

"Let's jet." Rachel scooted out of the booth, and we followed like guard puppies, throwing menacing squints on the way out.

I'm still at negative calories for the day, so I feel pretty good. Tonight please let me be back down to 110. I'm trying to only weigh myself once a day, but I'll never sleep if I don't know.

...

9:00 p.m.

I skipped dinner and I'm at 110. I'm starving and have no energy to write or do anything else, so I'm going to bed. Good night.

JANUARY 4 · WEDNESDAY

WEIGHT 110

in/out	description	calories
breakfast	toast & butter	200
lunch	coffee	0
dinner	Chinese food	600
exercise	none	0
	total	800

2:00 p.m.

This morning I let myself have a piece of toast with butter. I felt like I was on my way to ten pieces, but thankfully, Skye suggested we all four go to Cava. (She finished cleaning her room.) It's so much easier to not eat when I'm not home. My hands are still shaking from a million coffee refills, but I'll take being amped up over being hungry any day! Wish it would last forever.

THE MACKENZIE TIMES

Cava Java Edition

AND THE BIGGEST UNDERSTATEMENT AWARD GOES TO...

"I'm in serious trouble." Rachel flicked bits of her black nail polish on the floor.

"What happened?" London asked.

"The party."

"I thought your dad knew about it," Skye said.

"Yeah, he knew. That's not the problem."

We waited.

"I wrecked Lauren's car."

"How?" London asked.

"It's not exactly clear."

"I thought you passed out," I said. "Where'd you go?"

Rachel held up her index finger. "Well, that's the good news. Nowhere. I ran straight into the driveway gate." She cackled. "Mighta been good to open it first."

Skye and I chuckled half-heartedly.

London cracked up. "Glad you forgot! Were you hurt?"

"I'm fine, but the car's totaled. I can just hear my therapist, 'Do you think you subconsciously sabotaged your stepmom?' Gee, Doc, I've consciously thought of driving her off a cliff, but never such an indirect attack."

We all laughed.

I know Rachel sounds like a mess, but you have to cut her some slack. Her mom died when we were in fourth grade. It has been seven years, and sometimes it still doesn't seem real.

When her dad married Lauren two years ago, Rachel started to spiral. Lauren is in her thirties and looks more like an older sister than a step-mom. She tries to be nice, but we don't like her, even though it's not her fault Rachel's mom died. Fortunately, Mr. Dorian travels a lot for work and he takes New Mrs. D with him.

I kind of like this food-record/life-story. I might even keep it up—unlike my sixth-grade diary, or my fourth-grade list of the best Full House episodes, or the face-washing log I start every summer that lasts a week at most. It's giving me power— the day is more than halfway done, and I've only consumed 200 calories! My coffee is starting to wear off, though. Hunger moving in. Not good.

...

Midnight

Well, the hunger is gone and I'm so full I want to cry. I was doing great, but then Mom brought home Chinese food. It smelled delicious, so I made just a little plate, but then I went back for seconds. Shit! I estimate about 600 calories and hope that writing it down will make it true. 600. 600. 600.

Chinese food comes up easily. Now would be the perfect

time to throw up, and I could start fresh tomorrow. But NO, I'm not going to do it. I said I wouldn't, and I won't. Good job, Food Journal, you're helping me through! Think I'll go scroll through celebrity photos for inspiration.

JANUARY 5 · THURSDAY

WEIGHT 111

in/out	description	calories
breakfast	nothing	0
lunch	tuna sandwich	300
dinner	salad	300
other	M&M's	540
exercise	ran 3 miles	-300
	total	840

Alexis spent the night, and she and Maddie made cinnamon rolls this morning. Curse those annoying, skinny girls. I'm up a pound, so I didn't eat any. I'm so grouchy. I know I said I liked this food record but I'm already getting tired of it. I thought it was helping me, but maybe not.

How can winter break be over already?! I'm excited to see everyone, but ugh, the homework! My classes are really hard, and it's practically impossible to get into the schools I want to go to. Maybe I'll go to community for two years and then transfer. Maybe I'll take a gap year and just work. Who knows?

Wonder what London's doing...

Me: What's up?

London: Not much.

Me: Want to hang out?

London: Sure. Come over.

Me: Sweet.

London: Give me an hour.

Me: K. C ya.

Of my three best friends, London is my *best* best friend. Her mom, Jessica, is totally cool. In junior high she used to make us food all the time and tell us stories about Mississippi, but lately she's always at work. She's a human rights lawyer. London's dad moved away when we were in sixth grade. I never really understood what happened. I think he has another family somewhere else now, but London never talks about it. Makes me realize my troubles are stupid.

I parked my car and walked around the side of the house on flat stones surrounded by bright purple Mexican Heather. I know that's random, but London talks about plants like they're people so it's hard not to notice them when you're at her house. Her dad loved to garden, and London has kept things up more or less since he left.

She was sitting cross-legged on a lounge chair scrolling on her phone. "Party Saturday at Dax's. Wanna go?"

I stretched out on the chair next to her. "Sure." I had already seen the invite.

The crashing waves below made me feel like I was on a movie set. Except if that were the case, I would need to lose at least five pounds. Make that ten—camera adds weight. I was happy I hadn't eaten yet, even though my head was killing me. No pain, no gain.

"Remember Rachel last summer?" London's voice brought me back from the set.

"Hard to forget." It had been a miracle she survived jumping off the roof into the pool.

"Think Rachel and Dax will get back together officially?"

"Probably. He always asks me about her in class," I said.

"He's way too tame for her." She held out her phone. "He posts pictures of his dog."

"I know. Maybe he can be a stabilizing force?" I said.

"Maybe so. Been reading your Mom's magazines?"

I laughed.

London scrolled. "Ah, shit. Not what I wanted to see."

"What is it?"

"Niko and some girl at a party."

Niko broke up with London last summer, after they went out for over a year. Said he didn't want to be tied down in college. Really? JERK!

"Why don't you unfollow him?" I said.

"I should, but I think I'm hoping to see that he's miserable because he misses his ex-girlfriend." She zoomed in on the picture. "Those boobs cannot be real. Fuck this. Let's get something to drink." She reached over and picked a sprig of mint from the pot on the side table. "This will taste good in some iced tea."

I followed her inside.

She prepped the tea and handed me a glass. "So, what's up with Diego?"

"Not much, unfortunately." We sat at the kitchen table in big velvet chairs. The inside and outside of London's house are totally opposite—outside is all air and freshness, and inside is warm, southern hospitality. It's a perfect combination.

"I saw you dancing. I think he likes you."

"Doubt it." I was trying to keep my hopes in check. Seems like Diego likes everyone.

We watched makeup tutorials for the next hour, then Mom texted and said I had to come home for no reason. So annoying.

When I got home I ate a sandwich Mom had bought, then went for a run and took a shower. I wish I could always be that person, but she's not the real me.

The REAL me came out later...I was bored, so I went to the

kitchen. I ate a handful of M&M's from the bowl on the counter. No big deal. It was 3:00 and I was at 300 calories for the day. I was about to indulge in another handful when Maddie came in.

"Did you take my black sweater?" she asked.

"What black sweater?"

"You know, the short cotton sweater I got for my birthday?" She picked out a couple of blue M&M's and ate them one at a time. How can she eat just two M&M's?! I don't think we can possibly be sisters. Maybe she's adopted. Or maybe I am!

"Why do you always assume I took something if you can't find it?" I knew exactly which black sweater.

"Oh, I don't know. Maybe because that's usually the case?"

I walked away without a word.

For the next two hours I scrolled through before & after pics of fat people, and watched five episodes of *Vampire Diaries*. I would have watched a few more, but Mom called us in for dinner.

Dad came in from work just as we were sitting down. He served himself chicken salad from the bowl in the kitchen and joined us at the table.

"So, how was everyone's day?" Fake smile. Not even a glance at Mom.

"Boring." I gave an answer I know he hates. I get so annoyed when he acts like he's Mr. Sunshine Dad, but his grouchiness is simmering just below.

Maddie kissed ass, of course. "Good! Alexis and I made cinnamon rolls this morning. They were pretty tasty, huh, Mom?"

"Delicious," Mom said.

Dad stabbed his salad. "Well, maybe you can make some for me this weekend."

"Sure. No problem."

I scarfed down my salad and said, "I'm working on a project with London and she's waiting for me. Can I be excused?"

"Yes," Mom said.

I ignored Maddie and Dad's disapproving eyebrows, and tossed my plate and fork in the sink.

I can tell Mom and Dad aren't getting along. I wish they wouldn't pretend. Do they think we don't notice? I felt like throwing my dishes at both of them.

I'm so grateful for the sanctuary of my room. I flopped on my bed and stared up at the poster of the universe on my ceiling. Maddie texted.

Maddie: Mom wants you to clean up the kitchen.
Me: Why?

Maddie: It's your turn.

I didn't text back.

Maddie: OK?

I still didn't reply.

Maddie: Hello?

Me: K

I know I was being passive aggressive, but she drives me crazy! Why can't she just give me the message and leave it alone? If the kitchen doesn't get cleaned, there's proof she asked me to do it, so why does she need my confirmation? I think she has a problem.

Half an hour later, I dragged myself to the kitchen. While I slaved, the bowl of M&M's called to me. "Mackenzie, your family sucks. Eat us and you will feel better."

By the time I finished the dishes, I had eaten five handfuls. FIVE! I would have eaten more, but I didn't want to empty the bowl. There are 90 calories in 10 peanut M&M's. Whose idea was it anyway to keep a giant bowl of M&M's in the kitchen? Probably Dad's or Maddie's, the irritating, naturally skinny people in this family.

JANUARY 6 · FRIDAY

WEIGHT 112

in/out	description	calories
breakfast	nothing	0
lunch	nothing	0
dinner	nothing	0
exercise	none	0
	total	0

I don't know how I'm going to keep this up. I'm starving all the time, and I'm gaining weight. I want to feel full. NOT nothungry. FULL. Bursting at the seams, full. I want to eat M&M's until I can't eat one more. But the only way to do that, and stay skinny, is to throw up. So, what do I do? Maybe I should barely eat so I get to 105. Then I can eat whatever I want until I reach 110. Sadly, that would probably happen in one day. Eating nothing is easier than trying to be moderate. And I love documenting ZERO calories in my journal.

JANUARY 7 · SATURDAY

WEIGHT 112

in/out	description	calories
breakfast	yogurt	80
lunch	tortilla	120
dinner	nothing	0
exercise	2 miles	200
	total	0

11:oo a.m.

Just woke up. I'm back to 110, but I'm so hungry, I almost don't care. Not true—I definitely care.

Tonight the four of us are getting ready at Rachel's for Dax's party. Her room is crazy cool, complete with couch, bathroom, and walk-in closet. It's like being in a small apartment. They moved into this house about six months before her dad married Lauren. I think it was Rachel's consolation prize.

Heading out for a run now.

...

6:oo p.m.

My run sucked. Every time my foot hit the pavement I

thought my head might explode. So mostly I walked, but better than nothing. I showered and my hair is blown out. A blank canvas. London and Rachel will do my hair and makeup. I'm so over my clothes right now. Nothing to wear, no time to shop, and Maddie is on high alert so I can't raid her closet. Maybe Rachel will let me borrow something.

...

1:00 a.m.

I'm exhausted, but I have to write about our night.

Getting ready at Rachel's was a blast. She found me a sick (her word) outfit. In all that black, I almost felt thin. Not really.

Lauren brought us a tray of sodas. Rachel said thanks and closed the door before she could step inside.

"That was nice of her," I said.

"She's just being nosy." Rachel set the tray down on the coffee table.

"I think she wants to be your friend." Not sure what made me stick up for Lauren.

"I have enough friends, thank you very much."

Rachel got a makeup case from her bathroom, unzipped it, and took out a mini bottle of vodka. "My dad keeps a big box of these airline freebies under the bar. I like to keep a couple on hand. Anyone?"

Rachel and London each added a bottle to their soda.

"To friends." Rachel raised her drink like she was about to lead a military charge.

"To friends." We clinked.

The party started at 8:00, so we left the house at 8:30. Skye drives the cutest convertible—it's always immaculate. Well, *was* always.

THE MACKENZIE TIMES

Winter Break Closing Edition

MORE THAN A DANCE FROM DIEGO
RACHEL ON A ROLL
SKYE'S CAR DESTROYED

There were so many cars in front of Dax's we had to park halfway down the street. A good but bad sign. Last summer's bash only made it to 11:00 before the police broke it up.

We rang the bell, and Melissa opened the door and walked away without a word.

Rachel called after her, "Good to see ya, Mel." Under her breath, "Asshole."

People everywhere. The furniture was covered with black

plastic, and caution tape blocked the stairway. Low lights and music. We nodded approval to each other.

Skye waved to James who was standing in the family room with Arman. (Arman and I have been in the same classes since seventh grade. We went to Formal together last year, but we're just friends.)

"I'll catch you in a bit." Skye headed over to them.

Rachel, London, and I made our way through the crowd to the kitchen.

Dax was at the keg filling a cup for Eden.

"Hey, Dax," Rachel said. "Sweet décor."

Eden gave Rachel a cool once-over.

Dax handed Eden her cup without taking his eyes off Rachel. "Hey, Rach. Want a beer?"

Eden rolled her eyes and walked away.

"Sure. Unless you have anything else?" Rachel glanced around the kitchen.

"I don't know how to get you a drink without opening my parents' stash to the whole party," Dax said.

"No worries." Rachel took a mini vodka bottle out of her black clutch. "I'm always prepared. How about a soda?"

Dax's face relaxed. "Yeah, sure." He headed to the refrigerator.

London stepped up to the keg. "He's like a puppy."

"In a good way." Rachel blew him a kiss.

Dax was back with a Sprite on ice before London finished filling her beer.

"Thanks, Dax. You're the best." Rachel gave him a kiss on the lips.

"No problem." He cleared his throat. "London, I see you're all set. Mack, need anything?"

"I'm good. I'll grab a water."

London took a swig of her beer. "Careful girl, your halo's showing."

"Ha. Ha," I said. Was that comment necessary? I hate beer and I don't want to get fat. OKAY?

"Do your parents know you're having a party?" London asked.

"A few friends, but nothing like this. That's why we're inside."

"For Rachel's sake, I'm glad we're stuck in here." London said, clinking cups with Rachel.

"No shenanigans tonight." Rachel winked at Dax. "But, I wouldn't mind a private tour past the caution tape."

Dax raised his eyebrows and downed the rest of his beer. "I'm sure that can be arranged."

Maybe he didn't see the picture of her with Tyler on New Year's? Or maybe he's so in love he just doesn't care? It's not like they're exclusive, so why should it matter?

"Come on, Mack, let's go see what Skye's doing." London's voice broke me away from my thoughts.

We headed to the living room. My heart stopped. There was Diego, talking to Skye, James, and Tyler.

I made eye contact with Diego then quickly looked away. My cheeks were blazing.

London said, "Why the hell is Skye talking to Tyler? Let's go back to the kitchen. I already need a refill."

"Good idea." I fantasized Diego would follow.

No sign of Rachel and Dax in the kitchen. Private tour already?

London filled her cup. "Mack, you should at least carry a beer."

"Why? I'm not going to drink it."

"Because it makes other people comfortable, that's why." She filled another cup and handed it to me.

Her reason sounded stupid, but I took it.

Just then, Diego appeared!

And I have to admit I felt cool holding a beer.

"How's it going, girls?" Diego said.

I said, "Good, how have you been?" Cringe. What, are we at a cocktail party or something?

To make matters worse, I was so distracted, I took a sip of my beer and made a face. I wanted to die.

He laughed and said he was good too. I suppose he's used to girls acting like idiots around him.

"Catchya later," London said and walked away.

He flashed his beautiful smile. "Wanna dance?"

I nodded and followed, gripping my cup for courage.

Diego set both of our cups on the entry table, took my hand (sigh), and led me to the living room dance floor.

When the first song ended, he kissed me on the cheek. "Let's find some space."

He picked up our drinks and we made our way to the back of the room. We sat down and he handed me my cup. I could hear my dad, "Don't ever drink anything that has left your sight." I pretended to take a sip.

Diego leaned towards me. "Is this okay?"

"Sure. This party's great."

"I mean sitting over here with me, away from your friends."

"Um, sure it's okay." Please tell me that's not what I said. Ugh.

"Would it be okay if I kissed you?"

I was in a Disney movie. Diego wants to kiss me. Diego wants to kiss me. 😄

"Um, sure." *Really, Mack?!*

He tilted my chin up and gave me the sweetest, best kiss ever.

I have no idea how long we kissed. It was magical. Special. Amazing.

All of a sudden, I felt something hit my foot. I looked down, then up. London had kicked me.

"Hey, sorry to break up this tender moment, but Mack, I need your help."

Are you kidding me?

"It's important." London looked back over her shoulder.

I turned to Diego. "Sorry. Thanks for the dance."

He kissed my cheek. "No problem."

I floated down the hall behind London. She knocked on the bathroom door. "It's me."

Skye opened it, and I could see Rachel on the floor, curled around the toilet.

"What happened?"

"She's wasted." Skye washed her hands in the sink.

"How can she already be wasted?" I had been swept away kissing Diego, but it couldn't have been that long.

"She was probably drinking before we got to her house." Skye said.

"What if someone slipped her something?" I thought about Dad's warnings.

"Doubt it. Let's get out of here." London opened the door. "Skye, get the car, and we'll bring Rachel."

I kneeled down. "Rach, it's me. We need to get you up," I had to breathe through my mouth to keep from gagging.

She didn't move.

London filled a cup with water. "Here, splash her."

I dipped some toilet paper in the water and wiped her face. "Come on, Rachel, we have to go."

She stirred. London and I hoisted her up and put her arms over our shoulders.

"Hey, what are you guys doing? Are we gonna dance?" Rachel's breath was death.

London turned her face away. "Yep. Let's go dance."

We walked as fast as we could through the party. I don't think anyone noticed. Skye was waiting in her car, and we deposited Rachel in the front seat.

"Well, this sucks," Skye said.

I caught her eye in the rearview mirror. "Sure does. I was with Diego."

"Wait, you were with Diego. Like *with* Diego?" Skye slammed on her brakes.

"Not with-with, but we KISSED." Excited movie-girl scream. I couldn't help it.

Skye screamed too. "No way. I'm so bummed we had to leave."

At that point, Rachel woke up. "Why are we in the car?" She turned around in the seat to look at London and me. "You guys are no fun."

Then her face went gray and she quickly turned back around. She fumbled for the window control. If only the top had been down.

"Oh my God," Skye said.

Before anyone could do anything, Rachel vomited all over the dash.

Skye's face was expressionless. She rolled down the windows and drove in silence straight to Rachel's. London and I ducked our heads into our shirts the whole way. Rachel kept saying she was sooooo sorry.

Skye pulled into the driveway. "Get out. Everyone."

She took off as soon as we were clear of the car.

London and I used the keypad to get in the house. I helped Rachel take off her vomit-soaked clothes and threw them in the tub. London didn't come in the bathroom—said she'd barf if she did. I gagged a few times myself.

I tucked Rachel in bed, and London and I stared down at her like worried parents.

"What are we going to do about her?" I said.

"No idea." London sighed.

"I'm going home. Want a ride?"

"Nah. My car's here. I'll crash in the guest room."

"Okay. I'm glad you came and got me to help."

"Sure. We stick together, right?"

"Right." It feels like London's mad at me, but I have no idea why.

I can't stop thinking about kissing Diego. I've never kissed anyone like that. It was like the whole world stopped. He tasted like beer, but not in a bad way, which is weird, considering I hate beer. It made my heart pound and my head swim, and I never wanted it to end. But sadly, it did, with a projectile vomit courtesy of my drunk friend.

JANUARY 8 · SUNDAY

WEIGHT NOT LOOKING

10:00 p.m.

I'm not in the mood to write, but I have to so I can start fresh tomorrow.

Last night after I finished writing, I started to get hungry. Everyone was in bed. I found leftover Chinese food in the fridge! I decided I could have a little, since I barely ate all day.

I warmed myself a small plate in the microwave. It was warm and delicious, which made me realize how deprived I've been for the last week. I finished all of it and returned to the refrigerator for just one more bite. And then a switch flipped in my brain—I MUST FEEL FULL. I made an enormous second plate and gobbled it down. I washed it down with a ton of water. I might not be able to control what I put in my body, but at least I can control what comes out.

After I threw up, I sat on the floor and stared into the toilet and watched the food float around. I should have felt disappointed or disgusted, but I was only relieved. I simply cannot go for the rest of my life feeling empty every day. I decided that I can have one purge a month and still consider it sticking to my plan.

But then...this morning, I was lurking in the kitchen, and the M&M bowl called to me, "Tomorrow. Start tomorrow." I ignored it and went to the pantry. On the lowest shelf sat four enormous bags of peanut M&M's. There's not a single good thing to eat in this house and Mom buys four bags of candy?!

So much for once a month. I took a glass of water and a bag of M&M's to my room. I watched videos, and popped candies one after the other into my mouth. I pretended I was one of those naturally skinny people who eats everything they want. After I finished the entire bag, I embraced the reality of my not-naturally-skinny body, and threw up.

An hour later I was hungry again and that Chinese food was calling. And the cycle repeated. No one was home, so it's like it never happened. I don't know how I'm going to stop. I'm possessed. It's impossible to control my body. I don't want to be hungry, but I want to be skinny, and my body does not want to cooperate. I wish I could feel the way I do about ten minutes after I throw up, when I'm fresh and empty. It's the best feeling in the world. I'll have to settle for that feeling just once a month. Starting now.

JANUARY 9 · MONDAY

WEIGHT 110

I can't handle writing down what I eat anymore. I'm turning this into a Weight Journal and Life News Report.

THE MACKENZIE TIMES
Back to School Edition

DIEGO MAKES A SURPRISE APPEARANCE
SKYE PROVES HER SAINTHOOD
MACK AIDED BY MAGIC DRINK

I love the feeling of a new semester—empty folders and upcoming events. Winter Formal is February 11th. Please ask me, Diego! I know technically I could ask him, but he's a senior. No way.

Today he cruised past our lunch table and said, "Hey Mack."

I waved because I couldn't speak. After he passed, Rachel patted me on the back. "Someone's got a stalker."

"Very funny. How's your car, Skye?" I changed the subject.

"Detailer is coming today. Noah caught a ride back to school so I could use his truck."

"How nice." I wondered if I would do that for Maddie. Doubtful.

"Yeah, he's a good brother. But if my car still smells, I'm selling it."

Rachel raised her hand. "I'll buy it."

"You better." Skye smiled, but I don't think she was joking. I can't believe Skye isn't mad. Maybe she's just pretending to be over it.

London held up an energy drink. "Anyone want this?"

"Yes!" I took it from her hand.

"Geez relax. Didn't know you were such a fan."

"Just sounded good, thanks." I took a gulp. Disgusting, but I drank it all. So good to have something in my stomach.

The bell rang. I swear we get five minutes for lunch. So wrong.

The drink kicked in almost immediately. I could barely sit still in class—a nice change from trying to keep myself awake. I was happy-hyper for the rest of the day. When I got home from school I went for a run. Then I showered and worked on my homework until Mom called us for dinner.

AND I WAS NOT HUNGRY! My prayers have been answered.

At dinner, I finished half my sandwich, and all my carrot sticks, and didn't think too much about it—just like a normal person.

I'm still not hungry. I'm also not tired and it's almost 10:00. Think I'll read my book and try to get sleepy.

JANUARY 10 · TUESDAY

WEIGHT 109

I didn't fall asleep until after midnight, but I wasn't even tired when I woke up. I'm totally fired up because I have a new diet strategy. AND I LOST A POUND! I ate a small bowl of oatmeal and a banana for breakfast. Totally satisfied.

I don't know why I assumed London would bring another energy drink today, but she didn't. By the end of the day I was delirious with hunger. At 6:00 Dad walked in with dinner. Taco Tuesday—Dad's favorite night of the week. Two for $2, with all food groups represented. Best deal on the planet. For me it's a nightmare, but now I'm not worried because I discovered the magic drink that makes me not hungry, and in the future I won't need to throw up. So this is how I'm justifying eating six tacos tonight and barfing—because now I can be confident it's the last time. Tomorrow I'll buy some energy drinks on the way to school. I'm so glad I won't have to throw up anymore. Carne asada is beyond disgusting on the way out.

JANUARY 11 · WEDNESDAY

WEIGHT 109

So excited! Still in the single digits (following 100). My plan is working. I ate half a bagel for breakfast and had an energy drink on the way to school. I still wasn't hungry at lunch. Skye offered me some pretzels and I ate them just for fun. Skinny people probably do that all the time—eat a little something, then forget about food for the rest of the day. I feel free.

Mom just called us for dinner, and I notice I'm getting a bit hungry. Since I haven't eaten much today, I think I will eat a normal dinner, like a normal person.

JANUARY 13 · FRIDAY

WEIGHT 110

Where did that pound come from?! 😟

Yesterday I followed the same plan as Wednesday, although it required two energy drinks. The downside to this diet plan is I get all jacked up, scroll through everyone's posts, and end up feeling stressed. Yes, I know people are not as happy and beautiful as they appear on social media, but I feel like I need to make my posts extra-fabulous, since everyone knows they are better than reality. Authentic social media is such bullshit.

Today Eden came up to our table at lunch. She glared at Rachel. "New Year's Eve not enough for you?"

"What are you talking about?" Rachel looked genuinely surprised.

"I know Tyler was with you last night."

Rachel started laughing. "I wouldn't be surprised if he was with someone, but it wasn't me."

"Yeah right." Eden folded her arms.

Rachel said, "Tyler is a complete sleaze. Why do you want to be with someone like him?"

All of us were shocked, including Eden. Rachel and Eden are

arch-enemies. Why would she say something so compassionate?

The bell rang. Eden narrowed her eyes suspiciously at Rachel and walked away.

There may be hope for world peace after all.

I stopped by the store after school to stock up on energy drinks for the weekend. Dax and Rachel were walking out, holding hands. Aww, so cute.

Good luck, Dax!

Tonight we're sleeping over at Skye's and having a *Gossip Girl* marathon. We've seen every episode of every season, but it's fun to re-watch.

JANUARY 14 · SATURDAY

WEIGHT 111

11:00 a.m.

Another pound! 😫

We had pizza last night—the four of us, plus Skye's mom and her brother, Noah. Noah is three years ahead in school, and I've only spoken to him maybe five times in my life. He was home for the weekend. He's so different from the guys at school. He talked about his philosophy class like we might talk about a good party. It sounded interesting, but I was totally preoccupied with eating/not-eating the pizza. My energy drinks had completely worn off and it took all my willpower to only eat two pieces. To be honest, I would have eaten more if I thought I could have thrown up, but it seemed too risky. Anyway, Noah inhaled an entire pizza then said he had to go see what the locals were up to.

Rachel said, "Wish we had somewhere to go." She can be so rude.

I said, "What are you talking about? It's gonna be a great night."

"Oh, I know. I don't mean this isn't fun. Just love a good

46

party." Rachel said.

Mrs. Sato cleared the pizza boxes. "Nice to have a night in. You girls should treasure your friendship."

Rachel raised a soda can. "True dat, Mrs. S."

Skye's mom laughed. It's hard to tell what she's really thinking. She seems happy, but I wonder if it's real. Just like Skye.

We headed down to the basement to watch our show. London and Rachel spiked their sodas with Rachel's endless stash of vodkas—they poured from her purse like circus clowns out of a car.

After the first episode ended, Rachel jumped up on the coffee table. "Dance off!"

Skye changed the TV to a music channel.

London, Skye and I joined. You don't need to be drinking to get down with Rihanna.

"Come on, Mack. Let's see your moves." London and Rachel were twerking on each other.

I slapped my butt and acted a hundred times more confident than I really felt.

After a few songs, Skye and I were done, but Rachel and London showed no sign of slowing.

Skye changed the TV back to our show.

"Aww, come on. We're just getting warmed up." Rachel made herself another drink.

London sat down. "Let's watch for a while. We can dance again later."

"Okay." Rachel pouted.

Rachel was passed out by the time we had watched two more episodes.

When we went to the kitchen this morning Mrs. Sato and Noah were sitting at the table. Noah's hair was sticking up and he was eating pancakes like they might disappear if he took a breath. The pancakes looked good. As a matter of fact, so did Noah. Ooh, that's gross—he could be my dad. Not really, but kinda feels like it. Mrs. Sato asked if I wanted to join them, but I said no. How embarrassing to eat in front of Noah with his messy hair and me with no makeup. Too personal! I said thank you and headed straight to the drive-thru for a triple-shot non-fat latte. Not as good as an energy drink, but I didn't have the energy to get out of the car. Need to find a drive-thru that carries them.

So, thinking about the stupid pound I have gained, I think the problem is that energy drinks only hold back my hunger until about 8:00 and then I'm ravenous. I thought maybe I could eat what I wanted once a day and not gain weight. Obviously, not the case.

My family is going out to dinner tonight—must prepare and strategize. The caffeine is kicking in—heading out for my run.

...

8:00 p.m.

Dinner was a nightmare. As soon as I had my first bite of bread, I couldn't stop eating, even though I knew it was too risky to throw up at the restaurant. We stopped for ice cream, too, and by the time we got home, I was in a complete panic. Luckily, Maddie went straight to her room and blasted her music, so I had freedom to use the bathroom. I threw up as much food as I could. My once-a-month strategy clearly isn't working, so I'll have to figure out something else.

JANUARY 16 · MONDAY

WEIGHT 110

Back to 110! Yesterday, I survived on two energy drinks and five M&M's. Most of the day, I watched videos and crept around the kitchen to torture myself. I had zero energy to write.

Diego actually stopped when he passed our table today.

He stood next to me. "Energy drink, huh?"

I held up the can. "Mm hmm." Brilliant conversationalist, I know.

He put his cheek next to mine and peered at the can. "How can you drink that? It tastes like pee."

"How do you know what pee tastes like?" London said.

I took a swig. "It's not bad."

He laughed. "See ya 'round."

London rolled her eyes. "Tastes like pee?"

"Give him a break. He's just a boy," Rachel said.

"He's so lame sometimes." London wrinkled her nose. "He's right, though—energy drinks are disgusting."

Just then, a voice on the loudspeaker. "Skye Sato please come to the office. Skye Sato to the office."

Skye's face went white.

"Busted!" Rachel laughed. Skye is never in trouble.

She got up quickly. "I'm sure everything's fine."

We followed her to the office about fifty yards away. She gave us a terrified glance as the door closed behind her.

We heard a scream.

Rachel yanked open the door.

James was standing under a banner that read:

SKYE, LET'S DO IT...GO TO FORMAL, I MEAN!

He was holding a bouquet of roses. So sweet. So James. Wonder if they will actually do it? I think Skye and I are the only ones who haven't crossed over from the land of virgins, and it appears as if I will be the last. I'm not in a rush, but I wonder if Diego could be my first. Wonder how many firsts he has had. Do I want to be one of them? Do I care? Am I kidding myself that it's even a possibility?

JANUARY 18 · WEDNESDAY

WEIGHT 113

I forgot to buy more energy drinks and today was grueling. London and I hung out at her house after school...

London: I wonder if Diego will ask you to Formal.

Me: Doubt it.

London: I think I should ask Niko.

Me: Do you think he'd go?

London: Yeah, I think so. He always texts me.

Me: Texts that come in after 1:00 a.m. don't count.

London: Fuck off.

Me: I say he doesn't deserve to go with you, but that's just me.

London: Yeah, maybe.

She dropped the subject. Niko definitely doesn't deserve London. Period.

When I got home, I was greeted by the delicious aroma of pizza. Mom and Dad are super busy right now, so we just stood around the island and inhaled our food. I drank a lot of water since I knew what was coming next. I headed down the hall. Everything was going according to plan until Maddie started following me.

"Mack?"

"Yeah?" I didn't stop.

"Can we talk?"

Cue record screech sound from the movies. I can't remember the last time I heard those words from Maddie. Our recent conversations consist of random outbursts about me living in the bathroom or destroying her clothes.

I turned around. Her eyes were filled with tears.

"Yeah, sure. Let's go in my room," I said.

I sat on the edge of my bed and she sat in my desk chair.

She bit her cuticle. "I'm worried about Alexis."

"Alexis? I thought Rachel was the only one struggling in that house."

"If Mom died, don't you think both of us would be having issues?"

"You're right. What's going on with Alexis?"

"Did you hear she wrecked Lauren's car at the New Year's Eve party?"

"What? I thought Rachel did."

"No. Rachel just assumed it was her because Alexis never does anything wrong."

"Was Alexis drinking?"

"Yes."

"Were *you*?"

"Yeah." She folded her arms. "You're not the only one who can have fun."

I studied this alien who was pretending to be my sister.

"Drinking doesn't make you have fun." Yikes, I was channeling Mom.

"It makes it easier to blend in."

"I thought you were totally innocent, and so does everyone else."

"It's just that nobody notices us because you guys are so extra."

"Yeah right."

Her eyes welled up. "I don't know what to do."

"Is it something more than wrecking the car?"

She studied me. "If I tell you, do you promise not to tell anyone?"

"Yeah, sure." Just hurry up so I can get rid of this pizza!

"I think Alexis is pregnant."

"Shut up! No way. Who's the guy?"

Her eyes overflowed with tears. "Tyler."

"Tyler?!" My stomach lurched. "When was she with Tyler?"

"New Year's."

"That asshole sure gets around." It was bad enough when it was girls almost his age, but Alexis?!

"What do you mean?" she said.

"Well, you know he's technically Eden's boyfriend, right?"

"No, I didn't know that. I don't think Alexis does either."

"Well, he is. And he was also with Rachel on New Year's."

Maddie's face turned white. "Oh my God, that's so gross."

"Don't worry, I think they just kissed, but still. Why would Alexis be with Tyler?"

"Well, she was mad at Rachel because she wouldn't let us invite any of our friends to the party. So, at the end of the night when Tyler asked her if she was cooler than her sister, Alexis took the opportunity to get back at her."

"Poor Alexis." I wanted to kill Tyler.

"Why? It's what she wanted—a hot senior paying more attention to her than to her older sister."

"But *Tyler*? Gross. Was she a virgin?

"Yeah."

"Does she remember it?"

"She said it's mostly a blur."

"Too bad. I hope my first time isn't like that." I forgot I was talking to my little sister.

"Wait. You're a virgin?"

"My God, Maddie, I'm only sixteen. Please tell me you aren't drinking *and* having sex."

She laughed. "No, I'm definitely not having sex."

"Good." The pizza had completely left my mind.

"I don't think that's going to be an issue for me."

"What do you mean?"

"I just can't see me getting mixed up with some dirt-bag guy. Ever." She shook her head. "I can't believe you're a virgin."

"You don't know anything about me," I said.

"Well, how would I? All you do is sulk around and hide in the bathroom. I mean, what do you do in there? Drugs?"

"No, I don't do drugs. Sue me for reading my phone in the bathroom." It's amazing that in a millisecond I can go from wanting to hug my sister, to wanting to kill her. "Can we get back to Alexis? Did she take a pregnancy test?"

"No, but she was supposed to get her period last week and she's pretty regular."

"What's she going to do if she is?"

"Get an abortion, no question."

"Is she going to tell Tyler?"

"I don't think so."

"I think she needs to tell him. That jerk needs to know what he did." I wanted to choke him out. "I think you have to have an adult with you to get an abortion."

"Who's gonna go with her? Her mom?"

"That's harsh, Maddie." Sometimes Maddie acts like she's the only one who still feels sad about Mrs. Dorian.

"Sorry, but really, who?" Maddie said.

"Maybe she could tell Mom?"

Maddie chewed the side of her thumb. "Yeah, I thought about that, too."

"Or maybe we could tell Mom about it, but not say who it is. Then if we think she'll help, we can tell Alexis she should tell her."

"That's a great idea!" Maddie clasped her hands together.

Suddenly, it felt like we were kids, collaborating on a secret plan. I forgot how nice it feels to be on the same side.

We found Mom working in her office.

"Mom, can we talk to you?" I said.

"Sure. Is everything okay?"

"Sort of. I mean, everything's okay with us, but we have a friend who might be pregnant." I said it so fast, I'm surprised she didn't ask me to repeat it. Thank God, cuz I could barely say it the first time.

Maddie said, "We don't know what to do."

"Do I know this friend?" Mom frowned.

"No, no. You don't know her," Maddie said.

"If this friend is either of you, you can tell me. I won't get mad, I promise."

"No, no. It's not us," I said.

"You're both friends with her?" We should have known Mom would go into detective mode.

"Well, kind of. Not really." Maddie's a horrible liar.

"Can you tell me who it is?"

"It's Alexis." I was shocked Maddie told her.

Mom's eyes went wide and then she nodded. "I understand. She doesn't have her mom to talk to. Is there anyone else she trusts?"

"No," Maddie said.

"Well, she needs to talk to someone. Do you want me to talk to her?"

"Would you?"

"Of course."

Maddie threw her arms around Mom, and I put my arms around both of them. I felt so happy. It was like a little trip back in time. All of us together.

Maddie said. "You won't make her feel bad, will you?"

"Alexis is like my daughter. Don't worry, honey. We'll figure it out."

"Thanks, Mom. I gotta go text Alexis." Maddie ran out of the room.

"Mack, are you okay?" Mom squeezed my hand.

"Yeah, sure, I'm fine. Why?"

"You seem a little distant."

Part of me thought, "Out of my business, please." And another part was happy she noticed. Maybe Mom's not as clueless as she seems.

"Just busy with school. I'm fine." How was I supposed to answer? *Yeah, I feel like shit because I can't lose weight and I keep throwing up even though I keep promising myself I won't.* I probably could tell her, but then she'd be watching me. I can figure this out by myself.

I hugged her. "Thanks, Mom."

"I'm here if you ever want to talk."

"I know, Mom. Thanks." Exit!

I can't imagine how telling my mom would help anything. She'll tell me I look great, and that's not going to help anything. Because I don't.

I can't believe Alexis is in this mess. And with Tyler. 😫

JANUARY 20 · FRIDAY

WEIGHT 110

I'd like to give a shout-out to my savior, the energy drink, for its aid in my return to 110. It has been a stressful week.

Good news, Alexis is going to talk to my mom this weekend. And now for the weekly update...

THE MACKENZIE TIMES

Formal Proposals Edition

COLLEGE FRESHMAN ATTENDing HIGH SCHOOL FORMAL
CROWD WOWED AT SCHOOL ASSEMBLY
MILLIONS WONDER: WILL DIEGO ASK MACK?

London ended up asking Niko to Formal. He said yes, but I bet a million bucks he flakes.

Today there was an assembly to discuss the dangers of prescription drugs. After the informative lecture 😕, Dax walked on stage. I was freaking out because I thought he was about to confess he had a drug problem or something. The principal looked like she thought that's what was happening too.

"May I?" He held his hand out for the mic.

And she gave it to him!

He turned to face the audience. He set a portable speaker on the stage, and a slow beat started playing.

"It's really hard to say what I'm about to say." He put his head down.

Everyone looked around to see if anyone knew what was happening.

The music started pumping and he waved his hand over his head to the beat.

Ya'll know there's a girl who's way beyond fly

And I wanna know if she might be down with this guy.

Rachel, Rachel, is there any chance

You'll slum a little and go with me to this dance?

He pulled out a red rose and walked straight over to Rachel. They kissed and the gym went crazy! I can't imagine anyone other than Dax being able to pull that off. Everyone was laughing so hard they were crying. Even some of the teachers were smiling.

Out of nowhere, Diego zoomed across the gym floor in a hovercraft trailing a banner that said, "Mackenzie, Be Mine... Formal?" Everyone cheered, as I ran down the bleacher stairs, hopped on, and zoomed away...

Just kidding. I wish.

The four of us are going to the movies tonight. I asked

Maddie if she and Alexis wanted to come, and she hugged me. She was so grateful, I felt like a jerk that I never include her.

Fun fact: A lot of theaters have devices that display movie subtitles. When Mom used to take us to the movies, Alexis always got one, and sometimes Mom would let me get one too. Now I'm grateful I don't need it, but at the time it seemed like a privilege. It's just part of life for Alexis, and no one notices anymore.

JANUARY 22 · SUNDAY

WEIGHT 112

Yesterday Alexis talked to Mom. Maddie was there and said Mom was super cool. Alexis said there's no way she's telling her dad or Lauren, and Mom asked if would be okay if she talked to Lauren. Alexis said yes, so that's good.

Later in the afternoon, Maddie and I watched *Gossip Girl* for five hours. I didn't eat much all day, but then Mom ordered pizza and I gave in. After dinner, Maddie and I went to our rooms. She didn't turn on her music, and it was too quiet to throw up. I went for a run and might have burned off one slice. The other two pieces probably dissolved into fat and are plastered on my stomach.

Today, I snacked all day, and then tonight we had linguini, and again no opportunity to throw up. It's a miracle I don't weigh 120. At least I went for a run this afternoon.

Tomorrow will be a regimented day of diet soda, energy drinks, and starvation.

I have tons of homework I've put off to the last minute. Odds are I will do the bare minimum, if that. Community college, here I come.

Side note: Even though I'm not keeping an exact log of what I'm eating, I think my journal is still working. Well, maybe. I'm not exactly sticking to my resolution of not doing things that are bad for me. But I'm a little better. Anyway, I kinda like writing about what's going on. And it's a great way to procrastinate doing my homework.

JANUARY 23 · MONDAY

WEIGHT 113

And the pounds just keep coming. If Diego doesn't ask me to Formal, I plan to drown my sorrows in M&M's and Hot Cheetos.

The only thing that makes me feel any better about gaining weight is that I'm not pregnant. Maddie said Alexis isn't going to tell Tyler, but I still think she should. Not that he has any say in what she does, but he should know.

JANUARY 26 · THURSDAY

WEIGHT 112

THE MACKENZIE TIMES
OMG SPECIAL EDITION!

Diego sat down next to me at the end of lunch and handed me an energy drink. "Thought you might like this."

"Thank you." Crazy grin.

"Someone gave it to me, and you know I'm not going to touch it."

"Aww, you shouldn't have." I was so hungry, I think I was happier about the beverage than Diego.

"Do you like that kind?" he asked.

I held up the can to check out the label. In Sharpie, it said, "Let's go to formal!"

I almost flew out of my seat.

Skye was sitting next to me and saw it. She put her hands over her mouth and let out a little scream.

"Will you go with me?" he asked.

"Of course." I smiled (understatement).

"Awesome." He gave me a kiss on the cheek.

London, Rachel, and Skye looked like they were about to

burst. Diego grinned. His face was red. So cute.

The bell rang.

"I better go. I'll text you," he said.

"OK." I was so excited my brain went on meltdown.

He walked away and Rachel said, "I knew it!"

Skye did a tiny hand clap.

London gave me a thumbs up.

"We're all going to Formal!" Rachel squealed.

The second bell rang and we rushed off to class.

I better get serious about those extra pounds. There are exactly fifteen days until the dance. I want to weigh 105 and that is half a pound a day. Onward and ~~upward~~ downward.

JANUARY 29 · SUNDAY

WEIGHT 109

Back in the single digits!

London and I went dress shopping yesterday on Melrose.
We left early in the morning and had coffee at a sidewalk cafe.
We wore sunglasses and pretended to be famous. Not like
anyone noticed. It was killing me to keep the secret about Alexis.
London would absolutely freak out. I can't stop thinking about
it. Do I confront Tyler? Should Alexis consider having the baby?
I can't even imagine. It's just a mess. Makes me so angry.

But since I can't do anything about it right now, back to
fashion. I found an awesome black dress at the first store, but I
decided to check other places just in case there was something
better. At the next store, I stood on a raised platform in the
dressing area and twirled in a glittery turquoise dress. London
and I were both laughing, and I suddenly got dizzy and I fell
off the edge. For a minute I couldn't breathe or even remember
where I was.

London kneeled down. "Are you okay?"

"Guess I'm too old to be twirling." Might have been because
I hadn't eaten for 24 hours.

"Yeah, I guess." Her voice sounded irritated, not concerned. I wish she cared. I feel like she should have thought it was either funny or alarming, not annoying. It feels like we are becoming disconnected. We used to share everything, but all we do lately is talk about the weather and other people.

We checked out three more stores. London looked like a runway model in every dress she tried on. Oh, to be her for a day! I ended up buying the first dress I had tried on. I love it! Dresses are like impressions—the first one is usually right. I think I read that somewhere.

If Alexis doesn't tell Tyler by Friday, I swear I'm going to. Even though it's not really my business, it sort of is because Alexis is like my sister. The thought of having Tyler as the father of my semi-niece makes me want to scream. How do people deal with this kind of thing? I can't just let her get an abortion and pretend it never happened. I'm tired of thinking about it—think I'll give it a rest for now.

FEBRUARY 1 · WEDNESDAY

WEIGHT 108

I can't even remember the last time I weighed 108. I'm so happy I want to spin around like a kid. No—no spinning. But really, it's worth the occasional dizzy spell to watch the scale go down.

It's only Wednesday, and I have so much to write about.

First, Maddie and Alexis have decided to go to Formal together to avoid the hassle of dealing with boys.

My first question was, "Why would Alexis want to go in her condition?"

Drum roll please...

Alexis got her period! Now, I don't want to take too much credit, but I did pray/obsess pretty hard over that one. Just kidding, but it's truly a miracle.

On a related note, Mom is supposed to meet Lauren for coffee tomorrow to discuss the situation. I wonder if she'll still go.

Today Diego sat with us at lunch. When the bell rang he said, "Where's your next class?"

"Science building." I wondered if he could hear my heart

pounding.

"I'm over there, too. Can I walk with you?"

"Sure."

I gave a little wave to Rachel and Skye. Rachel put her hand over Skye's mouth and pretended to make out. God she's funny. So glad Diego didn't look back.

Diego put his arm around me. "I was thinking maybe we could drive to Formal with Tyler. He's got a Porsche—it's crazy fast."

I stopped.

"What's wrong?"

"Are you friends with Tyler?"

"Uh, yeah, sure."

"Like actual friends?"

"Well, I mean we hang out at school and play video games—stuff like that."

"How well do you know him?"

"I don't know. Why?" He frowned.

I folded my arms. "I don't want to go anywhere with Tyler."

"Yeah...okay...sure. We don't have to go with him. I just thought the Porsche would be cool."

"Good. I'll talk to you later." I walked away towards my classroom.

I think it's amazing how I can get so strong when something strikes me in just the right way. Even if Diego had promised I would weigh 100 pounds for the rest of my life if we drove with Tyler, I wouldn't have considered it for a second. Maybe half a second.

After school, London, Rachel, and I went to Cava. Skye said she had too much homework. Pretty sure Skye won't be attending community college.

I launched right into my story—I couldn't wait to see Rachel and London's faces. "You know who Diego wanted to drive with to Formal?... Tyler!"

"Diego is friends with Tyler?" London said.

"I don't think they're really friends, but they hang out. If you hang out with a scumbag are you a scumbag?"

Rachel said, "I know he's a total scammer, but he was pretty cool when we went out last year."

"I can't believe you're saying that," London said. "Mack, am I right?"

"One hundred percent. Tyler sucks, Rachel."

I felt like such a bad friend. If Rachel knew about Tyler and Alexis, there's no way she'd be defending him. I so wanted to tell her, but Maddie would never forgive me.

"Well, maybe you're right. Good thing I'm going to Formal

with Dax. I think we're driving with Skye and James," Rachel said.

I said, "London, do you want to go together?"

She kept her eyes on her phone. "Yeah sure, maybe. As long as Tyler's not there."

Stomach punch. The old London would have been excited. Who is this person?

Rachel held up her phone. "We've got a party!"

I checked my phone. Eden had just sent an invite for party at her house tomorrow night. She included Rachel in the group! My hope for world peace increases.

FEBRUARY 2 · THURSDAY

WEIGHT 107

Being anxious and over-caffeinated does wonders for your appetite. I would be a stick if I felt like this all the time. Diego texted me last night. 😜

> Diego: Still cool for Formal?
>
> Me: Yep
>
> Diego: Just making sure
>
> Me: Why?
>
> Diego: You seemed not into it at lunch
>
> Me: Just don't want to drive with Tyler
>
> Diego: OK

Did Diego really think I wouldn't want to go? It blows my mind to think he could ever have a shred of self-doubt.

Today, he walked me to class again after lunch. Sometimes he seems like he doesn't know what to say, which makes me like him even more. I asked if he wanted to drive with London and Niko, and he said that would be great.

Skye wasn't at school today and she hasn't returned my text. It's very unlike her.

FEBRUARY 3 · FRIDAY

WEIGHT 107

5:00 p.m.

Skye finally texted me back and said she's sick. Guess I'll be the designated driver tonight for Eden's party. Probably better than driving in Skye's car anyway. She says it's good as new, but she gave me a ride home the other day and I'm not so sure. I'm probably oversensitive though. I wonder if Maddie's going to the party. We haven't really talked since our brief reunion over Alexis. Business as usual.

Mom said I could take her car so I'm picking up Rachel and London at 8:00, but I have to go out to dinner with my family first. Fortunately, we're going to a seafood restaurant, so I can eat sensibly without much effort. And I still don't have much of an appetite—miracle of all miracles! Must go for a run now.

...

1:00 a.m.

Exactly one week away from Formal and I'm only two pounds away from my goal. I'm soooooo excited.

And on the topic of 105, tonight Dad said, "You should eat what you order. A little more food might be good for you."

Dad encouraging me to eat is even more incredible than my lack of appetite. But while I'm happy he thinks I'm thin, I wish he'd mind his own business. He doesn't pay enough attention to me on the daily to have the right to comment about my weight. Actually, I don't think he ever has that right.

But back to what is really on my mind—Eden's party.

Diego is either a total asshole or he's completely clueless. And my friends? Assholes all around.

At 11:30 Diego asked if I wanted to go with him to get burgers, and I told him I couldn't because I had a midnight curfew. I walked over to Rachel and London.

"Hey, I need to get going soon," I said.

Diego had followed me, and said, "A bunch of us are going to get food. You gals want to come?"

"Sure, I'll go," London said.

I laughed because I thought she was kidding.

London put her arm around Rachel. "Come on Rach, let's go. I'm hungry."

Rachel tilted her head at me. "You're not going, Mack?"

"I have to be home at 12." Were my friends seriously getting food with the guy I like without me?

I left before I could start crying. I heard Diego calling after me, but I sprinted up the stairs and out the front door.

Am I overreacting?

FEBRUARY 4 · SATURDAY

WEIGHT 105

London: OMG Rachel got a DUI

That's the message I woke up to.

Me: Is she OK?

London: Yeah

Me: Let's go see her

London: She's on permanent lock-down

Me: That SUCKS!

London: So bummed

Me: EMOJI (sad face)

I wished she would say, "I'm sorry I'm an asshole and went out to eat with your boyfriend." (I know, he's not really my boyfriend.)

But that was the end of our convo.

I'm so sad for Rachel. Not exactly surprised though.

On the bright side...105!!! I took a picture of the scale.

FEBRUARY 6 · MONDAY

WEIGHT 105

News of Rachel's DUI spread through school like wildfire. She filled us in on the details at lunch. Apparently, after my friends all went out to eat—*without me*—Rachel and Dax stopped by the store to get some candy.

In Rachel's words:

...Guess I put the car in drive, instead of reverse. My bad.

...Owner called the police, I failed the breathalyzer, and off to the slammer I went.

...I think it's fucked up that Dax got to go home, considering I had to drive because he was too wasted.

...Took forever for my dad to get there, and I had to chill with some super badass chicks.

...But I'm a badass too. They were probably more scared of me than I was of them.

...The thing that really sucks is I can't go to Formal, or anywhere else. EVER, according to my dad.

I feel really bad for her. Wish we could turn back time and erase it.

FEBRUARY 8 · WEDNESDAY

WEIGHT 106

It's impossible to stay at this weight. I'm starving!

Last night, tacos arrived like clockwork and I ate six of them.

Dad checked my plate. "Nice to see you eating a bit more."

Here's what ran through my head: Are you going to tell me to eat less if I get fat? What do you know? You don't notice anything!

Fortunately, dinner was quick. I went to my room and took out the M&M's I bought to replace the one I ate before. I devoured the entire bag in under ten minutes while I watched a Blake Lively shark movie on my phone. She has a perfect body.

I went into the bathroom, ran the shower to hide the sound, and threw up. Relief washed over me. I felt like a new person. Back in control.

But today, school was more of the same—I downed two energy drinks, didn't eat, and felt pretty shitty. I thought maybe a little Formal accessory shopping would cheer me up, so on the way to class I asked London if she wanted to go the mall. She was super snarly and asked why she would want to go shopping when she's not even going to Formal.

"What are you talking about?" I put my hand on her shoulder.

She jerked away. "Niko texted me last night and said he can't go because he has a huge test."

"I'm sorry, London. That sucks."

"He couldn't even call? What a chicken shit."

I went to give her a hug and she backed up as if I had the plague.

The bell rang and that was the end of it. Maybe she's being so rude because she knows I was right about Niko. I was going to call her on it, but now I feel bad since she can't go to Formal. Guess it can wait.

Skye texted about an hour ago and asked if Diego and I want to ride with them. I texted Diego and he's cool with it. So much better than being with London and Niko!

FEBRUARY 9 · THURSDAY

WEIGHT 106

Today is Operation 105. I discovered a new brand of energy drink—an enormous can with zero calories. I'm going to drink one for breakfast and go for a run before school while I'm still flying high. That pound doesn't stand a chance.

I'm so happy we're driving with Skye and James. We're going out to dinner first. Secret destination. Fun!

FEBRUARY 10 · FRIDAY

WEIGHT 104

104! Not since I was twelve, and probably never again. Getting here has been torture. I feel like I'm writing an Oscar acceptance speech.

Rachel brought me a necklace today. She said it's perfect for my dress and someone might as well get some use out of it. How nice is she? Skye and I are going shopping together tonight. I want to find a purse.

FEBRUARY 18 · SATURDAY

I'm so grateful to be in my own bed.

My last journal entry was a week ago—the day my world collapsed.

I wish I could write about Formal, but I have no memory of it.

The first thing I remember is waking up and seeing my mom sitting next to the bed. I don't quite trust my memory, but this what the conversation felt like:

"Mom?" I couldn't lift my head.

She leaned over me. "Hi, sweetie."

"Where am I?"

"In the hospital."

"Why?"

"You fell at the dance and hit your head."

"Tonight?"

"No. It's Sunday. You've been here for almost twenty-four hours."

"Have I been asleep the whole time?"

"Mostly."

She sat with me and held my hand. The next time I woke up, the room was sunny and my mom was still there.

"What day is it?" I asked.

"Monday."

I could remember getting ready at Skye's, James's shiny black Tahoe, the teppanyaki chef tossing knives in the air, and that's it.

Over the next few days, I mostly slept. I had no say about what I could or couldn't do. No decisions about what to eat. No sneaking. No plotting. No starving. No arguments with myself. It was a relief.

It seemed like Mom never left the room. Dad, Maddie, and Skye visited. Rachel and London texted. Not a word from Diego, but London texted on his behalf. Thanks, asshole, for the effort. And I gave that guy candy.

I don't want to write the next part, but here goes...

Yesterday, Mom brought me a green juice and a breakfast sandwich. Sometimes she's just the best.

"How are you feeling?" she asked.

"Better. This tastes so good. Thank you."

"I need to talk to you about something," she said.

I waited.

"The doctor has some concerns about your health."

"Like what?"

"Well, when you arrived, you were dehydrated, and your

heart was beating irregularly."

"Probably too many energy drinks." I thought about how amped up I had been that night, trying not to eat until dinner.

"Yes, they can have an effect, but not as severe as your tests showed."

"What does that mean? Am I okay?"

"If you start taking care of yourself, you'll be fine."

"Wait, what? I was joking. Take care of myself? Like take my vitamins?" Part of me knew what was coming, but I thought if I played dumb, it wouldn't happen.

"Honey, the doctor said she thinks your electrolyte levels are a sign of chronic vomiting."

"Oh." I tried to think of some excuse and burst into tears.

She wrapped her arms around me. "I'm so sorry."

"Why are you sorry?"

"I kept telling myself you were fine."

"Well, how would you know I wasn't?"

"I should have paid more attention. You were thin, but I didn't think it was anything like this."

I studied my hands to see if I was still thin.

Just then the doctor came in.

"How are you feeling, Mackenzie?"

"Better."

"You sustained a major concussion."

Pause...

"Mackenzie, there is something I need to discuss with you."

I felt my face flush and I held back tears.

"Do you know what an electrolyte imbalance is?"

"Not really. Sort of."

"Electrolytes help your body function properly. When the levels of electrolytes in the body are too high or too low you can have serious problems. Several of yours were severely low."

"But, they're okay now?"

"You have had five days of IV hydration and nutrition, and their levels have returned to normal."

"So, I'm all better?" I was thinking, "Good, I can just go home. I promise I won't throw up anymore."

The doctor was stone-faced.

"Your heartbeat also was irregular when you arrived. This could have been caused by the concussion, but it could also be an indication that your heart is not functioning properly."

This was bad. Maybe I did need to be worried.

"It has returned to normal, but I am concerned about what will happen when you leave the hospital."

"Why?"

"Mackenzie, while your symptoms may indicate a number of

things, I believe they are most likely caused by frequent, forced vomiting."

My face burned. Hearing the words out loud, from someone else, somehow made it real. It was a thousand times worse than the dream where you are naked in front of the school.

"I know this is hard for you, Mackenzie. Am I correct in my assessment?"

"You mean you aren't sure?" I was still thinking maybe I could fool her.

She said nothing.

I looked down and nodded. I knew she knew. I couldn't bring myself to make eye contact.

Mom put her arm around my shoulder.

The doctor continued. "When a person consumes food, then vomits intentionally, we call it bulimia, which is an eating disorder. Are you familiar with the term?"

"Yes."

"Bulimia has serious health risks. If you continue to purge, your body will break down, and your heart could fail."

"Fail? Like completely?"

"Yes, you could have a fatal heart attack. Do you know who Karen Carpenter was?"

"No."

"She was an amazing singer who died from heart failure caused by years of bulimia and anorexia."

"That's sad."

"It's tragic. It's also completely avoidable. Is that what you want?"

"To die? Of course not." That's what I said, but there's a part of me that likes the idea of being so thin I die. Like the ultimate goal. I know that sounds crazy.

"Mackenzie, no one can make you take care of yourself. You are the only one who can control your actions."

I started crying. I didn't want to tell her how hard I had tried. I didn't want to even admit I had been throwing up at all. I just wanted it to all go away. I wanted no one to know and be able to start over with a clean slate. I shouldn't have nodded. She couldn't be absolutely certain I have been throwing up, she just suspected it.

The doctor squeezed my hand. "I have the name of a psychologist who specializes in eating disorders. I will give your mom his card. Summon your strength, Mackenzie. I'm sure you can do anything you set your mind to. Right now, your vitals are good. If everything remains stable, you can go home tomorrow."

"Thank you."

After the doctor left, Mom gave me a kiss on the forehead.

"Do you want to talk more?"

"Not right now." I didn't want to share with the doctor, but maybe, just maybe, I could tell my mom. Someday.

When I woke up, it was still light. Mom was brushing my hair from my forehead.

"Time to go home, sleepyhead."

"I thought the doctor said tomorrow."

"Yes, she did. It is tomorrow."

I could have jumped out of bed. Best moment of my life! It's tomorrow! I'm going home!

"You're the best, Mom."

"I wish." She sighed.

I stood up to change into the fresh clothes Mom brought, and my head started spinning. A normal person would think, "I hope I'm okay." But my first thought was, "I wonder if I've lost weight."

A nurse came in with a wheelchair.

"Don't you think that's a little extreme?" I said.

"It's hospital policy."

Mom went ahead to get the car. It was cool being wheeled through the hospital. I imagined I was so thin, I couldn't even walk. Kind of impressive.

When we exited, I took a deep breath. Aahh, fresh start!

Being home is the best! I'm ready. It's Groundhog New Year's Day, in a good way. Stay skinny, but don't throw up. Now that I know it's really affecting my health, I will have more motivation not to do it. Plus, Mom knows, so I won't be able to get away with being in the bathroom.

I wonder what I weigh. I haven't eaten much this week, but I also haven't moved.

Just weighed myself: 109. Still in the single digits! Think I'll go see what there is to eat.

FEBRUARY 20 · MONDAY

WEIGHT 109

Mom made me breakfast this morning. An egg, slice of toast, and a tangerine. Very nice.

She sat down next to me. "When do you think you'll be ready to go back to school? No pressure—I'm just wondering."

I answered with my mouth full. "Oh, tomorrow for sure."

I swallowed. "Mom, does Dad know about my issue?"

"No, I haven't told him yet."

"Oh, I'm so glad."

"I'm not sure it's a good thing. He thinks you were in the hospital for so long because of the concussion. I haven't had a good opportunity to talk to him about what's really going on."

"Oh, please please don't tell him. Can't we just keep it between us? What good will it do if he knows? He'll just watch what I eat and make me feel self-conscious."

"Dad loves you." She touched my shoulder and I pulled away.

"I'm sure he does, but he's not helpful in this area."

"Maybe you're right. For now, I guess we can keep it between us. But you have to promise you'll tell me if you're struggling."

"I promise." I put my hand over hers.

Only having Mom and the doctor know my secret is as close as I can get to no one knowing. If I can just stick to my plan, it will be like it never happened.

FEBRUARY 21 · TUESDAY

WEIGHT 109

First day back at school.

I'm totally famous. Infamous. Rumor is I passed out from too many energy drinks. This has piqued the interest of the administration and prompted an all-school assembly to discuss the danger of energy drink consumption. I wonder if they'll put up posters of me. Everybody's making jokes about it. When kids are drinking, smoking, and taking pills, it seems crazy to have an assembly to discuss caffeinated drinks. If you ask me, it's just going to give kids a new idea for combining their drugs.

Just as I expected, Diego ran up to me when he saw me at school and swooped me into his arms. Sure he did. Right after he sent me this text:

Glad U R okay.

Fucker.

Mom already made an appointment this Friday with the psychologist, Dr. Martian. Wish I didn't have to talk to him. Total waste of time since I know I'm not going to throw up anymore. Yes, I know I've said it before, but it's different this time. A trip to the hospital does wonders for one's motivation.

FEBRUARY 24 · FRIDAY

WEIGHT 110

THE MACKENZIE TIMES
Post-Hospital Back-to-School Edition

CELEBRATE ENERGY DRINKS, ROOT OF ALL EVIL
SUSPICION RAISED OVER LONDON & DIEGO
DR. MARTIAN ESCAPES FROM THE WONDERFUL FLIGHT
TO THE MUSHROOM PLANET

What a week. I don't even know where to start. Today I saw
Dr. Martian, but I'll get back to that. London is barely talking to
me, even though she pretends she is. She hasn't asked me once
how I'm feeling. And here's the real issue...Guess who she is
talking to. Diego! 😡

I get so mad when I think about Diego, I want to scream. He
didn't come see me in the hospital and never even texted me. I
only heard about his concern through London. And apparently,
this incident has brought them closer, because I saw her walking
with him at break twice this week. I asked Rachel what was
going on, and she said she had no idea. But it's hard to talk to
Rachel about anything since she's been on lock-down. When
that girl's low, back off. My only friend right now is Skye.

Dax is having an Energy Drink party tonight to celebrate

our informative school assembly today. He's hilarious. I'm not up for a party, Rachel isn't allowed to leave the house, Skye is going to an art installation with her mom, and London just isn't going (according to her). I'm sure it will be fun though. I miss my energy drinks. I have not thrown up, nor consumed an energy drink, for two weeks. I'm proud of myself—but still kind of empty at the same time.

This brings me to Dr. Martian. Mom and I went together for the first visit. That is, the last visit. When I was younger, I read *The Wonderful Flight to the Mushroom Planet*, and Dr. Martian looks exactly how I pictured the little alien scientist in the story—thin hair and round spectacles. However, I tried at first to be open-minded.

He asked questions and made notes. I felt like a lab rat. When did you vomit for the first time?...Do you take laxatives?... Do you feel judged?...Have you ever considered suicide? It was like a quality assessment. And over and over, *How does that make you feel?* The final time he asked, I almost said, "It makes me feel like punching you in the face."

After an excruciating hour, our interrogation ended. He opened his calendar. "To start, I should probably see you twice a week."

"I will call to make the next appointment," Mom said.

"Very well." He snapped his calendar closed.

When we got in the car, we both let out a sigh.

"Mom, he's so awful. I can't go back there."

"It wasn't exactly what I was expecting," Mom said.

"Please don't make me go back."

"Mackenzie, I want to help you."

"I can do it without him. I'll ask you for help if I need it. The Martian would make things worse. I would stress-eat every time I had to see him."

She laughed. "I miss talking to you."

"I miss talking to you, too. We're both just so busy."

"True, but I can make time. I can make healthy meals. I'll do whatever it takes."

"Mom, the best thing you can do is trust me and not make a big deal out of it. I promise I'll get better."

"I do trust you."

"Please don't tell Dad and Maddie. If they start watching me, it's going to be impossible."

She was quiet.

My stomach dropped. "Wait, you didn't already tell Dad did you?"

"No, I haven't, but I'm really conflicted about it. I think he should know."

"Please give me a chance to prove I can do it. Please don't tell him."

"Well, at a minimum, we should find another therapist."

"I don't want to be studied and analyzed. I'll be totally fine if I talk to you. YOU are the best therapist."

She smiled and raised her eyebrows. "You might be getting a little carried away there, but I understand how you feel. I guess we could try it for a little while and see how it goes. Do you promise you will talk to me if you're having trouble?"

"I promise!" I reached over and hugged her. She rested her head on mine.

I like having a secret with my mom. But I still wish nobody knew, so I could fix everything and move on like it never happened. At least I won't have to go over it again with a total stranger.

FEBRUARY 27 · MONDAY

WEIGHT 112

This morning I scrolled through my phone in bed and mentally prepared for (I mean delayed) school. I'm totally behind from missing a week. I was greeted by a picture of Diego with his arm around London at Dax's party. I knew she was lying when she said she wasn't going! She's such an asshole! I want to confront her, but I never see her at school anymore. She's doing an off-campus internship and she leaves right before lunch. Maybe I should screenshot the pic and send her a text: WTF!

I ate a homemade turkey sandwich, thanks to Mom, while I chatted with Rachel and Skye.

"Do you know what's going on with London and Diego?" I asked.

"I saw the pic," Rachel said.

"Do you think they hooked up?" I studied her face for evidence of conspiracy.

"Nah, I think they're just friends." Rachel sounded less than sure.

I studied the photo on my own phone. "Looks like more than friends to me."

Skye touched my shoulder. "I don't think London would do that."

The bell ended our discussion.

I grouched my way through the rest of the day and managed not to eat until dinner.

Mom made chicken, broccoli, and rice, and we sat down to a civilized meal.

Dad said, "So, how's school going, girls?

Maddie got all bright and cheery. "Good. Got an A on my history test."

"Good job. How about you, Mack?"

I decided to be polite. "Good. A's and B's so far this semester."

"Way to go." Unlike the usual response where Dad doesn't even pause between bites, tonight he made eye contact.

My heart swelled. As mad as he makes me, I guess I still want his approval.

"Good dinner. Thank you." Dad got up from the table with his plate.

"Thank you." Mom looked surprised.

It seemed genuine. No fake smiles or passive aggressive comments. A perfect dinner. If our meals were always like this, I might be a completely normal person.

My stomach is satisfied, and I'm going to do my
now. This seems so easy, it's hard to remember why some
have such a problem.

ıappy family dinners—tonight normal dysfunction returned. Mom had to yell twice for Dad before he came to the table.

We inhaled our food while Maddie chattered and tried to make everyone happy. Mom listened to Maddie, pretended not to watch what I ate, and glared at Dad. I finished as fast as possible.

"Can I be excused?" I asked.

Mom said, "Sure, honey." Dad stared at his plate.

About an hour later, a knock on my door.

"What?"

Mom's voice. "Can I come in?"

"Yes."

She opened the door and sat on the edge of my bed where I peeked out from under the covers.

"How are things going?" She smoothed my hair away from my face.

"Fine." I turned my head away.

"Are you feeling okay?" She folded her hands in her lap.

"I guess."

"Are you still not…"

I said nothing. I didn't feel like helping her have this conversation.

"Honey, I'm sorry, I don't know what to say." Her eyes welled.

"It's okay, Mom. I know what you mean."

My feelings about Mom are complicated. I'm glad she cares, but it's also none of her business. Just because she's my mom, doesn't mean she can control my body. It's my body, not hers. My life. Sometimes I feel so angry at her, Dad, and Maddie, I want to disappear in a puff of smoke. Watching them be fake and angry makes me insane. I wish I could live by myself and not answer to anyone. And yet, sometimes things are happy and I love them, and that's almost harder, because you never know what's coming.

"No, I haven't thrown up."

"That's good." She fidgeted.

"Mom, I wish you would just say what you think instead of saying what you think I want you to say."

"That's what I'm trying to do, but I don't want to say the wrong thing."

We sat there in silence for a minute.

"I want to help, but I don't know how," she said.

"Mom, I'm doing fine. Thanks for checking in."

"Is there anything I can do for you?"

I thought for a second. "I liked the sandwich you made me for lunch yesterday. Will you make one for me tomorrow?"

"Sure! Anything else?"

"Will you buy more diet soda?"

"Didn't the doctor say you shouldn't drink them?"

"No, she said I shouldn't drink energy drinks. Mom, if you take that away from me, I'm going to die."

She pursed her lips. "I'm proud of you, Mackenzie. You're doing a great job."

She didn't add a "but." Amazing.

"Thanks, Mom."

She closed my door.

I know I wasn't very nice. Does she really think I'm doing a great job? I'm not so sure I am. I guess I'm glad she came and talked to me even though our conversation was irritating and unproductive. I'm a tiny bit less angry than I was at the table. Teensie tiny.

MARCH 3 · FRIDAY

WEIGHT 112

4:00 p.m.

Today Diego talked to me for the first time since I came back to school—TWO weeks ago. I guess it was the second time, if you count that lameass text he sent the day I came back.

He sat down next to me. "Are you feeling better?"

"Yes."

"That's good. I'm sorry I haven't checked in."

Silence.

"That was crazy what happened at the dance."

"Yeah? I don't remember much."

"I'm really sorry I didn't come see you. Hospitals freak me out. London let me know you were okay."

"I know, she told me."

Those eyes.

"Anyway, I'm sorry."

"That's okay." Not okay.

"So there's a party tonight. You wanna go?"

"Are you serious?" Talk about a 180.

"Yes. I've missed you."

Those lips. He's such a jerk, but still I was flattered. He missed me! Maybe he and London are just friends, after all.

"What party?" I asked.

"Beach bonfire. Just a last-minute thing."

"Sounds fun."

"Really? Cool. I'll text you later." He left before I could say anything else.

Skye threw a wrapper at me. "I can't believe you're going to a party with him."

"I didn't say I was going, I said it sounds fun."

"Didn't sound like that," Rachel said.

"Yeah, I got tongue tied."

"Mack, the guy totally abandoned you at Formal," Skye said.

"I know. Thank you for saving me."

"My pleasure. Please don't go out with him."

"I'm not planning to. I was just flustered."

"Yeah, right." Skye huffed.

"Anyway, I haven't heard of any party. Did you guys know about it?"

"Nope," Skye said.

Rachel was texting someone. "I did. I think Tyler is one of the planners, so I'm out."

"Wait! Could you go if you wanted to? Are you off

restriction?"

"As of this weekend, YES!" Rachel raised both fists above her head.

"That was fast," I said.

"I know. I think they're sick of seeing me moping around the house."

So awesome, Rachel is free. "We should celebrate! You guys want to spend the night?" I knew Mom would say yes.

Rachel said, "Do you care if we go to my house instead? I need to blow off some steam and your house is too cozy."

"Good with me," I said.

"Sounds fun," Skye said.

I wasn't offended. My house is like being in a tent compared to the freedom we have at Rachel's.

"Come over around eight. I'll let London know."

The bell rang and we went to class.

...

5:00 p.m.

Diego: Are you going to the party?

I had been thinking of a million ways to tell Diego I didn't want to go with him, but his text threw me off. Was he revoking his invitation? I mean, if he was asking me to go to the party, wouldn't he say something like, "Are you up for the party?" It was insulting enough that he invited me as if nothing ever happened, but now un-inviting me was too much.

Me: Not sure. Are you?

Diego: Probably

This would be the logical place for him to ask if I wanted to join him, and the logical place for me to say no. But he didn't, so I wrote nothing.

I keep checking my phone for a proper invitation that I can refuse. So far, nothing. *Jerk.*

I'm skipping dinner tonight and going for a run before I go to Rachel's.

MARCH 4 · SATURDAY

WEIGHT 112

8:00 p.m.

I'm home with nothing to do. 🙁

Rachel's was fun last night—we listened to music, watched videos, and ate pizza (ugh).

Rachel doctored her sodas with the contents of her tiny vodka bottles. "My lame DUI class says I shouldn't drink alone. Cheers! You guys are drinking too—yours just isn't as good as mine."

Skye and I exchanged a worried glance.

London texted us:

> London: Love you guys, but I'm going to the party.
>
> Rachel: Who with?
>
> London: Eden
>
> Rachel: Be careful
>
> London: LOL

"Since when does London hang out with Eden?" Rachel asked.

"My thought exactly," I said.

"Hey, maybe we should go to the party too!" Rachel turned the music up.

Skye said, "I thought you said Tyler was organizing it."

"Yeah, but I'm over that. We should go."

"That's the vodka talking. Let's just hang out here," Skye said.

"Oh, come on. Don't be such a downer." Rachel danced around.

Skye's face turned red. "I want nothing to do with Tyler, and I also don't want to take you to a party when you're already drunk."

"Chill out, girl. You need to lighten up. Come on, I'll make you a Rachel-special."

"No thanks."

I started dancing with Rachel to break the tension, then Skye joined us, and it was like the conversation never happened.

That was the first time I've ever heard Skye speak up. If she hadn't, I bet I would have let Rachel talk me into going, just so I could see Diego. I wonder if Diego un-asked me because he found out London was going. 😠

I wish London would give me some explanation for why she went to the party instead of coming to Rachel's. Maybe if I start the conversation, she will say something to make me feel better.

Here goes...

> Me: What's up?
>
> London: Nothing. Tired.
>
> Me: Fun party?
>
> London: Yeah

End of conversation. I'm SO MAD!

MARCH 5 · SUNDAY

WEIGHT 113

BREAKDOWN!

My eating has been fairly moderate, but my weight is going up. Exercise only helps so much. Last night my mom and Maddie made chocolate chip cookies to take to the swim meet today. I didn't eat any. This morning, when I woke up the house was empty. Mom left a note reminding me they would be home late.

On the counter sat a large plastic container filled with extra cookies. I made a plan:

1. Eat breakfast – ONE cookie and a cup of coffee

2. Go for a run

3. Do my homework

I filled my cup from the coffee pot and sat down at the table. I chewed the cookie slowly and sipped my coffee. It was so absolutely delicious, I can't even explain it. I decided two cookies wouldn't be bad if I didn't eat until dinner. I got another cookie and returned to the table to eat it. And then, it's hard to explain, but that switch flipped in my brain and I had to have more. I absolutely HAD TO HAVE MORE.

I brought the container to the table and inhaled deeply. I ate another, thinking maybe three would be enough. Then another and another and another and another. Then I started crying because I could not stop. I don't know how to explain it, but I could NOT stop. I was sobbing and eating.

After I ate at least twenty cookies, I started to slow down. I was still crying. I sat at the table and felt all those cookies in my stomach and I made a choice: I decided not to throw up. Instead, I went to my room and started typing and here I am.

Here's the truth: I have a problem I cannot fix by myself. I really thought I could, but I can't. I refuse to see the horrible Dr. Martian again, but maybe there's someone else, or something else. I wish Mom would get home.

The thought that I'm going to get help is making me feel not as bad about all those cookies in my stomach.

MARCH 6 · MONDAY

WEIGHT 114

Amazing, only one pound up. Don't get me wrong, 114 freaks me out, but I didn't throw up yesterday and I didn't eat any more cookies, so I'm kind of proud of myself.

When everyone got home last night, we gathered to eat sandwiches around the island. Ten minutes later, the trash was tossed, and everyone had relocated to their separate stations. I went into Mom's office and asked her if we could talk. She came down to my room and we sat on the edge of my bed.

"Mom, I need help."

"Oh, honey. What can I do?"

"I can't control myself. I know if I don't get help, I'm going to start throwing up again."

"Do you want to see Dr. Martian?"

"Are you crazy? No way."

"Sorry, that was a stupid question." She thought for a minute. "When I had lunch with Lauren, she mentioned she sees a therapist. Maybe she could give us a referral."

"Is it the same person Rachel sees?"

"I don't know. I'll call her first thing in the morning and

ask."

She checked her watch. "Actually, it's only eight. I'll call her tonight."

"Thank you."

"Mackenzie, I'm so sorry. I should have already found another therapist. I should have known you needed help."

"Maybe I had to realize it for myself."

"If I had paid more attention, I could have helped you sooner."

"I don't know, Mom."

She hugged me. "I love you, Mackenzie. I'm always here for you."

"Thanks, Mom. I love you too."

About thirty minutes later Mom came back.

"Lauren said she'll call her therapist in the morning."

"Did you tell her the whole story?" I hated the thought of Lauren knowing my business.

"No, just the minimum. Her doctor's name is Katherine Skyler."

"A woman! That's great. And it's not the same person Rachel sees—that's good too."

"Do you feel like talking more right now?"

"No. Thank you so much, Mom."

"It's the least I can do." She closed my bedroom door.

I'm going to be saved! I just have to hold on a little longer.

MARCH 7 · TUESDAY

WEIGHT 114

I have an appointment with Dr. Skyler this Wednesday at 4:00. I'm nervous, excited, and miraculously, not hungry!

MARCH 8 · WEDNESDAY

WEIGHT 114

4:00 p.m.

This morning I bolted awake in a panic about my skyrocketing weight and my (ex) best friend, London.

I went to sleep trying to erase the picture that showed up of London and Diego KISSING at the beach party Friday night. I knew it was only a matter of time before my suspicions would be confirmed with photographic evidence.

At school, I found London at break. No surprise she was talking to Diego.

I ignored him. "Hey, London. Can we talk?"

"Yeah, sure." She kissed Diego on the cheek, and he walked away.

"Are you and Diego together now?" I asked.

"Yeah, so?"

It took all my power not to cry. "Who *are* you? I've liked him for so long and you acted like you hated him. And he treated me like shit and now you guys are together. I don't get it. I thought we were best friends."

"I never *hated* him. You bailed at the dance, and Diego

118

asked me how you were doing, and we became friends. And then it developed into more. Simple as that."

"Excuse me, did you say, I *bailed*? Are you under the impression that I went to the hospital on purpose?"

"Sounded like you drank too much, so it's not like you are totally without blame."

"I *drank* too much?"

"Yeah, energy drinks or alcohol or both. I know you don't usually drink, but special occasion, whatever."

"Is that what Diego said?"

"He said you guys were partying."

"And you believe him?"

"You know, I don't care what you were doing. I feel like I haven't really talked to you since Rachel's New Year's Eve party. Actually, way before that."

The bell rang.

"I gotta go." London walked away.

My best friend has betrayed me, and I'm gaining weight by the minute. This therapist better be a miracle worker.

...

9:00 p.m.

DR. SKYLER

Dr. Skyler's waiting room has comfy chairs with colorful pillows, and a coffee table with books and magazines. So much better than Dr. Martian's sterile laboratory.

She opened the door to her office and greeted me with a smile.

"Hi. I'm Katherine Skyler. Are you Mackenzie?"

"Yes. Hi." I shook her hand.

"It's a pleasure to meet you. Please come in." She held the door open for me.

Her office is bright and open with a huge paned window facing a courtyard.

She gestured to four stuffed chairs. "Would you like to sit? Chose any seat you like."

I sat down in the closest one and swiveled it towards the window.

She sat down in the chair next to me. How old is she? Forty? Fifty? Sixty?

"I'm glad you're here, Mackenzie. You can call me Katherine, or Dr. Skyler, or whatever makes you comfortable."

"Okay." So different from Dr. Martian. I wondered if underneath, all therapists were the same. Maybe she was just better at hiding it.

"Did you choose to come here on your own?"

"Yes. I mean, no. I mean, don't you already know?"

"I'd like to hear your story from you."

"You mean from the beginning?"

"Wherever makes the most sense to you."

Nothing makes sense to me! Of course, I didn't say that out loud.

"Well, my problem is I can't control my eating. I've tried different diets and exercise, but the only thing that works is throwing up. And for a while, it seemed like the perfect answer."

I was shocked how quickly the words came out. Was it because I had already told the other therapist? Maybe I just wanted to get it over with.

"But it's not the perfect solution anymore?" she asked.

"No. I can't stop. I think I might die if I don't get help. And sometimes, I think dying would be easier." I started to cry.

Dr. Skyler offered me a box of tissues. "Thank you for sharing, Mackenzie. It takes a lot of courage."

I wiped my eyes. Maybe she was different from Dr. Martian. I can't imagine him saying anything like that.

We were quiet for a minute.

Dr. Skyler broke the silence. "You said sometimes you think

dying would be easier. Easier than what?"

"Easier than having to control myself for the rest of my life."

"What would happen if you stopped trying to control yourself?"

"I would be fat." (Obviously!)

"Are you sure?"

"Positive. Self-control is the only thing that keeps me from being enormous."

"Is being fat worse than dying?"

"Yes. To me, it is."

"I see. You would rather be dead than fat."

"I don't want to be either."

"I understand."

She picked up a notebook from the table in front of us. "Sometimes it helps me to jot down notes about things I want to explore later. Is that okay with you?"

"Sure." Weird to have a doctor ask your permission.

"Let's be analytical for a minute. How do you know your body wants to be fat?"

"Because all I want to do is eat."

"You conclude your body eats because it wants to be fat, correct?"

"Yes."

"Is it possible your body does not actually *want* to be fat?"

"I don't know if it wants to be fat, but as long as it can eat, it doesn't care."

"Your body wants one thing, and your mind wants another."

"Exactly." She is listening. She gets it.

"Do you think it's possible that your mind and body could have the same goal?"

"No way. One wants to eat, and the other wants to be skinny." Maybe she doesn't get it.

"What if both parts have the same goal—to be happy?"

"I don't think so. Being fat won't make me happy."

She jotted something. "Are you interested in doing a little experiment?"

"I guess so." Curious.

"For one week, let your body be in control. When you find your mind arguing with what your body wants to do, take note of it, and let your body win."

"Let my body be in control of everything? Like when I don't want to get up for school, just let it stay in bed?"

She laughed. "You will have to decide, but when it comes to matters of eating, let your body be in control."

My body in control. Mayhem. Obesity. Destruction.

"That makes me really nervous. Do you know how much

weight I could gain in a week?"

"You might be surprised. Listen to what your body is telling you. Let it be your guide, just for one week."

Eating anything I want for a week sounds kind of fun. Terrifying, but fun.

"Do you keep a journal?"

"Yes."

"Write down what happens."

"Are you going to read it?"

"If you want me to." She closed her notebook. "Mackenzie, the future is filled with possibilities, but you're going to have to do the work if you want to get better. Are you up for the challenge?"

"I hope so." Doubtful if you put my body in charge.

"The most important task you face immediately is not throwing up. Can you stop?"

"I can try."

"Will you stop forcing yourself to vomit?" Her eyes locked on mine.

"Yes." My face burned.

"Good. That is your number one objective, above all else."

I started crying again. "I'm so embarrassed."

"There is no reason to be embarrassed. We each have our

own journey. Changing behavior takes practice. Every single time you resist the urge to vomit, you get stronger. Every time you listen to your body, you get stronger."

"But what if I can't do it?"

"If you find yourself overwhelmed, take a deep breath and think, 'I won't throw up for the next ten minutes.' When those ten minutes are up, take another deep breath and ask yourself if you could wait another ten minutes. Remember, each time, you have the power to decide."

Do I have the power? Doesn't feel like it.

"Would you like to come see me again?" she asked.

"Yes."

She went to her desk and opened an appointment book.

"How about one week from today, same time? That would be March 15th."

"Okay."

She wrote on an appointment card and handed it to me.

"You are welcome to call me, if you need support."

"Thank you." Her card was white with black lettering and an orange flower.

Dr. Katherine Skyler, Clinical Psychologist

She walked me to the door. "I look forward to seeing you next week, Mackenzie."

I wanted to throw my arms around her, but instead I shook her outstretched hand.

"Thank you, Dr. Skyler."

I can breathe. I'm going to be okay. Well, maybe. Put my body in control for a week? Insane!

When I got home, there were grilled chicken sandwiches and salad out on the counter, ready to eat. Go, Mom! My first thought was to skip the bread, but I really wanted it. I decided I might as well start listening to my body now and I ate everything, including an ice cream sandwich for dessert. All I can think about is how long it's going to take to undo the damage my body is going to cause this week. Won't take long to prove to Dr. Skyler that my body does NOT want me to be happy.

MARCH 9 · THURSDAY

WEIGHT 114

I ate an enormous bowl of granola for breakfast. Delicious.

At break, I drank the diet soda I brought from home and hoped someone would have a good lunch they felt like sharing with me. No luck.

My body was furious. "Hello? Help me out here. I need food! Tomorrow you better bring something good to eat. And you better feed me today when we get home."

My head pounded through my classes. My stomach growled my new rules like a mantra:

1. Don't throw up
2. Listen to my body

In a way, it was peaceful. No decisions. No arguments.

When I got home, I inhaled a blueberry yogurt and drank a glass of water. It was a nice change to drink water simply to quench my thirst.

I contemplated eating a grilled cheese sandwich.

Mind: Bad idea

Body: Grilled cheese. Grilled cheese. Grilled cheese.

Mind: Fine, you'll see.

As I was buttering bread, Maddie came in from the garage.

"What are you making?"

"Grilled cheese."

"Will you make me one?" She made a heart with her hands.

"If you clean up the kitchen."

"Deal." Maddie pulled up a stool and munched on M&M's.

I ate a handful too, acting like it was the most natural thing in the world. I enjoyed pretending to be casual about eating, but inside I was having a heated argument.

> Mind: You can't eat M&M's and grilled cheese and not get fat.
>
> Body: Why not? Maddie does.
>
> Mind: You're not Maddie.
>
> Body: (Folding arms and stamping feet.) Well, that's what I want.
>
> Mind: Fine.

I tossed a few more M&M's in my mouth.

I handed Maddie a sandwich, and she took a bite and stretched the cheese out like a commercial. "This is delicious. You should cook more often."

"Maybe *you* should cook more often."

"I just mean you're good at it. This is fun."

Maddie took a deep breath. "If I tell you something, promise not to tell anyone?"

"Promise." God what now?

"Alexis is secretly seeing Tyler again."

"What?...How?...Where?...WHY?"

"He drives her home after school and leaves before Rachel gets home from volleyball practice."

"After everything that happened? I can't believe it. We have to tell Rachel."

"No way! I told Alexis I would keep it a secret."

I thought for a minute. "What if we get Rachel to go home early, so she finds them?"

"I can't imagine doing that to Alexis."

"What other choice do we have? You obviously want to do something, or you wouldn't have told me. It's your duty as her friend."

She took a deep breath. "You're right, it is."

"Let's see...Rachel doesn't have practice on Fridays, so he won't go over tomorrow, but I'll work on a way to get her home early on Monday."

"Thanks so much, Mack."

It felt nice to be on the same side as Maddie. United, once again, to help Alexis. On a mission to destroy the evil Tyler.

MARCH 10 · FRIDAY

WEIGHT 115

7:00 a.m.

ONE HUNDRED AND FIFTEEN POUNDS!
Fuuuuuuuuuuuuck.

Body, you're a monster! Dr. Skyler has no idea what she is
unleashing by letting you run free.

"I'm not against you." That's my body talking. So weird. I
wasn't trying to stage a conversation like I did in the kitchen. My
body's voice came out of nowhere.

Since it feels the need to speak up, I feel the need to
respond.

> Me: Then how do you explain how everything you do
> takes me away from what I want?
>
> Body: Maybe you don't know what you want.
>
> Me: Maybe you're full of shit.

Stupid body. This is the first time I have talked to myself in
my journal. Or is that what I'm always doing?

Rachel just sent out an invite to her "Pre-St. Patrick's Day
Party" tonight. Her dad has a last-minute business trip to New

York. I'm going over after school to help set up.

MARCH 11 · SATURDAY

WEIGHT 115

1:00 p.m.

I just got home from Rachel's.

Hold on to your hats—or your seats—or whatever they say...

In preparation for the party, we filled a big dispenser with vodka and lemonade and added green food coloring. Rachel asked if I wanted to try it, just to make sure it was good.

Normally, my response would be no, but I stopped to question this time. I was sure I heard my body..."Come on, you should at least taste it."

Fine. Bring it on body. Cheers to you.

It was delicious, and I continued tasting throughout the afternoon. By the time people started arriving (whenever that was), I was hammered. My body made me do it. <u>The real me would never let that happen!</u>

THE MACKENZIE TIMES
Hazy Edition

CONFIRMED: FORMER BEST FRIEND IS AN ASSHOLE
MACKENZIE LETS CAT OUT OF THE BAG

SURPRISE TWIST: DOUBTS EMERGE REGARDING BEST FRIEND'S SUSPECTED STATUS ABOVE

I was dancing in the living room when London walked in the front door with Diego. She didn't even have the courtesy to pretend they arrived separately! I walked straight up to them and went bat shit crazy.

Skye walked over in the middle of my tantrum and moved us into one of the bedrooms. Snippets from our conversation:

London: You're self-absorbed and thoughtless.

Me: Where were you when I was in the hospital?

London: Where have you been for the last three months? I'm done with this shit, Mack.

She stormed out. I went to the kitchen, where I found Rachel doing shots at the counter with a bunch of people, including Diego and Tyler. Yes, Tyler.

Me: Rachel, why the hell are you hanging out with this asshole?

Rachel: Mack, it's time to let it go.

That was it. I couldn't keep the secret anymore.

Me: Tyler, do you wanna tell Rachel what's going on, or should I?

Tyler: What are you talking about?

Me: You know exactly what I'm talking about.

Tyler: Mack, you're drunk. I'm sure you're as clueless as always.

Me: Rachel, I promised Maddie I wouldn't tell, but I can't keep it a secret anymore. Tyler is sleeping with Alexis.

Rachel: No way. That's impossible.

Tyler: Where the hell did you get that one? What a joke.

Rachel: How could you make that up, Mack?

Me: I'm not making it up. I swear it's true.

At that moment, London came to my rescue. *That* I remember very clearly.

London: Rachel, you know Mack would never make that up. Tyler is lying.

I was totally shocked.

Tyler: You bitches are all crazy. I'm out.

We heard the front door slam.

"I have to find Alexis." Rachel walked out of the kitchen.

"Why did you do that?" I asked London.

She shrugged. "I know you, Mack. I also know Tyler."

I wondered if she did it more out of love for me, or hate for Tyler, but I don't really care. My best friend is back. I'm willing to forgive and forget it all.

"Come on," she said.

I followed.

We found Rachel talking to Alexis and Maddie by the pool.

"Thanks a lot," Maddie said when I walked up.

I rubbed my fist in a circle on my chest. "Alexis, I'm really sorry. Are you okay?"

Alexis was crying. She nodded and touched her thumb to her chest with her hand sideways. *I'm fine.*

London said, "Alexis, how can you be with someone like him? You're so much better than he is."

She put her fingers to her lips then pulled her hand to the side with her thumb out. "*Better?!* No guys ever talk to me. Better? How?"

Rachel said, "In every way. You're beautiful and smart and funny. Tyler is nothing." She put her hands together in front of her and moved them apart to draw an invisible line. *NOTHING.*

Skye had come up with James. He put his hand on Alexis's shoulder. "Alexis, you've got it goin' on. Don't waste your time on trash."

She had been rolling her eyes at our words, but James got through. I practically fell in love with him on the spot. Skye's lucky.

She said, "I get it. I'm fabulous and Tyler is shit." She put her hand to her mouth and out like she was blowing a kiss.

Thank you.

She and Rachel hugged, and we all headed back to the house.

I pulled Maddie aside. "I'm really sorry."

"It's okay. I'm glad Rachel knows." I could smell alcohol on her breath.

"Have you been drinking?"

"Like you have any right to ask. You're wobbling all over the place."

"Yeah, well, I make shitty choices. Don't be like me."

I headed straight to Rachel's room and passed out for the rest of the night.

Part of me is glad I told Rachel about Alexis, but I feel bad that I betrayed Maddie. Am I self-absorbed, like London said? I wonder how much I will weigh by Wednesday. I need to get ready to go out to dinner with my family. Dreading what my body has in store for me. 130 here I come!

...

9:00 p.m.

Back from dinner. I hadn't planned to write again today, but the evening's events are spinning in my mind and I must get them out.

We ate at the Fish House. My body wanted fish and chips—no surprise there.

> Mind: Are you sure you wouldn't prefer a nice grilled piece
> of halibut, with a side of asparagus?
> Body: Absolutely positive. Fish and chips!

I obeyed. Yum! I devoured the entire plate and was feeling pretty happy, until I noticed Dad staring at me.

"What?"

"Nothing. I just haven't seen you eat like that for a while."

"Oh." AND?! What the hell are you trying to say?

Mom was glaring at him.

"Are you proud of me for finishing my dinner?" I flashed my best fake smile.

"Always good to eat what you order. Wouldn't want to eat like that all the time, though."

"What's that supposed to mean?" I forced myself not throw my glass of water at his head.

"Doesn't mean anything. Fried food isn't good for anyone."

"Thanks for the advice. Very helpful."

Mom interrupted. "I'm glad you enjoyed it, Mack."

Maddie took a piece of bread from the basket and

concentrated on buttering it.

Dad turned to Mom. "You can't always do what you want. Sometimes you need to have discipline."

She spoke through her teeth. "Sometimes, but not when you go out to dinner on Saturday night."

"Any time is a good time for discipline." Dad held his fork up like a professor.

You could literally feel the anger rising.

"Anyway, my fish was good. Thanks for taking us out to dinner, Dad," I said.

Maddie waved her bread. "This is delicious."

Dad frowned. "You're still eating bread? Didn't you just finish your meal?"

My mom pushed her chair back from the table. "Excuse me, I need to use the restroom."

Maddie acted like nothing was happening. "Yeah, so? I'm still hungry."

"Sometimes you just need to stop," Dad said.

Mind and body were in agreement on this one: Shut the fuck up, Dad!

"Whatever." A crumb fell out of Maddie's mouth as she responded. She never buys into Dad's shit. Is she brilliant or clueless? Does she not realize he's warning her that she'll get

139

fat if she eats too much? She probably doesn't even consider the possibility of not being skinny. I envy her immunity to his words.

The car ride was silent, and I headed straight to my room when we got home.

A few minutes later, Maddie knocked on my door. "Can I come in?"

I grunted.

She opened the door and leaned on the doorknob. "After what happened last night, guess we don't have to worry about scheming to get Rachel home early, huh?"

"Guess not." Read my cues, Maddie. Go away.

"Alexis told me she's done with Tyler."

"That's good."

She took a step into my room. "I just wanted to say thanks for sticking up for me at the party."

"What are you talking about?"

"With Tyler? You don't remember?"

I sat up. "Remember what?"

"OMG! After you disappeared Tyler came back and convinced Alexis to come talk to him out front. I secretly followed them. I don't think anyone else knew he was there. He told her Eden wasn't his girlfriend and that your story about him kissing Rachel was bullshit."

"I can't believe he came back. He has zero conscience."

"Yeah, Alexis started crying and he said, 'Let's get out of here.' She started to follow him to the car and I ran up. I'm like, 'Alexis don't leave with him.' Tyler goes, 'Maddie, you're just like your sister—in everyone's business but your own. Leave us alone.'

Then all of a sudden, you burst out the front door. You held Alexis's arm and said, 'Tyler if you ever come near Maddie or Alexis again, I will make sure everyone at this school knows what a total sleaze you are.'"

"I did? Holy shit. Good for me!"

She laughed. "I thought for a minute he was going to hit you, but then he got in his car and drove away."

"Are you sure that's what happened? Were you drunk?"

"Yes, I'm sure. I only had a couple of drinks."

My head reeled. I thought back, and saw myself lying down on Rachel's bed. That's the last thing I remember. I started to think out loud. "Rachel's room faces the front of the house. Maybe you guys were loud and it woke me up." I could see little snippets.

I said, "This sucks not to remember. Don't think I'll be drinking again any time soon."

Maddie said, "I'm the opposite. Forgetting is my favorite part of drinking."

I laughed.

"I'm serious. Don't you wish you could forget things sometimes?" she said.

"I guess so. What's so bad in your life that you need to forget?"

"You act like you're the only person in the world with problems."

"What problems do you have? Other than me borrowing your clothes?"

"You're such a jerk." She turned to leave.

"No, wait. I'm sorry. I'm just kidding."

She folded her arms. "Do you know what it's like being your sister?"

"Obviously not."

"Imagine you have a nice friend who you play with all the time. Then, all of a sudden, she hates you and won't play with you anymore."

"You think of me as your friend?"

"Sure. I mean, I used to. Don't you remember all the things we did together? Clubs and plays, and sneaking to the kitchen after Mom and Dad went to bed?"

"Yeah, I remember." I couldn't help smiling.

"And now you're different."

"Don't you think we're just growing up? It's not like we're gonna put on a play for Mom and Dad and invite the neighborhood kids."

"Yeah, but just because we're older doesn't mean we can't be friends."

I was surprised. "I guess you're right."

I might need a little time to get used to this concept. It's not that I don't like Maddie, but I don't think of her that way. London, Rachel and Skye are my friends. Alexis is Maddie's friend. Maddie is my sister.

"Anyway, I didn't come in here to beg to be your friend, I just wanted to say thanks."

I was lost in the idea of having no memory of the event.

She huffed.

"What's wrong?"

"Nothing, you're just being you." Her eyes welled up.

"Maddie, you're my sister and I love you. I'll work on being a better friend." I stood up and gave her a hug.

"Thanks, Mack. Good night." She closed my door.

Maddie is very sweet. I wonder if that gene skipped me. Good night.

MARCH 12 · SUNDAY

WEIGHT 115

I can't believe I'm relieved to be holding at 115. Sad state of affairs!

I was just reading what I wrote about the party and contemplating whether or not to share it with Dr. Skyler. Maybe I will, maybe not.

This morning Maddie made pancakes. My body was ecstatic. Brain, not so much.

I sat down at the table. "Where's Dad?"

Mom patted my hand. "Good morning, Mackenzie. He went to check on a project."

"Good morning." I rolled my eyes. Mom has a thing about entering a room with a greeting. "What project?"

"Oh, I don't know." She sighed.

> Body: Hooray! No Dad. I can eat in peace.
>
> Mind: Don't go overboard. You ate fried food last night.
>
> Body: Pan-cakes. Pan-cakes. Pan-cakes!

I took a bite. "These are delicious."

"Thanks." Maddie smiled and returned her attention to her phone.

Neither Mom nor Maddie seemed to notice or care how

many pancakes I ate. I stopped counting at three.

Mom said, "I'll do the dishes, Mads. Thank you for breakfast."

"Awesome." Maddie put her plate in the sink and headed towards her room.

Mom squeezed my hand. "I'm sorry I haven't had a chance to talk to you."

"About what?"

"About how you're doing, about Dr. Skyler, about everything. Are you okay?"

"I guess so."

"You look good."

"Good, how?"

"Healthy."

"Healthy, as in fatter?" Anger rising.

"You know that's not what I mean."

"Are you sure?"

"Yes, I'm sure. Your cheeks have more color. Your face isn't as drawn."

"See? That means I'm fatter."

"Honey, you were frightfully thin before the dance."

"You think so?" My heart leaped in happiness, followed by instant panic that I was no longer thin.

"Yes."

I narrowed my eyes. "Why didn't you say anything if it was so frightful?"

"I keep asking myself the same thing. Sometimes you're hard to talk to."

"So, you're saying it's my fault you didn't say anything?"

"No, not at all. It's completely my fault. I'm just trying to figure out how I kept ignoring the signs. I convinced myself time after time everything was fine; that you were a normal teenager with normal struggles."

"If it makes you feel any better, I don't think it would have made a difference."

"No?"

I thought about it while I swirled a piece of pancake in syrup. "I don't know. I guess it depends on what you said."

"What should I have said?"

I have no idea.

"Is there anything I can say now that would help?"

"Mom, sometimes I want you to have the answer. I don't want to tell you what to say. Do you know what I mean?"

We were quiet for a minute.

She wiped her eyes with a napkin and took a deep breath. "I know exactly what you mean. I love you, Mackenzie."

I wiped my own tears. "I love you too, Mom."

Even though Mom has no answers, I'm happy she cares.

She stood up and kissed the top of my head. "I'll do the dishes."

"I'll help you." I think my body said that—it's a lot nicer than I am.

My body is like Santa Claus—jolly, nice, and fat. I like Santa Claus, but I don't want to BE Santa Claus. But, how can you not be what you are? Honestly, I would much rather be mean and thin. Nightmare Before Christmas-style!

MARCH 13 · MONDAY

WEIGHT 116

I'm having a serious problem with this number. One hundred and sixteen might as well be one hundred and twenty. The only thing preventing a total breakdown is knowing there are only two more days of my totalitarian body regime. Part of my brain is enjoying the time off, but mostly I'm terrified about what I'm allowing to happen. Miraculously my clothes still fit, but I'm avoiding the mirror.

Today, I was walking through the quad and I saw London and Diego arguing. I'm not sure what possessed me, but I walked over to them.

London's face was red. "So it meant nothing to you?"

I coughed. "Sorry to interrupt." Right out of a bad movie.

"I'm glad you did." London took my arm. "Let's go."

She pulled her arm away after a few steps.

The bell rang.

"Do you want to talk?" I knew she used me as an excuse to get away, but I still hoped it meant she wanted to be friends again.

"I have to go to class." She wiped her eyes.

"One tardy isn't going to kill us. Come on, talk to me."

"Fine."

We sat down on a nearby bench.

She put her head in her hands. "I'm such a fool."

I didn't say anything.

"I thought he loved me. He told me I was special."

I wasn't quite ready to be sympathetic. "Did you get together with him when I was in the hospital?"

"No! We were just talking about you."

"Is he the reason you didn't come visit me?"

"Not really."

Saying those words out loud brought back fresh hurt and my eyes welled with tears.

"Why didn't you come see me? I thought you were my best friend."

"Friendship goes two ways, Mackenzie. I have problems too, you know."

I started crying.

She stood up. "Don't turn this around and make it about you."

I faced her. "I'm not. You totally left me and you liked my boyfriend—or whatever he was."

"He liked me before I liked him."

"What the hell does that matter?"

"After Niko, it felt really good to have someone want me."

"You didn't care that I liked him?"

"I TOLD you I didn't get together with him." She raised her voice.

"You did eventually."

"I needed a friend. I couldn't stand being alone. No best friend, no boyfriend, no one."

Wave of guilt. "I didn't realize you felt so bad."

"Well, how could you? You're all, Diego, Diego, Diego, and me-this, and Maddie-that, and I'm so fat, and on and on."

Huge stomach punch. My cheeks burned.

A campus guard walked by and told us to go to class.

I walked away.

Right now I feel angry, guilty, and stupid. I guess when London stood up for me against Tyler, it was more about Tyler than me.

MARCH 14 · TUESDAY

I lost a pound. Spooky.

Skye wasn't at school today or yesterday. I texted her and she said she was sick. I told her I was going to bring her a get-well smoothie, and she said I shouldn't because she might be contagious. I did it anyway.

> Me: Check your porch.
>
> Skye: Yum. Thank you! 😊

See? I'm not a terrible friend to everyone.

London and I haven't talked since yesterday. Maybe if she had told me her problems in the first place, I would have told her mine. Or maybe if I had shared mine a long time ago, this never would have happened. Anyway, I'm still mad, but I hope we can work it out.

Tomorrow is the end of my body's reign! Truthfully, we've had some good times—grilled cheese and pancakes—but I'd like to get back to the business of being skinny again.

MARCH 15 · WEDNESDAY

WEIGHT 115

Lunch today was dismal. Rachel had to stay in the office because she got caught (for the millionth time) using her phone in class. Skye is still out sick, and London was at her internship. I munched on pretzels and tried to focus on my very important (non-existent) text conversation.

After school, I warmed up a frozen bean burrito and did homework until it was time to leave for my appointment.

Dr. Skyler

I was feeling pretty low when I arrived at Dr. Skyler's office.

We sat in the same chairs as last time. Her hair has a streak of gray in the front that makes her look young and old at the same time.

"How was your week?" Dr. S looks like she cares—she reminds me of Mom. I wonder if it's just an act.

"Okay, I guess. I gained a pound." I studied my legs.

"How do you feel today?"

"About my body?" I compared the size of my legs to hers (about the same).

"Is that what is most on your mind?"

"It's always on my mind." I studied my hands. Were they fatter?

"Is there something you would like to talk about?"

"What do you mean?"

"I sense you are preoccupied."

"Yes, I guess I am."

"Do you want to talk about it?"

"It has nothing to do with why I'm here. It's not about my weight or food or anything."

"I believe everything we think and do is connected."

I thought about that for a minute. "Well, I'm just thinking about my best friend, London. We got in an argument."

"What was it about?"

"Well, I was mad—still am—that she didn't come see me in the hospital. And then she started going out with the guy I liked."

"London is your best friend?"

"Supposedly. See—isn't that lame?"

"Sounds like you are angry with her."

"Very."

"Is there more to it?"

I thought about keeping the rest to myself. I still had the

153

chance to paint myself as the innocent victim, and have Dr. Skyler on my side.

"Not really."

I studied her and decided she probably didn't care if I was the victim or not.

"Well, what's really bothering me is, she said I'm a bad friend, and have been for a long time."

"Could she be saying this to justify her behavior?"

"Yes! Again, that's totally lame, right?" Vindicated! I knew Dr. S got it.

"But that's not what is really bothering you."

I nodded. "I wonder if she's right."

"Right about what?" Dr. Skyler made a note.

"That I'm a bad friend."

"How do you define being a good friend?"

"Loyal, trustworthy, supportive." I counted on my fingers.

"Do you consider yourself those things?"

"Yes."

"But?" She raised her eyebrows.

"I know I'm loyal and trustworthy, but maybe I'm not supportive. Not on purpose, but maybe I don't listen, or give my friends what they need."

"What makes you think that?"

"London said I only think about myself. My sister said the same thing."

"Is that true?"

"No. I mean, I'm always worrying about my weight, but I always think about my friends and my family, too."

"Maybe you are considering the way in which you think about them."

"What do you mean?"

"You said maybe you don't listen."

"Right. I keep wondering why London didn't tell me something was wrong. But maybe she tried, and I didn't listen. I wonder if my other friends feel the same way." It was all beginning to form a horribly clear picture. Please don't let this be me.

"Does London listen to you?"

"I don't know. Maybe. Sometimes."

"Was she able to help you?"

"She didn't know I needed help."

"Why?"

"I didn't tell her." And I'm mad she didn't tell *me*? Shit.

"Do you think if she were a better listener, you might have told her?"

"Doubt it."

Dr. Skyler was quiet.

I thought about it a little. "Maybe if she had asked me or said she was worried. Maybe."

"Mackenzie, we all have room to improve our listening skills. Communication, like friendship, goes two ways. Listening is only half of the equation."

"So, it's only partly my fault?" Oh yay!

"You might get closer to the truth if you stop trying to assign the blame."

"So, it's no one's fault?"

She chuckled.

"Do you want to know whose fault it is, or do you want to mend your friendship?"

"Mend our friendship. But I don't want it to be all my fault."

"I encourage you to suspend your judgment. Instead of assigning blame, examine your actions and intentions."

How am I supposed to do that, I'd like to know! She makes it all sound so simple.

"See if you can identify when your actions have supported your friendship with London, and when they have not. Making a list can be helpful. Examine the intentions behind your actions."

I wrote down a reminder in my notebook. (I was proud I had remembered to bring it!)

"Since we are talking about relationships, how are things going with your body?"

I had momentarily forgotten about that battle. "Good and bad."

"What is good?"

"I'm more relaxed not having to be in control all the time."

"In control of what?"

"Eating."

"Who controls it?"

"Right now, my body."

Dr. Skyler made a teepee with her hands under her chin. "How does your body control your behavior?"

"If I listen to it, it tells me what it wants, and I do it."

"Does your body ever listen to you?"

"Only when I force it to."

"Do you think your mind and body could ever be in agreement?"

"I doubt it. They never have been."

"Never?"

I considered.

"Well, maybe when I was little, I did what I wanted. I didn't

157

know any better, so I wasn't trying to control myself."

She opened her notebook and wrote: C-O-N-T-R-O-L. Then she tore the page out and handed it to me.

"Will you hold on to this for me?"

"Sure." I took the page. For now? Forever? Why?

"Are you open to trying a quick visualization exercise?"

"Okay." Bring it on, Dr. S.

"Close your eyes and inhale deeply. On your exhale, picture all your control exiting with your breath."

I inhaled and exhaled. I pictured my control floating away. Scary.

Her voice was matter-of-fact, not like a hypnotist from a movie, like I had expected.

"We are going to visit your body. On your next inhale, enter your body with your breath. As your breath travels down into your lungs, let it carry you inside your body. Keep traveling down until you reach your stomach."

I took a deep inhale and imagined myself swimming down my esophagus like a frog.

"On your exhale, picture yourself sitting comfortably in your stomach. Look around and notice how it feels and sounds. It is perfectly fine if it isn't clear to you."

I exhaled and pictured myself taking a seat. It was pitch

black and silent.

"Now picture your body walking in to greet you."

I could see my body. She was smiling and had a bounce in her step. When she hugged me, I automatically hugged her back. Warm and loving.

Dr. Skyler continued, "Your body says, 'I hope you will come see me again soon.' Then she squeezes your hand and walks away."

She paused.

"Now inhale deeply, and on your exhale, travel with your breath up and out of your body. When you are ready, open your eyes."

I inhaled, then exhaled slowly, picturing myself swimming up, up, up, and out. I opened my eyes.

Dr. Skyler was gazing out the window. "How did that feel?"

"Interesting." Bizarre. Silly. Cool.

"Do you want to talk about your experience?"

I was quiet.

"Do you have a question?"

"I do...When I visualized meeting my body, it was friendly."

"Yes?"

"But my body is actually against me. I weigh a pound more than last week, and I if I keep eating like it wants me to eat, I'll weigh at least another pound more next week."

She sat forward on her seat. "Would you consider not using the scale for a week?"

"The scale is the only thing that keeps me thin—or not gigantic, anyway."

"I know I'm asking a lot."

"I don't know. I'll think about it." I pictured myself at 200 pounds and felt on the edge of hysteria.

"Just consider the possibility. That's all I'm asking. Our time is almost up."

Phew! My head was about to burst with all these new concepts.

Dr. S rose from her chair. "Next week, same time?"

"Yes. Thank you." I followed her to the door.

The sun was still shining, and I had a new kind of "fresh start" feeling—like the beginning of something completely different.

MARCH 17 · FRIDAY

WEIGHT 100

5:00 p.m.

I don't really weigh 100 pounds, but it was fun to write.

I decided to take Dr. Skyler's scale challenge. Depending on the minute, I'm either scared to death, or inspired. I moved it to my closet shelf so I won't be tempted to step on it, and I felt a fleeting moment of happiness. I might weigh less just not having the weight of my weight on my mind. Ha! I'm considering extending my body's reign for one more week—it's a nice break to not fight with myself.

There's another beach party tonight. I asked London if she wanted to grab dinner before. I'm not totally over Diego, but I can't let a stupid guy come between us. And he's not the only problem, so I guess we just have to figure it out.

Lunch convo today:

Skye: I'm not feeling up to the party.

Rachel: Are you sick?

Skye: No. Just don't feel like going.

Rachel: A party will lift your spirits.

Skye: Yeah, maybe.

Rachel: Maybe? Totally! (puppy dog eyes) Pleeeease?

Skye (laughing): All right.

Rachel: Yay!

Me: Want to come to dinner with London and me?

Rachel: Sorry, plans with Dax.

Skye: I'll probably go with James. He'll be glad I changed my mind. He says I'm no fun lately.

Me: Okay.

I'm picking up London in an hour and I'm talking to myself about what to eat tonight.

Mind: Zero interest in consuming alcohol, thank you very much.

Body: That was you, not me.

Mind: Silence

Could my body be right? Who's in charge of this shitshow anyway?

MARCH 18 · SATURDAY

9:00 a.m.

THE MACKENZIE TIMES
Drama Drama Drama

SUSHI STRAIN
DIEGO AND LONDON: A NEW CHAPTER
RACHEL TORNADO STRIKES AGAIN

Last night I picked up London and we drove to dinner in silence. She texted the entire ride.

We ordered three sushi rolls to share.

> Brain: These have a million calories!
>
> Body: Ignored.
>
> Brain: YOU'RE GOING TO GET FAT!
>
> Body (humming to itself): Not listening.
>
> Brain: You still have time. Control the damage!
>
> Me to Body: Since you're in control here, will you please tell my brain to shut up?
>
> Body: Don't worry, you're fine.
>
> Brain: 😶 (Remained eerily quiet for the rest of the meal.)

"Nice work, body!"

But who said that? Not my brain. Not my body. I have created a third personality.

I wish I could explain these thoughts more realistically—all that took about twenty seconds in my head. When I write, they sound sequential and logical, but inside it all happens practically at once, like a bunch of people talking over each other.

After I finished the conversation with myself, I tried to talk to London.

Me: How's your internship going?

London: Good.

Me: Did you finish that history packet?

London: Yeah, nightmare.

Me: Who do you think will be there tonight?

London: The usual suspects.

Me: Is Diego going to be there?

London: Yeah.

At that point, I couldn't take it anymore.

"I hate talking to you like this, London."

She took a drink of water. "Like what?"

"Like we're strangers. Like we haven't been friends since we were five."

"I feel like you don't know anything about me," she said.

I was quiet.

"I think Diego knows more about me than you do."

I blinked back tears.

"Sorry. It's just, I've been mad at you for so long."

"Why didn't you say anything? What did I do?"

Silence.

"I'm not a mind reader, London. I get you think I'm selfish and I don't listen, but how am I supposed to fix it if you won't talk to me?"

"I don't know. I'm just not ready to talk to you yet."

"Am I supposed to keep trying to be your friend while you sit around righteously holding a grudge?"

"Hey, I agreed to come to dinner."

"Wow, I should be so honored."

We ate the rest of our food in silence. The conversation killed my appetite, so I suppose you could consider that a silver lining.

I thought to myself, "Hey, body, did you know this would happen? Is this why you said I was fine?"

I was grateful to have myself to talk to.

When the server came by, I asked for the check. She asked if we wanted a box. We answered "no" at the same time. In the old days, we would have laughed at that, but we didn't even make eye contact.

We split the bill and headed down the street for my car. London lagged behind and texted (Diego, I assumed). I wanted her to trip.

On the drive, I blared the music and she stayed glued to her phone. We got off the main highway and drove down a hill to find the party. It's the perfect hiding spot. If we had a bonfire in plain sight, the police would break it up before we could even get started.

I parked, and London immediately got out of the car and headed towards the beach. I stayed and applied lip gloss to show I wasn't even remotely interested in walking with her.

Dax and Rachel pulled in. I got out and Rachel opened her door.

"Daaahling, it's so good to see you." She hugged me and stumbled when she let go.

Dax caught her. "Take it easy there."

She pulled her arm away. "I don't need any assistance, thank you very much."

She weaved towards the beach and called over her shoulder, "You guys coming, or what?"

Skye and James pulled up.

James and Dax performed a slide-grip handshake. "What up?...Hey, bro."

Skye and I hugged.

"Is that Rachel?" She squinted.

"Yep."

"Where's London?"

"She went ahead."

Skye searched my face. I shrugged.

James put his arm around Skye. "We gonna stay in the parking lot all night?"

The full moon made it easy to see as we walked down the path to the party. We found Rachel talking to Eden and some other people.

Dax put his hands around Rachel's waist, and she leaned her head back and gave him a long kiss.

I struck up conversation with Eden in an attempt to distance myself from their PDA. "How's it going?"

"Good. How's it going with you?"

"Fine. Do you know who got this party together?"

"Yours truly." Eden gestured like a benevolent queen.

"Nice. Tyler too?"

"Nope. I've had enough of Tyler. You need anything to drink? I have a secret stash."

"No, thanks. I'm glad you're not with Tyler anymore."

"Yeah, I'm glad I found out what he was up to. Or, I should

say, finally believed it. Thanks. I'm glad you came tonight."

Eden is definitely growing on me.

Rachel and Dax disappeared, and I walked over to the bonfire where Diego was sitting alone. I don't know what came over me, but I sat down right next to him.

"Hey Diego."

"Hey Mack."

"Where's London?"

"I'm not sure." He squinted into the darkness, face glowing like a Greek god—an otherworldly commercial for camping. I hoped my red cheeks were disguised by the firelight.

"Mack, I'm really sorry about everything that happened."

I was stunned.

"I know it was lame not to go to the hospital. I was totally freaked out, and Skye seemed like she knew what to do. I just let her handle it."

I said nothing.

"And then I was too embarrassed to come see you, and then so much time had passed I didn't know what to say."

Happiness and anger flooded me. "Let's see...How about... oh I don't know...maybe, *Are you okay, Mack?*"

"Agreed." He sighed. "But I did ask London to tell you for me."

"Yeah, let's talk about London."

Silence.

"I never meant this to happen," he said.

"What do you mean?"

"I mean, London and me—we just happened."

"How do you just happen?" If you could literally turn green from jealousy, I would have been neon.

"I don't know. She's easy to talk to."

"And I'm not?"

"Not really. Well, not for me anyway."

"Oh." I let that sink in. "Why not?" I squeezed my hands together to hold back my tears.

"I don't know. You just always seem like you have a plan, and I'm always trying to figure out what to do."

"But London isn't like that?"

"No, she's different. Most girls are confusing, like you. But London is straightforward and kind of doesn't give a shit.

"So that's what guys want—a girl who doesn't give a shit?"

"See what I mean? That's not what I said."

"Whatever."

"I'm only talking about me and London. That's it. Not you. Not other guys. Mack, you're great. Everyone likes you. I just don't think we go together."

I couldn't hold back my tears. The pitiful movie played in my head. If everybody likes me, why don't you like me? Pull your shit together, Mack!

He put his arm around my shoulder. "Come on. We can still be friends."

"You really care about London?"

"Yeah, I really do."

Just then, a blast of sand hit me in the face. My first thought was wind, but then I saw London.

"London, what are you doing?" Diego stood up.

"What am I doing? WHAT THE HELL ARE YOU DOING?!" She pushed his shoulders.

"Nothing. We were just talking about you."

"Yeah, right. Mack, you're such an asshole. Do you have to have everything?

I stood up and brushed sand out of my eyes. "Shut up, London. He wants you, okay?"

She turned to face Diego. "You want me?"

"Yeah, I want you." He kissed her on the forehead.

She put her arms around his neck and they started kissing.

Her sleeve slid up and I saw evenly spaced cuts on her forearm. My heart raced—I was pretty sure they were self-inflicted. At camp, I had seen cuts like that on Shayla.

Everything was falling into place. I walked away, towards the ocean. How could I be so blind? If London is cutting herself, there's some bad shit going on. And I had no idea. She probably has every right to kick sand in my face. I sat down and cried until I was out of tears. I could hear Dr. S: *What are your intentions?* I brushed off my jeans and walked back to the party. Ready to be a better friend.

"Mackenzie, there you are!" Rachel came out of nowhere. "I've missed youuuu."

I steered her over to the ice chests and she plopped down on the sand.

I handed her a water.

She squinted at the bottle. "No thank you." She started to pour it out.

I snatched it back. "Stop! Rachel, you're a mess."

"I know you are, but what am I?" She turned her head and threw up into the sand.

I held her hair back and was so glad I wouldn't have to do any cleanup. After she stopped heaving, I shook out a nearby towel and handed it to her.

She wiped her face.

"Can you stand?" I asked.

"Suuuuure I can."

I put her arm over my shoulder. Dax came up.

"Where have you been?" I snarled.

"Rachel said she was going to find you. It hasn't been that long. Chill out."

"Yeah, well it was long enough for her to puke all over the place. I'm going to put her in my car."

"Good idea," he said.

"Don't just stand there, help me."

"Yeah, sure, sorry." He put his shoulder under Rachel's other arm and we started walking.

I said, "Do you think maybe we can put her in your car instead of mine?" Flashback to Skye's dashboard.

"No, your car is better. I shouldn't drive."

"Brilliant."

We laid her down on my backseat and locked the car. I knew how stupid this was, but I wasn't ready to leave. Why should my night have to suffer?

We headed back to the beach.

"Dax, aren't you worried about Rachel?" I asked.

"Why? Cuz she threw up?"

"No, because she's always wasted."

"Well, I'm pretty much always wasted, so no, not really."

Someone yelled, "Hey Dax, we need you."

"Duty calls. Thanks, Mack." He jogged away.

I sat down by the fire next to Eden, London, and Diego.

"Where'd you go?" Eden asked.

"Nowhere."

"I wish we had marshmallows," London said to no one in particular. "Doesn't that sound good?"

"Sounds awesome." I felt embarrassed at how excited I sounded.

London smiled at me like, "We're friends again." It's hard to explain how happy it made me. It's easy to convince yourself that you hate someone—even your best friend—but when they come back, you know it was all a bunch of bullshit. I love London.

Eden stood up. "I just remembered! I DO have marshmallows. But we need sticks or something."

"Diego, you're a Boy Scout. What should we do?" London said.

"I'm not a Boy Scout."

"Duh," London said.

We all laughed.

"I think I have some dry cleaning hangers in my trunk," Eden said. "I'm on a mission." She waved over her shoulder.

London put her hand on Diego's leg. "Can you give me and

Mack a few minutes alone?"

"Yeah, sure." He kissed her cheek. "I'm sure someone around here wants my company." I swear his teeth gave off one of those glinty starbursts you see in old toothpaste commercials.

"God, he's cute." The words came out of my mouth before I could stop them.

London turned to face me. "What are we going to do?"

"About what?" I said, even though I knew what she meant.

"I'm really happy, Mack, but honestly I feel terrible. I swear I didn't try to take Diego from you. Remember how I was always rude to him? I didn't want to like him."

I studied her face in the firelight. "I believe you."

A million pounds flew off my chest.

We both started crying and hugged for a long time. Then we let go and stared at the fire.

"I've missed you so much." London said.

"I've missed you too. I'm sorry I haven't been there for you." She was quiet.

I reached over and put my hand on her sleeve. "Are you okay? I saw your arm when you hugged Diego. I'm sorry I didn't listen. I'm ready to listen now."

London hugged herself and rocked. Tears fell onto her jeans.

I put my arm around her shoulder, and we rocked together

in silence.

All of a sudden, Eden ran up. "Mack, you have to come quick." She put her hands on her knees to catch her breath. "Rachel is screaming and pounding on the windows. What'd you do—lock her in there?"

I jumped up and ran.

I could hear Rachel from the path. "Get me the fuck outa here!"

I pressed my key. The car beeped and Rachel flew out the door—a crimson demon with huge, black-ringed eyes.

She lunged at me. Her vomit-alcohol breath hit me full force and I held up my hands. She stumbled backwards and fell. Shiiiiiit!

I kneeled down to help her. She propped herself up on her elbow. Then her eyes rolled into her head and she fell back to the ground.

London came running up. "What happened?"

"She fell." That was true, right? I didn't push her over, did I?

"Let's move her before everyone sees," London said.

Dax came up. "Here, I'll take her shoulders and you guys take her feet."

In hindsight, it was probably stupid to pick her up.

A small group of partygoers gathered.

Dax smoothed Rachel's hair from her forehead and closed the car door. He put his hands on his hips and swaggered through the crowd. "Nothing here to see. Run along now." Jedi mind trick...*We don't need to see his credentials.* Everyone dispersed like magic.

Crowd: What happened to Rachel?...Did she OD?...I think she and Mack got in a fight.

Dax-Wan herded everyone back to the beach.

He returned a few minutes later and checked on Rachel. "She's gonna feel like shit tomorrow, but she's fine."

I exhaled the breath I felt like I had been holding for twenty minutes.

I had lost interest in festivities. "Think I'll take her home."

"Do you want me to go with you?" London asked.

"No thanks." I knew she didn't want to, but I was happy she offered.

"That's cool of you, Mack," Dax said. "I would, but there's no way I can drive right now."

"No problem." 😟

"You're a good friend," London said.

"Thanks. You have no idea how much that means to me."

When I got to Rachel's house, I couldn't wake her up, so I drove home, parked in the garage, and left her in the backseat.

(unlocked!)

Around 2 a.m., I felt someone shake my shoulder.

Rachel was standing over me. "Why are we at your house?"

"You passed out. I couldn't get you to wake up." *You're welcome.*

"Can I sleep with you?" She sounded like a little girl.

"Sure." I scooted over.

I gave her one of my pillows and rolled over to face the wall.

She snuggled up to my back and hugged me.

"Thanks, Mack," she whispered.

"No problem." I felt like her mom. Poor Rachel.

When I woke up this morning, she was gone.

> Me: Where are you?
>
> Rachel: Ubered home
>
> Me: You OK?
>
> Rachel: Fine. Thanks for last night.
>
> Me: No prob

No texts from London or Skye. I called them both, but neither answered.

...

3:00 p.m.

I showered, then decided to drive over to Skye's. Mom has been so cool lately about letting me take her car.

When I rang the bell, Noah opened the door.

My heart stopped. Since when was Noah this cute?!

"Hey, Noah, is Skye home?" I pretended to look for something in my purse.

He stepped onto the porch and closed the door. It was so unusual, it snapped me out of my embarrassment.

"Is everything okay?" I asked.

His voice was just above a whisper. "Yeah, everything's fine. My dad's not feeling well, so it's better if we talk out here."

I looked at him more closely and my heart pounded out of my chest.

"Skye didn't answer her phone, so I decided to come by." I was talking twice as fast as normal.

"Why don't you wait here, and I'll go see if she's up."

"Okay."

I sat on the bench and scrolled. Rachel rumors had started to emerge, the most popular being *overdose*, followed closely by *knocked out in a girl fight*.

Skye came out, still in her pajamas. "Hey, Mack." She closed the door behind her.

"Hi. Is everything okay?"

"Fine. Everything is always perfectly fine around here." Her eyes were puffy.

She tied her hair in a knot on top of her head. "So why'd you come over?"

"Just wanted to get the scoop on the rest of the night."

"Nothing exciting. Someone threw up in the ice chest. People danced. The usual."

"Your dad must be really sick." Sometimes I'm as abrupt as Maddie!

"Uh, yeah he is."

Not a good question. "Want to go get coffee?" Subject change!

"For sure. I bet Noah wants an excuse to get out of here too. Mind if he comes with us?"

"Sure, that's fine." Way more than fine. I hoped she didn't notice my burning cheeks.

"I'll be right back." She opened the door just enough to squeeze through.

As I walked back to the car, my head was bursting with thoughts. Noah is coming with us! What's going on with Skye's dad? I wish I had spent more time getting ready. At least I showered. Does Noah have a girlfriend? Would he ever like someone who's still in high school? Am I his type? Does he have a type?

I checked my face and put on clear lip gloss. I didn't want to look like I was trying too hard. I started sweating. Calm down, Mack! I rolled down my window and tried to take deep breaths. Thankfully it took them a while to come out.

Skye got in the front seat, and Noah hopped in the back.

He leaned into the front seat. "You guys want to go to Cava?"

He smelled clean—just a hint of soap.

"Sure, that sounds awesome." I answered as if he had just asked me to take a tropical vacation. I prayed the acoustics were bad in the back seat.

"Great." He leaned back.

"Have you talked to London?" I asked.

"Nope," Skye said.

"Should we go by and see if she wants to come?"

"We could," she said.

I looked over at her. "Why do you sound so weird?"

"I think she stayed at Diego's last night."

"Oh." A twinge of jealousy. "It's okay, I'm cool with it."

I checked my rearview mirror and saw Noah's reflection.

"I'm totally over him," I added, and imagined Noah was listening as he stared out the window.

"Wow, that was fast."

Face on fire. "Well, I think they really like each other. Diego's not such a bad guy after all."

"If you say so."

"Really. He just freaked out. He told me he was sorry."

"Well, he still owes me an apology for leaving the whole situation in my hands."

"You're right, he absolutely does," I said. "I'm so grateful to you for calling the ambulance and my parents. Thank you, Skye. Really."

"I'm just glad I could help and that you're okay." She patted my leg.

We got to Cava and found an open table.

"This is a miracle," Skye said.

"It was meant to be." I met Noah's eyes and felt my cheeks go red. "Be right back." I tried to walk slowly towards the restroom.

I stared at myself in the mirror. "Get a grip. Noah is too old for you. You're rebounding from Diego. STOP." I wondered for a brief second if my mind or body was talking, but decided it didn't matter.

I took a deep breath and returned to the table—cool, calm, and collected.

"Did you order?" I didn't sit down.

"No, we were waiting for you," Noah said.

I felt my cheeks burn again—my personal pep talk had been totally useless. Why can't I control the color of my face!?

"Thanks. I'll go order." I was desperate for an excuse to leave the table again.

Noah stood up. "No, I'll get it. My treat. I crashed your party."

Skye said. "Thanks. I'll have an almond milk latte."

"Mackenzie?" Hearing my name come from his lips caused near paralysis.

"Hello?" He raised his eyebrows.

"Oh, sorry. Just thinking. I'll have the same as Skye, thanks." I sat down. I don't even like almond milk.

"Be back soon, I hope."

I watched him walk away. Confident. Strong.

"Mackenzie, what's going on in that head of yours?"

"What do you mean?"

"You know what I mean. I've seen that face before."

"What face?"

"The dreamy face. Do you like my brother?"

"Shhhh," I hissed.

"Oh my God, you do!"

"Shut UP!" I whispered.

She started laughing.

"Stop it. It's not funny."

"I'm sorry, it's just so weird. You've known him since you were five, and all of a sudden you like him?"

"I've practically never talked to him until the other night at your house. You make it sound stupid."

"I'm sorry, it's not stupid, but it's weird to imagine you liking him. And I feel like yesterday you were still in love with Diego."

I sighed. "That's fair, but I'm not now. And I'm not in love with Noah either. I just happened to notice he's cute, that's all. Can we please drop it?"

Noah was returning with our coffees. He set down the tray. "Here you go."

I took a sip of my coffee and grimaced.

He was watching me. "Did I order the wrong thing?"

"No, it's perfect. I was thinking about something else." How can Skye like almond milk?

"I hope your dad's okay. If you ever need anything, you know my family would help," I said.

"I don't think anything will help at this point." A tear rolled down Skye's cheek.

"Is it serious?" I blurted.

Noah put his arm around Skye's shoulder. "It's going to work out."

She pushed his arm off. "Easy for you to say. You get to go to school. You don't have see it all the time."

"I'm trying to come home more. I'm trying to help," he said.

Skye took a deep breath. "I might as well tell you. My dad has a drinking problem."

I was shocked. "It's so hard to believe. Your family seems perfect." I regretted it the minute it came out.

Skye scoffed. "Yep, that's what we're going for. Perfect."

"Come on," Noah said.

"What?" She raised her voice. "Don't you get sick of pretending?"

Noah bowed his head.

"Sorry." She put her head in her hands. "We should probably get back home."

I didn't know what to say, so I just put my hand on her arm as we stood to leave.

Noah held the door for us.

I made eye contact. "Thank you."

"You're welcome."

I know I could be imagining it, but I felt like he meant, "You are welcome." It wasn't, "No prob," or "Sure," or a little nod. He made total eye contact. My heart did a flip flop.

We didn't say much on the way home. I pulled into the driveway.

"Thanks, Mack. I'll text you later." Skye headed to the house.

Noah got out, then peeked his head back in, both hands on the top of the car. "Thanks for the ride, Mackenzie."

"Thanks for the coffee, Noah." Saying his name made my cheeks flush.

"Anytime. See you around."

"Bye."

I keep playing his goodbye over and over in my head. I know he would never like someone in high school, but I'm pretty sure I saw something. Something.

Now I'm home, writing in my journal, dreaming about Noah, and munching on pretzels in my bed.

London hasn't texted. I hope it's all good between us now.

MARCH 19 · SUNDAY

10:00 a.m.

CRISIS. We went out to breakfast this morning and I had pancakes because my body was demanding them. Now I feel fat and horrible and all I want to do is throw up. Just this once. I haven't done it for so long.

But before I do, I'm going to follow Dr. Skyler's advice and wait ten minutes. This way, I will have proof her strategy doesn't work.

To pass ten minutes, I'll write about our remarkably pleasant breakfast: Dad read the paper. Mom did a crossword. Maddie and I talked about going to the beach, which sounded fun until now, because I feel like a fat cow.

Let's see. Wait ten minutes. Listen to my body. I'll move on to what my mind and body are discussing.

Me: What's going on in there? Busy getting fat?

Body: Just chillin'. The pancakes are pretty happy in here.

Me: Well, they might be, but I'm not.

Body: Why?

Me: Because you're making me fat.

Body: Did you enjoy the pancakes?

Me: Yes, they were delicious.

Body: I'm glad.

Me: But not so delicious that it's worth being fat.

Body: The pancakes are turning into energy.

Me: That sounds better than fat.

Body: Think of them as sparkly energy.

Me: I'll try.

So that's my body, living in la-la land, pretending pancakes are sparkly energy and aren't making me fat. Where did that come from anyway? I guess it's what I wish the pancakes were turning into. Even though it's not true, I do feel a little better.

Ten minutes have passed, and I still want to throw up, but I don't feel quite as panicked. Even if I got half of these pancakes out of my body, that would still be helpful, so maybe I can wait another ten minutes.

...

8:00 p.m.

Just as the second ten-minutes ended this morning, Maddie knocked on my door. I'm pretty sure if she hadn't shown up, things would have gone in a different direction.

Somehow Maddie convinced me to go to the beach, and Rachel and Alexis came with us. Neither Rachel nor I brought up Friday night's fiasco. I wonder if she even remembers.

It was overcast, so I wore my big sweatshirt. I was comfortable and unselfconscious, and by the end of the day I had stopped obsessing over the pancakes. I could actually almost see them as sparkly energy.

Tomorrow is Rachel's birthday. I'm sure she'd rather party, but we're going to the movies since it's a school night.

MARCH 20 · MONDAY

11:00 p.m.

No weird vibes at all with London at the movies tonight. But as happy as that makes me, I'm miserable.

I ordered popcorn, candy, and an Icee. I told myself I would only have a little bit of each. It's Rachel's birthday—I should celebrate, right?

> Delusional mind/body chant: I am moderate. I am moderate.

It only took about twenty minutes to finish all of it, and I couldn't stop thinking that I probably weighed at least 120 pounds.

> Brain: Get rid of that food. You're getting so fat. Throw up!

I had a flash of brilliance—I remembered the theater has a single restroom where I could throw up and no one would know.

I felt the familiar sensation of the switch flip, and self-control flew out the window. Or maybe self-control had returned, if self-control is keeping me from being fat. Either way, I felt compelled.

No one paid any attention when I said I needed to use the restroom, and I took this as evidence I was doing the right thing. The stars had aligned.

After I finished, I was filled with relief. It felt so good to be empty, but not hungry (yet). But the relief was quickly followed by disgust and disappointment. After abstaining for so long, the sheer nastiness of vomit was overwhelming. I couldn't believe I did it. I promised I wouldn't. But I did.

"Who are you?" I asked my reflection.

No reply.

I returned to my seat, totally distracted by my mental chatter.

> Body: Why did you throw up? You didn't need to.
>
> Brain: Why did you make me eat all that crap?
>
> Body: I didn't make you.
>
> Brain: Well, I certainly didn't make me.

I don't know who is right. I'm losing this battle. It's like I'm a spectator watching myself being controlled by the shifting of power.

I know Dr. S is going to be mad at me. Maybe I won't tell her.

MARCH 22 · WEDNESDAY

7:00 a.m.

I can't stand myself. I don't even want to see Dr. Skyler today because this is hopeless. I was sure the movies would be a one-time thing, but the floodgates have opened.

I need to get ready for school, but I can't move. Maybe if I write down what happened last night, I will feel better, and I can move on and stop doing this!

Last night was the beloved/dreaded taco night. I ate a couple, then a few more, and a handful of M&M's. The familiar feeling was creeping in. I didn't want to be moderate, I wanted to eat and eat and eat until I didn't want to eat anymore—until it was *impossible* to eat any more.

I had a yogurt, a handful of granola, a slice of cheese, another taco, and more M&M's—all the while, telling myself I just needed to feel satisfied. I would not throw up!

No surprise, as soon as I was so full I felt sick, I convinced myself that throwing up would actually be helping my body. Not only because it would help me not get fat, but also because I was so uncomfortable, I would never be able to sleep if I didn't get rid of the food.

Since I had just thrown up two nights before, I was prepared for the unpleasantness, and I successfully blocked it out. I feel like I'm right back where I started. If I weren't going to see Dr. S today, I know I would be headed straight back down the rabbit hole.

...

9:00 p.m.

Dr. Skyler

I'm back from my Dr. S visit. On the way to my appointment, I decided I would tell her I was struggling, but not admit I had thrown up. I brought my notebook as proof that I've got my shit together.

She opened the door to the waiting room and we shook hands. I felt tears spring to my eyes and I quickly looked away.

We took our same chairs.

"How are things going?" Her voice sounded concerned. Could she tell? Maybe the stupid tears.

"Fine." I tried to remember what I had planned to say.

"Were you able to make a list of actions?"

"No." Totally forgot.

"Have things improved with London?"

"Yes, they are actually a lot better." I realized I hadn't

thought about London since the movies. In fact, I had not thought about anything, except being fat and throwing up.

"I'm glad. Did you talk?...Mackenzie?"

"Sorry. What?" I couldn't focus. Why was I here?

"What's on your mind?"

"I don't know." How was I going to make myself sound like the person I wanted to be?

Dr. S waited.

"Things are a lot better with London, but I'm struggling."

"You seem upset."

"I do?" I thought I was putting on a good show.

"Do you want to talk about it?"

"Yes and no." I wasn't ready to give up. Maybe she was just guessing I was upset. She's not a mind reader. She doesn't know everything.

"Tell me about your conversation with London."

I didn't want to talk about London.

"Mackenzie, you are safe here. You don't have to talk about anything you don't want to. I'm here to help you."

Did she read my mind? I started to cry.

Every time I tried to talk, I would burst into a fresh set of tears.

"It's okay to cry. Take your time."

After a while, I finally composed myself.

"I don't know if I can do this," I said.

"Whether you think you can, or think you can't, you are probably right."

"What do you mean?" Where was her sympathy and encouragement?

"The life you desire is here, if you decide you can have it. You must start with your thoughts."

"But my thoughts are the problem. The thoughts of my brain, the thoughts of my body—I have no control over them."

"Actually, it is possible to control your thoughts. Thoughts disappear unless they are nurtured. If you are consumed by negative thoughts, it means you are providing them with an environment where they can thrive."

She pointed to a picture on the wall I hadn't noticed before:

Our THOUGHTS become our BELIEFS

Our BELIEFS become our WORDS

Our WORDS become our ACTIONS

Our ACTIONS become our HABITS

Our HABITS become our REALITY

"It all starts with our thoughts," she said.

"I feel like my thoughts aren't even mine."

"Maybe we need to start with your thoughts about your thoughts. In order to claim or release your thoughts, you must own them. Whether you feel like they come from your body, or your brain, or somewhere else, they are your thoughts. You can nourish them, or you can let them go. The choice is yours."

I nodded.

"In your notebook I would like you to write down the first three thoughts that come to your mind."

"Right now?"

"Yes."

"Anything?" I had a lot more than three thoughts at the moment.

"Yes."

I unhooked my pen from the notebook cover and wrote:

1. I have no self-control.

2. I am fat.

3. This feels pointless.

"May I see?" Dr. S asked.

I handed it to her.

She read my statements out loud and handed it back.

"Okay, let's start with number one: *I have no self-control.* In this area, if you were exactly how you wanted to be, how would you describe yourself?"

"Maybe...'I'm disciplined'?"

"How do you feel when you say, 'I'm disciplined'?"

"Tense."

"Do you want to be tense?"

"No." Who would want to be tense?

"This time, try to say something about your ideal self that makes you feel happy."

I studied the ceiling and had an inspiration. "I would say, 'My body and brain work together, and I don't fight myself.'"

"Excellent," Dr. S said. "Now cross out the original sentence you wrote and write your new one below."

I did.

"Does every part of that sentence make you feel happy?"

I studied it. "The first part does, but the fight part makes me remember how I feel now, so that doesn't feel as good."

"Would it still be a good sentence if you took out the second part?"

"Yes. Better, actually."

"Cross out your first sentence and write the new one."

I did.

~~My body and brain work together and I don't fight my-self.~~

My body and brain work together.

"Now say it aloud."

"My body and brain work together," I said.

It was missing something. "Can I add to it?"

"Of course—it's yours."

I wrote,

~~My body and brain work together.~~

My body and brain work happily together.

"What did you add?"

I read her the new version.

"How does that feel?"

"It feels good. But, it also feels ridiculous because it's not true."

She gestured to her sign again. "Will you add that to your notebook too?"

I wrote:

Our THOUGHTS become our BELIEFS

Our BELIEFS become our WORDS

Our WORDS become our ACTIONS

Our ACTIONS become our HABITS

Our HABITS become our REALITY

"At the risk of sounding like a teacher, please read it to me," Dr. S said.

I did.

"I never get tired of hearing those words," she said.

"I like them, too."

"May I give you an assignment?"

"Sure."

"I would like you to revise your other two thoughts in the same way you revised the first one. First, let's write down the steps you took today so you can reference them."

I wrote as she said them:

1.   Cross out the negative thought.

2.   Revise the thought in your head and say it out loud.

3.   If the revised thought makes you feel happy, write it down.

4.   Check to see if you can make improvements to the thought.

5.   Continue the above steps until saying the thought out loud makes you feel totally happy.

"Do you think you can do this for the other two thoughts you wrote down?" she asked.

I flipped back the page, and read what I had written:

1. ~~I have no self-control.~~

    ~~My body and brain work together and I don't fight myself.~~

    ~~My body and brain work together.~~

    My body and brain work happily together.

2. I am fat.

3. This feels pointless.

"Yes, I think I can," I said.

"Excellent work, today, Mackenzie."

"Thank you." I was amazed how much better I felt. An hour ago, I had been hopeless and didn't want to tell Dr. S anything. Now I couldn't wait to go home and write delusional sentences about myself.

"Healing starts with our thoughts," she said.

I followed her to the door. I was so glad I came to my appointment.

MARCH 23 · THURSDAY

I revised my other two thoughts tonight in my notebook. It's easier to cross things out with a pen, but I also like to see them all neatly formatted on the computer.

Here's what I came up with:

Original:

1. ~~I have no self-control.~~

2. ~~I am fat.~~

3. ~~This feels pointless.~~

New and Improved:

1. My body and brain work happily together.

2. I am beautiful.

3. My thoughts create my reality.

At first, I replaced "I am fat" with "I am skinny," but when I gave it the feel test, it made me tense and worried about whether I could stay skinny. So, I changed it to "I am beautiful," and even though I don't really believe it, it does pass the happy test. It was easy to fix number three. I feel powerful when I read it.

Tonight Dad was like an alien, in a good way. He ate his dinner slowly and stayed at the table until we were all done.

He asked us if we wanted to go to a new shrimp restaurant tomorrow night.

Mom said, "What's the occasion?"

"No occasion. I heard it's pretty tasty."

"I heard it's good, too," Maddie said.

I think Mom and I must have had similar expressions on our faces, because he said, "Not into shrimp?"

I said, "No, that sounds great."

"Jane? What do you think?"

I can't remember the last time Dad asked Mom for her opinion, or the other way around. I wanted to say, "Hurry, Mom. Please be nice. Don't ruin this."

She said, "Sure, I'll go."

I hoped her lack of excitement wouldn't make him mad. Amazingly, he stayed nice the rest of the dinner.

I have a strange mixed feeling of happy and worried. I feel like something horrible is going to happen, like he's taking us to dinner to tell us he's leaving. Or maybe he has cancer. I take that back! My thoughts create my reality. I'm sure everything is just fine.

MARCH 24 · FRIDAY

The Mackenzie Times

DAD'S SECRET

By Mack Stewart, on special assignment

"What do you think about putting our phones away for the rest of dinner?" Dad said.

My stomach dropped.

Maddie and I put our phones in our laps.

"I would like you to physically separate yourselves from your phones. Put them away."

We tossed them in our purses.

Dad took a deep breath. "Now doesn't that feel better?"

It felt the same.

"What shall we talk about?" he said.

Here it comes…The hammer. The bombshell. The other shoe.

"I read an article about how phones prevent us from connecting," Dad said. "Hence, the phone-free meal tonight." He waved his arms like a magician.

Since when is Dad concerned about connecting?

"What does everyone have going on this weekend?"

"Swim meet Sunday," Maddie said.

"Movies tomorrow night," I said.

Was this Dad's clever way of throwing us off-track? He didn't look like someone who was about to leave his family.

"Mom and I have an announcement to make."

Silence.

"I'm going to be taking some time off work."

"Why?" I braced myself.

"I have a building design I want to work on, and I also want to be around more."

"So, you're leaving work? I don't get it," I said.

"Are you sick?" Maddie had read my mind.

"No, nothing like that."

I studied him. He was relaxed, no evidence of a terminal disease. My mom looked happy and she's a terrible bluffer. My stomach unclenched a bit.

"You're just taking a break from work?" I needed one more confirmation.

"Yep."

"Can I take a break from school?" Maddie asked.

"Sure," he said.

"Really?"

"In about two and a half months, you can take a break for the summer." He and my mom laughed.

"Hilarious," we said at the same time. Maddie, my sister, my friend—I could feel it for a minute.

"Speaking of summer," Mom chimed in. "We have something else to tell you."

Paaaause... "We're going to Hawaii in June, right after school gets out."

Maddie and I both let out a scream. People turned.

"Sorry," we mumbled. So embarrassing.

We spent the rest of dinner talking about snorkeling, scuba, and luaus. It was possibly the most perfect dinner ever. Delicious food. Not a single comment about what I was or wasn't eating. No silent battle between my parents. Just all of us eating and talking like a totally normal, happy family.

MARCH 25 · SATURDAY

Tonight we went to the movies: Skye, James, Rachel, Dax, Maddie, Alexis, and surprise-guest, Noah, who was home for the weekend. Not sure how, but I ended up sitting next to him. He smelled just like he had in the car. Fresh and clean. The movie was scary, and we jumped at all the same places and laughed each time. You know, his smile might be better than Diego's. London and Diego didn't come with us because they had other plans. 🤢 I take back the barf face. I really don't care. Well, maybe a little. It still annoys me. I'm not perfect, okay?

After the movie, predictably, we decided to go to Cava.

"Let's text London," Rachel said.

Yikes! I'm almost comfortable with the idea of being with London and Diego, but the thought of being near Diego and Noah at the same time is a whole different story.

Two seconds later, Rachel said, "Cool. They'll meet us there."

As we headed to the parking lot, I hoped Noah would say he was tired and going home.

Instead, he said, "Hey Mack, want to ride with me?"

My stomach flipped. I know that is an expression, but it literally turned upside down.

I could feel my face turn bright red. I had driven with Rachel and Dax, so I turned to them.

"See ya there," Rachel said.

As soon as Noah turned around, she moved her eyebrows up and down like a cartoon character.

OMG! Could Noah actually like me? Why else would he want to drive with me?

He held open the passenger door of his black truck, and I stepped up into the cab. New car smell. Spotless.

He jumped in the driver's side and started the engine. The music blasted, and he reached over to turn it down.

After a minute he said, "Does Skye seem okay to you?"

I thought about it. "I think so. She's missed school a lot lately, but she seems like the same Skye."

"She missed school?"

"Yeah. Maybe, like, ten days since we came back from break."

"Huh." Noah tapped his steering wheel.

"Do you think something's wrong?" I asked.

"No, she just seems withdrawn."

"Well, it seems like you have a lot going on with your dad. That could explain it."

"Maybe," he sighed. "I just wonder if there's something else too."

"Something going on with James?" I offered.

"Nah, they seem fine. I asked him about Skye, too. He agrees she seems down."

"Honestly, I think she's just upset about your dad."

"You're probably right." He turned the music back up, and my selfish heart sank, as I realized Noah had asked me to drive with him to ask me about Skye, not because he liked me.

We pulled into the parking lot at the same time as London and Diego.

Shit shit shit. I jumped out, waved, and walked quickly towards the front door.

My heart was pounding. There was no way I was going to stand there between two guys who don't like me. Humiliating.

I went straight to the restroom.

Brain/body/whoever else: You're such a fool.

"Your thoughts create your reality," Dr. S's voice said in my head.

I repeated, "My thoughts create my reality. I am beautiful, and my brain and body work happily together."

I felt ridiculous, but a tiny bit better too. I took a deep breath and opened the door.

London was in the hall.

"Oh, hi." I held the door open for her.

"I don't need to go, I was just waiting for you."

"Why?"

"I wanted to say thanks for being so cool about me and Diego."

"No big deal." I immediately felt defensive and self-righteous. Proof positive I am indeed a fabulous friend.

"It is a big deal, Mack. I'm really sorry." Her eyes welled up.

I realized how much I had wanted to hear those words.

I hugged her. "I love you, London."

"I love you, too."

We stood in the hallway hugging, until we heard Rachel's voice, "You girls gonna get a room?"

We laughed, and wiped our eyes.

Rachel put her arms around us.

Then Skye walked up. "What are you doing?"

"We're having a reunion," Rachel said. "Come on."

Skye put her arms around us too, and we stood there in a huddle.

"This is how it should always be," Skye said.

"Amen." Rachel put her arms down.

We all walked back down the hall to where our group was

sitting.

"Did you fall in?" Diego asked.

We laughed. I waited for everyone else to sit first, and the only remaining seat was next to Noah. I felt so happy about patching things up with London, I wasn't worried about Noah anymore. So what if he doesn't like me? He's too old anyway.

Diego and James offered to get the drinks.

Diego to London: Latte, no foam?

She gave him a thumbs up.

Diego and London actually make a pretty cute couple. He totally paid attention when she talked, and at one point, he tucked her hair behind her ear. It was so sweet, it was embarrassing.

When we were leaving, Noah offered to drive me home. I'm sure he felt obligated.

"No, that's okay, Rachel lives so close." I said.

"Sounds good," he said. "See you around."

I was sad he didn't protest.

In the car Rachel asked, "What's up with turning down Noah's ride?"

"He was just being nice. It's totally out of the way."

"Didn't seem like he was just being nice to me."

"I promise, he was."

MARCH 26 · SUNDAY

This morning:

> London: Beach today?
>
> Me: Who's going?
>
> London: You and me
>
> Me: Sounds great
>
> London: Pick you up at 12

We're really back together! I'm so happy.

I wore shorts and a loose t-shirt over my bathing suit.

I wanted to get the scale out of my closet, but I knew I'd be miserable if the number was high, so I didn't.

> Mind: You're in total denial if you think you aren't fatter.
>
> Me (not exactly Mind or Body): I'm beautiful.
>
> Mind: You're such a fraud.
>
> Me: My thoughts create my reality. I am beautiful.
>
> Mind: 😶

The good thing is the beach has a way of making everything better. And London and I are friends again. I wouldn't give that up to weigh 105. And that's saying something!

It felt just like old times as we settled into our chairs and snuggled our toes in the sand.

"How's your mom?" I was determined not to talk about myself.

"Fine, I guess. Why?"

"Just asking."

London was quiet.

I offered her a granola bar from my bag.

"Thanks. Know what I brought?"

"What?"

"Mom's pasta." She held up a cooler bag. "She made me bring a huge container, along with two forks." She rolled her eyes. "She was so happy I was hanging out with you today."

"Really?"

"Yeah, she loves you."

I wondered what her mom had said.

"I don't get it," London said.

"Get what?" I asked.

"My mom acts like she cares, sending me food and shit. Asking me how you are..."

"But?"

"But she doesn't really care. She's never home. She works all the time, and now she's seeing someone, so she's gone at night sometimes, too."

"I'm sorry," I said. "How long has she been seeing someone?"

"She told me about him in January, but I think since before Thanksgiving. I know she can't stay alone forever, but I just want my dad back. Not someone else."

London was right—I didn't know anything about her. I had to bring up what I saw at the party. My heart was pounding out of my chest.

I touched her sleeve. "Is that why you cut yourself?"

London pulled away. "What are you talking about?"

I panicked and wondered if I had imagined it.

"The bonfire, remember? When you were hugging Diego?"

"What does that have to do with anything?"

"Your arm. The scars. I know what they're from, London."

London dug her toes deeper in the sand. "Have you ever done it?"

"No."

"How would you know, then?"

"You know Shayla who works at summer camp with me?"

"Yeah."

"She used to cut herself."

"She doesn't anymore?" she asked.

"I don't think so, but actually, I don't know."

She pulled up her sleeve to reveal evenly spaced lines that ran along the inside of her bicep. They were scabs, not scars.

I winced. I had seen different lines at the party.

She put her sleeve back down. "Pretty, huh?"

"Did you tell Diego? Is that what you mean when you said he knows you better than I do?"

"I didn't tell him, but I think he knows. I wouldn't be surprised if he does it, too."

I couldn't imagine perfect Diego cutting himself. Then again, I couldn't imagine London doing it either.

"I can't stand the thought of you hurting yourself. Is there anything I can do?" I asked.

"Kill the guy my mom is seeing?"

I laughed. "Anything else?"

She gazed out at the ocean. "Just be you. That's all I need."

We spent the rest of the day going in the water and making up stories about people on the beach. Best friends forever.

MARCH 29 · WEDNESDAY

Dr. Skyler

"How are you feeling?" Dr. Skyler asked.

"Not bad." I tried to block out how much I ate last night.

"How are things with London?"

"So much better. Turns out she has issues, too."

Dr. S waited.

I didn't feel like going into it.

"Were you able to rewrite your thoughts?"

I sat up straight like a good student. "Yes, I did. Do you want to hear them?"

"I would love to."

I read, "1. My body and brain work happily together. 2. I am beautiful. 3. My thoughts create my reality."

"Powerful," she said. "Did you find it difficult to write them?"

"No, it was pretty easy."

"I'm glad. Some people find it quite challenging."

"Writing them was easy, but believing them is another story. I like the idea that my thoughts create my reality, but where's the proof?"

"Good question. Would you say you shifted your thoughts this past week?"

"When I could, yes."

"Would you say your reality has changed since last week?"

I thought about it. "Well, I'm friends with London again, but that's because she apologized."

"Do you think anything you did made it easier for her to apologize?"

"Maybe, but can you say that's because I changed my thoughts?"

"I could," she said. "Can you say it's absolutely not because you changed your thoughts?"

"Probably not."

"Are you willing to stay open to the possibility?"

"Yes."

"How are you feeling about your body?"

"I haven't weighed myself, so I'm not sure about that part, but I'm not as worried about how I look. I'm not freaking out anyway."

"How is the relationship between your brain and your body?"

"Not total enemies at the moment. My body mostly controls what I eat, and my brain is trying to chill out a little."

I couldn't keep the truth inside any longer. "I have to tell you something."

She waited.

"I threw up."

She was quiet.

"I didn't tell you last week because I was pretty sure this whole thing was going to be pointless, and I didn't want to hear a lecture."

"Why tell me now?"

"Because I feel different. I feel like I might actually be able to get better and be a normal person, if I work at it, and I don't want that secret to get in the way."

"I'm glad you told me."

I felt lighter.

Dr. S wrote something in her notebook. "You said you might be able to get better. How do you feel when you say that?"

"Hopeful. Skeptical."

"Can you think of how you might revise that thought? Maybe try writing it down."

I opened my notebook.

~~I might be able to get better.~~

I will get better.

She said, "When you're finished, say the new thought out loud."

I said, "I will get better."

"How does that feel?"

"Uninspiring."

"Try again," she said. "Read aloud when you are finished."

I wrote:

> ~~I will get better.~~
>
> ~~I will be healthy.~~
>
> I am healthy.

I said, "I am healthy."

"How does it feel now?"

"Good."

Whose idea was it to change "better" to "healthy?" My body's? My brain's? That other entity I haven't named yet?

"You're frowning," she said. "Why?"

"I feel frustrated. I don't know what part of me is controlling me."

"Do you still have the paper I gave you last week?"

I pulled it out from under the front cover of my notebook and unfolded it.

C-O-N-T-R-O-L

"Write down the first three words that come to mind when you think of the word on the paper."

> Force
>
> Perfection
>
> Tense

"At the risk of sounding repetitive, how do those three words make you feel?"

"Anxious."

"You said you don't know what part of you is controlling you. Do you want to be controlled?"

"No."

"But you think you are being controlled."

"Well, something is making me think and act, isn't it?" It seemed obvious to me.

"Philosophers have long discussed this issue, but for our purposes, let's approach it practically. Try revising your thought, 'I don't know what part of me is controlling me.' Say it out loud when you're done."

> ~~I don't know what part of me is controlling me.~~
>
> ~~Nothing is controlling me.~~

~~I am controlling me.~~

~~I am in control.~~

~~I think and act.~~

I think and act in healthy ways.

I said, "I think and act in healthy ways."

She smiled. "I think you've got the hang of this."

I felt giddy with the unexpected change of perspective.

"I would like to point out you didn't specify your body or your mind, only the single entity, I. What was the first thought you rewrote last week?"

I turned back a few pages in my notebook. All these new thoughts weren't easy to remember—I had just made them up!

I said, "My brain and body work happily together."

"No mention of control," she said.

"True."

"You might consider keeping a separate list of the thoughts you want to nurture. Practice saying them every day."

I nodded. I can do this.

"Our time is almost up. Is there anything else you want to discuss?"

"No, this was really helpful. Thank you."

"Keep up the good work."

Dr. S is my savior. I can't even imagine where I would be right now without her. Actually, I take that back, I know exactly where I'd be...staring into a toilet full of food. I'm so grateful that's not where I am!

APRIL 1 · SATURDAY

3:00 p.m.

April Fool's party tonight at Dax's. It's supposed to rain, so I guess we'll all be packed inside. We probably would be anyway, because the last indoor party was so successful—no neighbor complaints. I'm glad it's cold because I can wear something baggy and comfortable. I'm curious about my weight, but not enough to break out the scale.

We all ate together this morning, including Dad. He's full of surprises lately. After breakfast, he asked me if I would run an errand with him. Huh?? That's as weird as asking me if I would help him with an architecture plan.

He said, "Come on, humor me."

"Where are we going?"

"To get some drawing supplies."

"All right." I didn't have anything else to do, other than sit around and obsess over what to wear tonight.

Dad was almost smiling as we drove. "What's going on?" I asked.

"Not too much."

"Why do you look so happy?" Secret mistress? Secret life?

Secret agent? Super spy?

"I look happy?"

"Well, you're not frowning, like you usually are." I enjoyed having the opportunity to point out this fact.

"I usually frown, huh?" He frowned.

"Yep."

"I guess I'm always thinking."

Guess I'm not the only one.

"So what's new in your world, Mack?"

Trick question? Dad and I never talk like this. It was so weird.

"Not much." It was going to take more than a father-daughter trip to the store to make me want to share with him.

"I remember being a teenager. Did you know I didn't talk to my dad for an entire year when I was in high school?"

"You didn't talk to him at all?" Impressive.

"Not once." He shook his head.

"Why?"

"I got in trouble for cheating in school."

"*You* cheated?" I couldn't imagine.

"Well, we had an assignment, and three of us decided to split up the problems and share our answers. At the time, I thought of it as being efficient, not cheating."

"It's a good idea." Why hadn't I thought of it?

"No, grasshopper, it was a bad idea. You should always do your own work."

I rolled my eyes.

He looked over at me. "That's how I felt about it at the time."

I laughed.

"Anyway, I got suspended and my dad went ballistic. It was the end of my junior year and he said I was throwing my life away."

He took a deep breath. "We yelled and got physical."

"You mean you hit each other?" It was mind-blowing.

"Mm-hmm. And we didn't speak again until my graduation."

"Wow, that's terrible".

"Yeah. There were times I wanted to tell him something, but I wouldn't give in. When I got accepted to college, I could only share my excitement with my mom. I was too stubborn to break the silence."

"He should've broken the silence. He's the dad," I said.

"You're right."

I was? I am? I had expected him to disagree.

"It's hard being a teenager. My dad should have tried to bridge the divide," he said.

Dad found a parking spot and turned off the engine.

"The thing is, Mack, when you get to be a parent you don't know how to make it better. You get wrapped up in being an adult, and it's hard to remember what it was like when you were young. And things have changed so much."

"You and mom did kind of grow up in the stone age."

"We're pretty hip, now, though, huh?" He moved his neck in and out, I assumed trying to be cool.

"Totally."

He laughed. "I'm trying to tell you I'm here for you. For anything."

"Why now?" Part of me was happy, the other part doubtful and still angry.

"Why not?"

"It's just weird. You're not exactly the easiest person to talk to." I flashed back to what Mom had said. And Diego. Ugh. Was I just like my dad?

He sighed. "I know. Your mother has told me that many times."

He reached over and touched my arm. "What I'm trying to say is, I'm trying. I know I need to work on it."

Even though I felt softer, I wasn't quite ready to let go of the awesome feeling that I was holding something over my dad. It was like our roles were reversed.

"Let's go in," he said.

I wandered around and found some notepads and journals.

Dad walked up. "Whatcha got?"

"A journal. I like the cover." It read, *Reality emerges from our dreams*. I was thinking I could use it for my new and improved thoughts.

He tilted his head to read it. "I can see why. Want to get it?"

Shock. "Yeah, I'd love to."

He smiled. "I'm ready. Let's go check out."

Back in the car, I took the journal out of the bag and studied its brightly colored sun. I thought about Dr. Skyler.

"Do you know I'm seeing a therapist?" I said.

"Yes."

"Do you know why?"

"You have some things you are working out." He sounded like he was reading from a script.

"But do you know what's wrong with me?"

"Nothing, I would guess. You're just a normal teenager with normal teenage problems."

Flash of anger. "Do normal teenagers go to the hospital?"

"If they drink too many energy drinks, they do." He chuckled.

"That's not funny at all." I started to cry.

He looked over at me. "I'm sorry. I was just kidding."

"You don't get anything, Dad. You might be trying, but you suck at it."

He drove for a minute, then pulled into a parking lot and stopped the car.

"Mack, please tell me what I don't get."

"Everything." I held myself.

"Kids didn't end up in the hospital too often when I was young, but these days it doesn't seem that unusual. Energy drinks are not good, but I was relieved you weren't drinking or doing drugs. You had a concussion."

"But it wasn't just energy drinks. Didn't mom tell you?" Even though I had begged her not to tell him, for some reason, I thought she had anyway.

"Drugs?" His eyes went wide.

"No. Drugs and alcohol aren't the only teenage problems, you know."

"Can you tell me?"

His obvious relief that I wasn't on drugs made me mad.

"I don't know if I want to."

He sighed. "I understand."

He looked genuinely confused. I wanted to hold onto this moment where I knew more than he did.

I heard myself thinking, "I'm in control here," which reminded me of Dr. S.

I took a deep breath. "Dad, I have an eating disorder. I'm bulimic."

I corrected myself. "I *was* bulimic."

He frowned.

"Do you know what that is?"

"I think so, but I thought only fat people were bulimic."

The implication that he thought I was not fat made me want to hug him.

"Anybody can be bulimic. The goal is to be thin, so you might or might not already be fat. I'm always worried I'm going to be fat."

"Well, everyone has to watch what they eat." He patted his belly.

My heart sank. "You don't get it, Dad."

"No, I don't suppose I do."

We sat there in silence.

My dad squeezed my hand. "Thank you for sharing with me, Mackenzie." His eyes welled up. "Maybe, gradually, you can help me understand. Or maybe I never will. But, I'll read about it too. I'll try to be a better listener."

All of a sudden, I heard my own words to London. I had

been as clueless and self-absorbed as my dad. For a flash, I could see him as a person. Just as quickly, he was back to Dad.

I put my other hand on top of his. "Thanks, Dad. I love you."

We tilted our heads together. We stayed like that for maybe five seconds, then my dad cleared his throat, sat up straight, and wiped his eyes with the back of his hand. He put the car into gear.

When we neared our driveway, he said, "Thanks for coming with me, Mack. This might be one of the best days of my life so far."

I touched his shoulder. "Mine too."

APRIL 2 · SUNDAY

9:00 a.m.

Ugh...I have a black eye from last night's party. I'll start from the beginning...

1. Dax opens the front door and greets guest with a shot glass topped with whipped cream
2. Guest smiles and tilts it back
3. Guest coughs and swears (because it's lemon juice)
4. Dax laughs hysterically
5. Scenario repeats without variation until Dax loses interest (20 times maybe?)

It was pretty funny, like twice. I think Dax is a five-year-old stuck in a seventeen-year-old body.

Dax made an indoor slip-n-slide and we were standing around, cracking up as people slid into cushions lined up along the wall.

All of a sudden, there was a huge crash in the kitchen. I ran in to see what happened.

Rachel was lying on the floor next to a toppled chair and a broken bottle of vodka.

Dax made it over to her first.

"Are you okay?" he asked.

She propped herself up. "Yeah, I'm fine. Do you have to keep your stash up so high?" She laughed like that was the funniest thing she had ever heard.

"Shit, Rachel, that's messed up. Why didn't you just ask me?" Dax said.

"You would have said no." Rachel tried to stand.

"Yeah, maybe. For good reason."

He offered her his hand. "Here, let me help you."

"Don't bother." She pushed herself up on her knees, then held onto the counter and stood.

"What's everyone staring at? There's a party going on." She started moving to the music and danced out of the kitchen.

Arman came into the kitchen and kneeled down to help Dax. Arman is not exactly social, so it was weird to see him at the party.

"This is why I never come to these things," he said.

"Small price to pay to the party gods. I gotta go check on Rachel. Can you finish this for me?" Dax asked.

"No prob."

"Thanks bro. I totally owe you."

I was standing there, trying to decide whether I should

follow Dax, or help clean up.

"Hey, Mack." Arman nodded at me.

"Hey, Arman." He looked cuter at the party than he does in class.

"You always go to these things, don't you?" He brushed broken glass into a trashcan with a dishtowel.

"Sometimes." I tried to find something helpful to do.

"How can you stand the idiocy?"

"I guess I mostly ignore it."

"What else is there to pay attention to?"

"I don't know. Dancing. Fun people."

He seemed to be considering. "Yeah, I guess some people are cool—like Dax."

He put the trashcan back under the sink, and met my eyes. "And you, Mack. You'd be worth dealing with a bunch of idiots."

I laughed and turned red. The only time Arman talks to me is for clarification on an assignment.

Just then, Tyler walked in. "Hey, Arman. To what do we owe the honor?"

"Hey, Tyler," Arman said.

Tyler glared at me. "What are you doing here?"

"I could ask you the same question," I said.

"You know, because of you, Eden and I broke up, and Alexis

won't talk to me."

"Because of ME? You're the one who cheated on your girlfriend."

Dax and Rachel walked in.

"Everything okay?" Dax asked as he opened the fridge.

"Perfect," Tyler smirked at me.

Dax offered Rachel a bottle of water.

Rachel waved it away. "Water's for wimps."

He set it down in front of her.

"Fuck your water." She picked it up and threw it.

The bottle bounced off the wall and hit me smack in the face.

I bent over and held my head in my hands.

"Oh my God, Mack. I'm so sorry. Are you okay?" Rachel put her hands on my shoulders. I wondered which one of us she was trying to steady.

"Get off me." I flicked her hands away.

"I just wanna make sure you're not hurt. I didn't mean for that to happen."

"I'm sure you didn't."

"Shit, Mack, I'm trying to apologize."

I pushed past her. "You can apologize when you're sober."

I went outside and flopped down in a chair.

A minute later Arman walked up and handed me a bag of

frozen peas. "Hold this on your face. It'll help."

"Thanks." Slight heart melt.

"Can I join you?" he asked.

"Sure." I slouched forward and rested my throbbing cheek against the peas.

"Are you okay?" I felt him peering at me.

I nodded. "How can you be friends with Tyler?"

"I wouldn't exactly consider us friends."

"Oh."

He leaned towards me. "Here, let me see." Cologne. Nice. Different from Noah. Not better, just different.

I sat up and lowered the peas.

"You're gonna have a shiner. As the youngest of four brothers, trust me, I know."

"How old are your brothers?" Nice to think about something else.

"Nineteen, twenty-one, and twenty-two." I wonder if they're cute, too. Stop, Mack! One older man in your life is enough. Like Noah is really in my life. As if.

"Do you guys get along?" I asked.

"Pretty much. Do you get along with your sister?"

"You know I have a sister?"

"Uh huh. We talked about it last year, on the way to

Formal."

"Oh yeah, that's right." Zero recollection. Maybe I really don't pay attention to anyone. I pressed the peas to my throbbing face. "Thanks so much for these."

"No problem. Did you see the announcement for Prom?"

"Yeah. My dance days might be over."

"Because of what happened at Formal?"

"Yeah. It's so embarrassing."

"I wouldn't worry about it. No one even remembers anymore. It's so yesterday."

I brightened. "You think?"

"Sure. I mean who really cares if you had too many energy drinks? It's pretty boring actually."

"Huh. I think I feel insulted."

He laughed. "I just mean it doesn't matter."

"Thanks."

He rolled a water bottle around in his hands.

"So, I was thinking..." He threw the bottle up and caught it. "I know we're just friends, but...maybe when it gets closer, if neither of us is going to Prom, maybe we could go together."

"Sure, that'd be cool." Last year Arman and I kissed after Formal, but we went back to being friends like it never happened.

"Great. So it's a plan," he said.

"It's a plan," I echoed. Not a very romantic one, but a plan nonetheless.

"Think I'll get going," he said. "Do you need a ride?"

"I drove, but thanks anyway."

"Are you sure you're okay?"

"I'm totally fine. Thanks. Really."

"No problem." He smiled and walked towards the house.

I texted London.

> Me: Going home. Do u need a ride?
>
> London: Diego can take me. U OK?
>
> Me: I'm fine.

I snuck out without saying goodbye to anyone.

I thought Rachel might text me to apologize, but the weekend is almost over and I haven't heard a peep.

APRIL 3 · MONDAY

Rachel greeted me at lunch with, "Thanks for throwing me under the bus, Mack."

"Excuse me? I'm pretty sure you're the only one who's been doing the throwing," I said.

"Very funny. Everyone is talking about how I hit you in the face with a bottle."

"I doubt that, but news flash—you did hit me in the face with a bottle."

"Eden told me you told Melissa I hit you."

"We have first period together. She asked about my eye, and I told her what happened."

"She made it sound like you said I did it on purpose."

"Well, that's not what I said. How about you saying, 'I'm sorry?'"

"I already tried to apologize and you wouldn't let me."

"I'll take an apology now that you're sober."

"Fuck off, Mack." She stormed away.

"Skye, am I wrong?"

"Girl, you're waiting for an apology that's never coming. I guarantee she has a completely different story made up in her head."

"What, someone else threw it?"

"Who knows, but I promise you, sober Rachel will protect drunk Rachel."

"I don't get it. How can she not apologize? Even if it was an accident, she still did it."

"Here's how it works. Just for example, let's say my dad throws a glass against the wall. In his mind, the reason the glass is broken is because someone put it in the wrong place or because someone made him mad. Not his fault. End of story."

"I'm so sorry. That's hard."

"Thanks. Do yourself a favor and don't hold your breath waiting for that apology."

I unwrapped my turkey sandwich. "Do you want to spend the night Friday?" I asked.

"Sure. That sounds great!"

London has Diego, and Rachel has Dax and alcohol. I'm so lucky I have Skye.

...

9:00 p.m.

Mom brought home pizza for dinner.

Body: Eat what you want.

Mind: You're getting fat. You can't eat what you want
and stay skinny.

I ate three pieces and tried to stay calm. I went to my room
and read through my positive thoughts, but they were drowned
out by the noise in my head. *I am fat. I am fat. I am fat.* I'm too
depressed to try to transform the thought. It's an un-revisable
fact.

But even though I feel terrible, I didn't consider throwing up
for even a second. I can't imagine doing it. Not an option. I guess
that's a bright side.

APRIL 4 · TUESDAY

I went to bed grouchy, but I woke up happy for no reason.
The only thing I can think of was that I didn't want to throw up
last night. I honestly didn't want to.

I'm transferring my improved thoughts to my new journal.
Dr. S will be so proud.

- My body and brain work happily together.
- I am beautiful.
- My thoughts create my reality.
- I think and act in healthy ways.

These thoughts actually do make me happy. But on the other
hand, I have a black eye and Rachel isn't speaking to me. Did my
thoughts create that reality? Or did stupid Rachel?

Maybe I need to rewrite my thoughts about Rachel.

She's selfish and drinks too much. She doesn't care
how her behavior affects anyone else.

Are my thoughts creating this reality or am I having
accurate thoughts about reality? I would say the second is true.
But, let's say I change my thoughts about Rachel, then in theory
it will change Rachel's reality. Or maybe just my reality with

Rachel. Is that the same thing?

Rachel thought revisions:

> ~~Rachel is selfish, drinks too much, and doesn't care~~
> ~~how her behavior affects anyone else.~~
> ~~Rachel misses her mom.~~
> ~~Rachel needs support.~~
> Rachel misses her mom and needs support.

I guess I should support Rachel. But, how do I not get mad? I'll add my Rachel thought to the list and we'll see what happens.

Now I'm inspired. Even if it doesn't change my reality, it feels nice to have a positive thought about Rachel. I don't feel as angry. Hmmm...What other negative thoughts are spinning around in my head?

1. Diego doesn't like me.
2. Noah doesn't like me.
3. Arman only likes me as a friend.
4. I'm afraid of the scale.

I'll work on the first three:

> ~~Diego, Noah and Arman don't like me romantically.~~
> (Depressing)

~~Diego, Noah and Arman are all in love with me.~~ (Too much! Also, I don't want Diego to be in love with me—I want him to be in love with London.)

~~Noah and Arman are in love with me.~~ (Makes me anxious. Arman is just a friend.)

Noah really likes me. (Keeper!)

Last one:

~~I am afraid of the scale.~~ (I don't want to be)

~~The scale is my friend.~~ (Feels ridiculous)

~~I don't need the scale.~~ (Sounds stupid)

~~My health does not depend on the scale.~~ (So so)

The scale has nothing to do with my beauty. (Better, but not great)

I can't seem to get the scale thinking right. Maybe Dr. S will have a suggestion.

APRIL 5 · WEDNESDAY

Lauren picked Rachel up for lunch today. Could this be the result of my new thinking? Ha!

After school I did homework until it was time for my appointment.

Dr. Skyler

I told Dr. S about my revised Rachel thoughts and asked if she thought they could change things.

"I do believe our thoughts affect others," she said.

That wasn't the question! I wanted her to say, "Yes, Mackenzie, your positive thoughts are making a wonderful impact on Rachel's world."

Instead she said, "How are your thoughts affecting you?"

"Helping, I think." I studied my thighs. Fat? Skinny? Neither?

"Can you be specific?"

"Well, throwing up is no longer a dieting option."

"That's major progress, Mackenzie." She jotted something in her notebook.

"I suppose."

"Go on," she said.

"I still feel bad. It's like I don't know how to feel about myself if I don't know how much I weigh. I tried to make up a good thought about the scale, but nothing worked."

"Do you want to walk through it?"

"Sure."

Dr. S: Explain how you think about your weight.

Me: If I weigh a certain amount, I know no one could say I'm fat.

Dr. S: Is that because they know how much you weigh?

Me: No, but it's a low number so I feel confident I'm not fat.

Dr. S: Do you like your appearance when you are at that specific weight?

Me: Well, I like it better than when I weigh more.

Dr. S: Are you satisfied with your appearance at that weight?

Me: I guess. I mean, not really. I always think I could be skinnier. My legs are okay, but my stomach always needs work.

Dr. S: I see. I think I know what you need.

She went to her desk and took out a small white notepad. "I'm going to give you a prescription."

Appetite suppressant? Fat burner?

She wrote something then tore off the sheet and handed it to me.

Gratitude. Ingest daily. Increase frequency when symptoms flare.

I felt disappointed. "How is gratitude going to help me lose weight?"

"Gratitude is the key to achieving anything you want."

I had heard this babble before. Be grateful. Count your blessings. I didn't see the relevance.

"Do you want to be happy?" she asked.

"Yes."

"Then you must be grateful. Gratitude will help you transform any negative thought. And what do your thoughts do, Mackenzie?" She pointed to her sign on the wall.

I rolled my eyes. "They create my reality."

"Exactly."

Honestly, I was ready to stop listening. I think she read my mind.

"I know it sounds like fantasy, but if you follow the steps, I promise you will start to see a difference."

"Okay, what should I do?" I was willing to give it a try. Maybe.

"Every time you have a negative thought, replace it with a grateful thought: 'My stomach is fat' is replaced with 'I am

244

grateful my stomach can digest food.'

"What if I can't think of anything to be grateful for?"

"The object of your gratitude doesn't have to be the same as what you are having a negative thought about. *I feel ugly* can be replaced with *I liked the movie I saw last night.*"

Riiight, Dr. S...

"I know it sounds strange, but it works. When you are grateful, you raise your vibration. The more you think about what you like, the more things you like will come into your life."

"And what if it doesn't work? What am I supposed to do when I feel bad?"

"You remind yourself you're perfect just the way you are."

"But I'm not perfect."

She pointed to the wall again.

I folded my arms. "It's a fact. I'm NOT perfect."

She smiled patiently and continued to point at the wall.

"You're saying, if I change my thoughts, I will make myself perfect?"

"You already are perfect, just as you are."

I don't know why, but I started to cry. She looked sincere. But I'm not perfect. Nobody is perfect. How can she say I'm perfect? I mean, I want to be perfect, but that's impossible.

"How can you say that? I feel like you're lying."

245

"Mackenzie, you ARE."

"But, I'm not."

"Listen to what I'm saying. You ARE. Perfection lies in being who you are. You are unique, you are present, you ARE. That is perfection."

I felt overwhelmed. This wasn't my idea of perfection, but I wanted to believe what she was saying.

"This week, repeat to yourself, 'I am perfect as I am.' When you can't think of anything to be grateful for, put that thought at the top of your list."

I wasn't exactly on board, but as usual, her words made me feel better.

We talked a little more. When it was time to leave, I impulsively hugged her. She hugged me back.

I AM PERFECT AS I AM. I AM PERFECT AS I AM. I AM PERFECT AS I AM.

APRIL 8 · SATURDAY

Skye and I had the house to ourselves last night. We sat on my bed while we waited for our face masks to dry.

"How's your dad?" I asked.

"He went to rehab."

"Really? That's great!"

She pursed her lips.

Stomach drop. I said the wrong thing. "Isn't it?"

"Yes, it's great."

"You don't look very happy." Why can't I just shut up?

"No, I'm happy."

"But?" Mackenzie, enough!

She was quiet.

I wanted to apologize for asking, but I was afraid I'd say the wrong thing again.

"It's just, we've been through this before. When he came home from rehab the first time, I thought everything was fixed. And it was good for a long time, but then I had to watch the whole thing again."

I didn't really understand what she meant.

"And being with Rachel is the same. There's nothing I can do. I can't stand it." She started to cry.

I put my arm around her, and she leaned into my shoulder.

"It's going to be okay."

She pushed away from me. "You don't know that."

Tears sprang to my eyes. It makes me feel better when my mom says that, but I'm not Skye. I wished I could say the right thing for once.

"I guess I don't know for sure that it will be okay, but I think it will work out."

She hugged me. "Guess we should get this stuff off."

We rinsed our faces and went to the family room to watch a movie.

"I'm starving. Do you have anything to eat?" Skye said.

"We might. Let's go see."

She followed me to the kitchen.

I scanned the refrigerator. "Would you like an apple, a slice of cheese, or a soda?"

Skye laughed. "Are those my only choices?"

"Not all of us are blessed with stocked refrigerators." I closed the door.

She opened it to see for herself. "You're not kidding. Wanna order pizza?"

"That sounds so good." Hot, delicious, cheesy pizza.

"But maybe not, I don't know," I said.

"I'll buy," Skye said.

"Thanks. It's not the money." Should I tell her?

"Not in the mood?"

I handed her a soda, then opened one for myself. I inhaled. Aaah...Just the smell of diet soda makes me feel thinner and in control. I know that's crazy.

Right in the middle of this thought—out of nowhere—came, "I'm perfect as I am." And right after that, "Tell Skye. You can trust her." Who is this person talking to me now?

"Do you ever worry about getting fat?" Tiny baby step. Dipping my toe in the water.

"All the time," Skye said.

"Really?" Impossible.

"Of course. Who doesn't?"

"Well, how do you stay so perfect?"

"Perfect? You're crazy. I lose and gain the same five pounds every month. It's a constant battle."

"But you talk about having pizza like you aren't even thinking about it. Are you just pretending?"

"A little pizza isn't going to kill me," she said.

She's so sane. Will she understand?

"Are you okay, Mack?"

Will she think I'm gross?

"Yeah, I'm okay. Well, I should say, I'm getting better."

She didn't say anything.

"You know when I was in the hospital?"

She nodded.

"Did it seem weird to you that I had to stay there for a week?"

"Not really. A concussion can really mess you up."

Relief. Everybody else probably bought the story too. I still had a chance to keep my secret a secret. But it wanted to be free.

"The energy drinks weren't the real problem."

"You mean you took something else?" Her eyes widened.

"I didn't take anything. My electrolytes were all messed up."

She looked confused.

"I guess it's pretty common for people who binge and purge." I still couldn't say it!

"Do you know what I'm talking about?"

"Purge, like throw up, right?"

"Right."

"I tried it once. I couldn't do it." She shook her head like she was trying to get rid of the memory.

"I can't imagine you trying it."

"I'm sure I've done a lot of things you couldn't imagine."

I finished my soda and threw the can in the trash.

"I guess pizza does sound good," I said.

Skye smiled. "I'll order. What kind?"

"How about Canadian bacon and pineapple?"

"Yum. Anything else?" Skye tapped her phone.

"Can you order a medium maybe? Not a large." I felt my cheeks redden.

"Yep."

She hugged me. "Thanks for telling me, Mack. It means a lot."

I'm so grateful for Skye.

APRIL 9 · SUNDAY

9:00 a.m.

> Skye: Beach?
>
> Me: Sure!
>
> Skye: Care if Noah comes?
>
> Me: Sounds good

Beach with Noah!? 😜 I can hardly breathe. Must go get ready.

...

10:00 p.m.

> BEACH REPORT
>
> Weather: Sunny with a slight breeze
>
> Ocean: Medium swells
>
> Activity: Sunbathing. Bodysurfing. Flirting. Drinking. Fighting.

The afternoon started out great. Skye invited Rachel and London, and we all piled into Noah's truck. Skye sat in the front and I ended up in the back middle, which made it impossible not to see Noah in the rearview mirror. A couple of times we locked eyes, but then he adjusted the mirror.

We set up our chairs near the water, and I sat between Noah and Rachel. I don't know if I sat next to him on purpose, or if he sat next to me. I was so nervous and flustered, I just set my stuff down and started putting on sunscreen.

I took off my shirt but left on my shorts. I need to start doing situps again.

"Do you want me to put sunscreen on your back?" Noah asked.

My head went fuzzy. I know my face was redder than it has ever been.

"Sure, thanks." Totally casual, as if it were Skye, and not NOAH. I handed him the bottle and angled towards him.

"Sorry if this is cold." He. Put. His. Hands. On. My. Shoulders.

"Not cold at all." Not. At. All. Please, body, don't start shaking.

He applied the sunscreen like any of my friends would, but there was electricity coming out of his hands. Holy SHIT!!!

"There you go." He handed me back the sunscreen.

"Thank you."

"Wanna go in the water?" London was already down to her bathing suit.

"Sure." I took off my shorts and wrapped my towel around my waist (no way was I walking away from Noah in just my bathing suit), and followed her.

I set my towel at the edge of the wet sand and ran into the water. Phew...safe. Butt out of sight.

"Where's Diego today?" I asked.

"He had to work," London said.

"Bummer."

"No big. Let's swim out." She took off.

We ducked under whitewash and headed towards the second sets of waves. After a minute, I saw something out of the corner of my eye. My heart caught.

OMG. Shark?

Nope. Something infinitely more heart-stopping. Noah!

A perfect wave crested, and I took it. But I didn't duck out in time and ended up getting smashed in the whitewater. When I came up, my hair was all over my face, and my top had practically fallen off. London and Noah were laughing at me. We had all taken the same wave, but a they had managed to get out of it gracefully.

Mortified, I took a bow and started making my way back out to the surf.

There was a lull before the next set, and we bobbed next to

each other. I kept dunking my head under the water to cool off my cheeks. I think Noah might have tried to say something, but I kept going under water and pretending I didn't hear him. I felt like we were naked, which we practically were. I was paralyzed by stranded-on-an-island fantasies.

Another good wave came. I called out, "I'm heading in after this."

I caught the arc of the wave and streamed across. As it started to crash, I pulled back and stood. I wanted to put my hands up like a gymnast. Perfect ten! But, just in case Noah was watching, I casually walked to shore.

A little girl was sitting at the edge of the water, digging up sand crabs. "Want to see?"

I smiled at her. "Maybe later."

Her face fell. I walked a few more steps and turned around. Her sad face moved me more than my desire to hide my butt from Noah's view.

I kneeled down next to her. "Wow, did you catch all of these?"

"Yep!" She swirled her hand in her bucket.

"Looks like some are getting tired. I think sand crabs are happiest in the ocean. When I was little, I would collect them for a little while, and then throw them back."

"Maybe I should throw mine back in too!" Her big eyes reminded me of Maddie. Guilt. I haven't thought about Maddie much lately.

"That's a great idea," I said.

The little girl jumped up. "Want to go with me?"

"Sure."

We walked a few feet into the shallow water, and she dumped out her bucket. I casually scanned the water. No sign of Noah and London. What if London starts to like Noah? What if Noah starts to like London? Your thoughts create your reality. A big fat NO to those.

"Be free. Be free," the girl called to her former captives.

"Great job." We walked back towards the dry sand. "Are you going to collect more?"

"No. I think I killed that big one."

"Maybe he was sleeping?"

She narrowed her eyes. "Do you really think so?"

"I think you might have saved him when you threw him back in the water."

She beamed. "I saved him! I see my mom. Bye!" She skipped off.

I realized I had been totally absorbed in the moment and had not thought about my butt once. Such a nice change. I found my towel and headed up.

"Where were you?" London asked.

"I stopped to free some crabs. You must have walked right past me."

"I saw you," Noah said.

Whoosh...My unselfconsciousness washed out to sea. I sat down and pretended I didn't hear him.

Just then Rachel came up, holding a soda, trailed by a shirtless guy.

"Hey!" She flopped down cross-legged on the towel spread out in front of our chairs. "This is Mike."

"Hi. It's Makai." He held up his hand in greeting.

"Sorry, this is *Makai*." Rachel gestured towards him.

"Rachel, I'm going to catch some waves. I'll see you later." Makai was hot!

"See ya," Rachel called over her shoulder.

"Who was that?" Skye asked.

"Met him at the snack bar." She waved her drink in a semi-circle. "Anyone?"

"Sure," London said.

London took a big gulp. She coughed. "What is this?"

"Just a little beach juice—my signature recipe." Rachel stood up. "Come on, let's do something." She picked up the volleyball.

"Who wants to play?"

"I will," I said.

London stood up. "How about two-on-two? Skye? Noah?"

Please not Noah.

"Sure, I'll play." Skye said.

"Guess I'm out." Noah rested his chin in his hands.

"Don't worry, James will be here any minute," Skye said.

"Nice." He glanced at me. I was totally staring at him! I tried to make it seem like I was lost in thought. So embarrassing!

We found an open net.

Rachel said, "Skye and Mack vs. me and London." She took a big swig of her drink and set it down.

We had a good volley going and were laughing and joking. Then Rachel spiked the ball into Skye's chest and knocked her over.

"Are you okay?" I kneeled down.

"Sorry, I can't play for shit." Rachel offered Skye her drink. "Here this'll help."

Skye slapped it out of Rachel's hand.

"Hey, that was a good drink! What's wrong with you?"

"Wrong with ME?" Skye tried to stand up, and I gave her my hand.

Rachel shook her head at the empty cup lying in the sand.

"So lame, Skye."

"Rachel, I can't do this anymore."

"Do what? Play volleyball? It was an accident."

"An accident, right." She picked up the cup and pushed it into Rachel's chest. "Nothing is ever your fault."

London tried to take the cup from Skye. "Come on, let's just drop it."

"I don't want to drop it. See this?" She held it up. "This is the problem, Rachel. You don't take responsibility for anything."

"It was an accident. Chill out."

"That's enough." London stepped between them.

"Why are you defending her, London? I know you see it," Skye said.

"I'm not defending her, I'm supporting her. Skye, sometimes you and Mack are so clueless. You don't know what it's like to have half a family. You sit in your ivory towers and pass judgment on everyone."

"That's not true and you know it," I said.

"Says Miss Mack, Miss Sober, Miss Prude," Rachel said.

Tears of shock sprang to my eyes.

"Shut up, Rachel," Skye said. "You're drunk and you're going to regret what you're saying."

"First, I'm not drunk, and B, I'm not going to regret saying the truth."

I turned and ran away.

"Mack, stop." I heard Skye's voice behind me.

She jogged up. "Are you okay?"

"Is she right? Is that how I am?"

"No, of course not."

Her smile showed her perfect teeth. She's so pretty. I guess I don't usually notice (there's something new).

"Thanks. I know you wouldn't agree even if she was right, but I believe you," I said.

"You're the best friend I've ever had." Her voice caught. "I don't know what I'd do without you."

"I don't know what I'd do without you either."

As we walked back, my thoughts turned to Noah. Could he possibly like me?

- He drove me to the beach.
- He put lotion on my back.
- He went in the water at the same time I did.

"Is Noah going back to school today?"

"Don't get too hung up on him, Mack. He's a puzzle."

"What do you mean?"

"He's not a stupid high school guy. He'll be a junior next

year. He could practically be our father." She burst out laughing.

"I'm glad you find yourself so funny."

As we neared our spot, we could see Rachel, London, Noah, and James sitting in a semi-circle of chairs, laughing. Skye ran up, leaned over James's chair, and gave him a long kiss.

"Do you mind?" Noah grimaced.

They stopped.

I pretended to study the ocean to avoid making eye contact with anyone.

Rachel got up from her chair. "I gotta get home. I called an Uber. London, wanna come with me?"

"Yeah, sure."

"Anyone else?" Rachel lifted her drink from the cupholder in her chair, and swigged it. Where did she get another drink? She probably keeps little vodka bottles stashed in her ass.

"Hello? Anyone else need a ride?" She fumbled with her chair. "And can someone help me with this? Shit."

James stood and folded her chair for her. "No thanks, I drove."

"Nope," Skye said.

Rachel and London made zero eye contact with me.

"Thanks for the ride, Noah." Rachel blew a kiss to everyone and no one. "Catchya later." She and London weaved across the sand, laughing and bumping into each other. Hilarious. 😒

James said, "What was that all about?"

Skye and I shrugged.

"Whatever." James put his hands behind his head which made his muscles look particularly impressive. So glad we can't read each other's minds.

"I should get going too," Noah said. Maybe he did read my mind and he's jealous. Ha! Totally delusional.

Happy it was time to go, I started to fold up my chair.

"I didn't mean this very second." Noah laughed.

Of course, he didn't. Shit. I was in mid-chair-fold, completely paralyzed.

"How about if we leave in thirty?" Skye tried not to laugh.

"That works," Noah said.

"Sure, whatever." I unfolded my chair and sat down. Ugh!

James said, "I'm gonna catch one last wave. Anyone else?"

"For sure," Skye said.

"No thanks," I said. "I don't want to drive home in a wet bathingsuit." Does James care why I don't want to go in the water? NO! Guess I wanted to make sure I made a complete fool of myself.

Nah," Noah said. "I'm comfortable right here."

Skye gave me a quick eyebrow raise. My face was on fire

again.

James and Skye walked away, hand in hand.

"How does Skye seem to you?" he asked.

There it was again! I had blocked it out, but Noah's interest in me is because of Skye.

"Better. She hasn't been missing school lately."

He was quiet.

"But, maybe that's because..."

I almost said, "BECAUSE YOUR DAD IS IN REHAB." But I didn't. One star for me today.

"Because we've been hanging out more. Having fun, you know?"

Noah stood up. "I'm going to get a snack for the road, and I'll meet you guys in the parking lot. Do you want anything?"

"No thanks." Mack, get it together. You cannot cry just because your friend's brother doesn't like you.

Further evidence:

- Noah went to the beach to spend time with Skye and ask her friends about her
- He sat next to me because it happened that way
- He went in the water because he felt like it
- He walked away because he has shit on his

mind, and couldn't care less about me

- I am in high school
- He is in college

Conclusion: Noah doesn't like me. Don't need to be a professional detective to figure this one out.

APRIL 10 · MONDAY

I ate lunch with just Skye today. London was at her internship and Rachel didn't come to school.

"Have you talked to Rachel or London since the beach?" I asked.

"No. Have you?" Skye ate a piece of her California roll.

"Nope. Thanks again for sticking with me." I munched on a protein bar.

"Always. Hopefully we'll all work it out by Spring Break. This Saturday is Mrs. Dorian's anniversary. Should we do something for Rachel?"

"Like what?" I was not feeling like doing anything for her.

"Last week I picked up an unfinished ceramic skull at the craft store, and I thought maybe we could paint it together."

"That's a really thoughtful gift. I'd be afraid I would ruin it," I said. Skye is super talented in all things crafty.

"The pattern is already drawn, we just have to follow the lines. Since my dad's not home, you could come over any time."

I never realized Skye's dad had ever been in the way of me coming over.

"I guess I could."

"Want to come over after school today?"

"Okay." I'm mad at Rachel, but when I think about how I would feel if Mom died, I'm ready to forget it.

Skye is such a good friend.

APRIL 11 · TUESDAY

Rachel was back today and she acted like the beach never happened.

"So, what'd I miss?" she asked.

Skye and I said nothing.

"What? Now you guys aren't talking to me either?"

"Who else isn't talking to you?" I asked.

"London. She got mad at me Sunday because I ended up hanging out with that guy I met, instead of taking the Uber with her. I still don't get why she got so mad. And now you two. What's everyone's problem?"

Skye said, "My mom says when you think everyone else has a problem, the problem is usually you."

"Right, I'm sure it's all me," Rachel said.

"Do you even remember our argument at the beach?" I asked.

"Yeah." She scanned the sky. "Sort of."

"Do you remember what you said to me?"

"Not really. I was having a good time."

"*That's* why you're the problem." Skye said. "While you're having a good time, the only person you care about is yourself."

"That's not even true. Maybe if you relaxed and enjoyed

yourself once in a while, you wouldn't be so quick to judge."

Skye stood and picked up her bag. "I'll see you later, Mack."

"What crawled up her butt?" Rachel said.

I was silent. Did she think I would agree with her?

"Mack, don't tell me you're in on this too."

I said, "Rachel, you were a complete asshole on Sunday. London supported you, and you bailed on her with some random guy. I'd like to know how this isn't your fault."

"I was an asshole?"

I glared at her. *High and mighty. Miss Sober. Miss Prude.*

"Mack, I really don't remember what I did."

"Doesn't it bother you that you can't remember?"

"I guess, but it bothers me more that everyone is so uptight and judgmental."

"Rachel, I'm done with this conversation." I got up and walked away.

The skull we made Rachel turned out awesome, but I don't even want to give it to her now.

APRIL 12 · WEDNESDAY

Dr. Skyler

"How are you feeling this afternoon?" Dr. S asked.

"I'm fine." Conversations were replaying in my head. Do I judge? Am I high and mighty?

"Would you like to share what's on your mind?"

"My mind is full of everyone else."

"Anyone in particular?"

"I'm having trouble with Rachel."

She waited. Sometimes I don't want to talk when I get to my appointment, but once I start, it all seems to pour out.

"We're all mad at her, and she doesn't even remember what she did because she was drunk."

"Sounds like her behavior upset you."

"It upset everyone, not just me."

"Does it matter if it upset other people?" she asked.

"Well, yeah, I think it does matter. It shows I'm not being judgmental or overly sensitive. She hit me in the face with a water bottle and also said the rudest things to me. I don't think she meant to hurt me, but I'm still so mad."

Dr. Skyler's expression was neutral. Say something! Tell me,

"You're totally right. Her behavior is unbelievable. Why are you even friends with her?"

"That must have felt bad." Dr. Skyler's face was sympathetic.

Tears sprang to my eyes. "That's an understatement."

"Do you think of Rachel as a close friend?" Dr. S passed me the tissue box.

"We've been friends since we were five—we're like sisters."

"If you could make your relationship exactly how you wanted, how would it be?"

"Probably like it was before her mom died. We would have fun and talk." I pictured us lying on the ground eating tomatoes in their garden. It was so long ago—almost like it never happened.

"But her mom did die."

"Yes." Dr. S, Master of the Obvious.

"Were you close to Rachel's mom?"

"She was like my second mom."

"So, you lost someone too."

"Yes, but Rachel lost the most. I tried to be there for her and not think about myself."

"Sounds like you were being a good friend."

"I tried." Maybe I wasn't there for her. I started crying.

"Mackenzie, sometimes anger is a mask for pain.

Acknowledging your pain is the first step towards understanding your anger."

I let my tears fall. "I can't get it all straight. I don't know how to figure out everything I'm feeling."

"Remember how I said you don't need to strive, or improve, or do anything to be perfect?"

"Yes." Haven't reminded myself of that lately.

"You can take a similar approach to emotions. We don't have to sort them out, we simply need to pay attention to them. You said your mind was full of everyone else. Would you be open to doing a brief mindfulness exercise to bring you back to yourself?"

I had serious doubts, but I said, "I'll try." I could hear Shayla in her Yoda voice, "Do or do not. There is no try."

"First, take a deep breath and close your eyes."

I did.

"Now bring your attention to your left hand. Notice how it feels. Is it warm? Cold? Tense? Painful? Neutral? Breathe deeply and when you exhale release any pain or tension. Take your attention to the tips of your fingers and thumb, then slowly pull your attention down into the center of your hand. Feel your attention gathering in your palm. If you drew a picture, it would look like the center of your hand was glowing. Take a deep breath and feel into the sensation. Now let your attention go."

"You can open your eyes."

I did. Dr. S was facing the window. I was glad she wasn't watching.

"Now, shake out your hands. Do you feel a difference between your left hand and your right hand?"

"I do. The left one feels lighter than the other."

She turned to face me.

"I don't understand how this helps," I said.

"It is a grounding tool. When you are anxious or worried or thinking about everyone else, a mindfulness exercise can stop the mental merry-go-round. You can focus on any part of your body, or your entire body as a whole. As you practice more, it will help you discover the heart of what is upsetting you or making you uncomfortable."

"Feels like I'm going to need a lot of practice."

She smiled. "Life is one big practice. Would you like a little exercise to try at home?"

"Okay."

"Interview yourself in your journal. Ask questions like, 'How do you feel?' and 'Why do you feel that way?' Answer honestly— it's only for you. The key is to step out of your head and *feel* your response. You might be surprised at what you discover."

I nodded. I was in no mood to consider interviewing myself, but maybe I'd give it a try later.

"I admire your commitment to working on your health, Mackenzie."

"Thank you." As always, Dr. S makes me feel good, but I have doubts about my commitment.

APRIL 13 · THURSDAY

London texted me this morning to see if I wanted to go to Cava. First time we've talked since the beach. (I considered saying no, but in my quest to be more compassionate and less selfish, I agreed.)

When we walked in, we saw Eden sitting at a table. We waved as we got in line.

"Should we ask if she wants to sit with us?" I asked. I didn't really want her to, but she looked so lonely.

"Hell no." I appreciate London's simplicity. Wish I could be more like that.

Just then, Arman sat down at Eden's table with two drinks. Sympathy flew out the door. Eden pointed to us and Arman waved. Were they a couple? What would they talk about? Eden throws parties. Arman hates parties. I waved back.

"Let's sit on the patio." London headed for the door.

"Sure." I stole a quick glance at Arman and Eden—no evidence they were more than just friends.

"Thanks for the coffee." I sipped my latte and waited. I knew we weren't here just to hang out.

"No prob. I'm really sorry about the beach."

I didn't say anything.

"I think I just get jealous about your family. I didn't mean it."

I brushed her arm. "It's okay."

I changed the subject. "How's Diego?"

"Fine." She looked around—you never know who might overhear your conversation at Cava. "I mean, things have been good lately. He even shared a few personal things."

"Nice."

"It feels like we're getting closer. I asked him if he wanted to come over this weekend and meet my mom. Just casual, you know?"

I nodded.

"And he got all weird on me—fidgeting and talking about things he had to do. So I was like, 'Hey, no big deal. Maybe some other time.' He totally relaxed and said, 'Yeah, another time, for sure.'"

"Maybe he really had things to do."

"Come on. Give me a break."

"Really, you don't know. Guys are weird. It doesn't mean he doesn't like you."

"I know, but he's the first guy I've ever wanted to introduce to my mom."

Sharing secrets, just like the old days.

"There's lots of time to have him meet Jessica the Great."

That got a little laugh out of her.

"Maybe you should come over this weekend, since Diego is such a butthead," she said.

"Sure! Maybe she'll make us some more pasta."

"Maybe, but if you want to see her, you better come over during the day. She spends all her evenings out with what's-his-name."

"Sorry."

"I met him the other night. He's not horrible, I guess." She sat back in her chair and folded her arms. "She said I should give him a chance. Hell to the NO."

She looked in the window. "What's up with you and Arman?"

"Arman?"

"Don't play dumb with me. I saw you two chattin' it up at Dax's."

"Yeah, well, looks more like he's got something going on with Eden," I said.

"Is someone jealous?"

"No." I confirmed my answer with a swig of coffee.

"He's not a bad catch." She sounded like she was talking to herself. "If you like the studious type."

"I don't think I can catch anyone these days."

"You could have anyone you want. You want Arman? Go get him."

Pursue Arman? Pursue anyone? I'm waiting for them to come to me.

The patio door opened and Arman peeked his head out. "Taking off. See ya tomorrow, Mack." No sign of Eden.

"Told you so." London smiled as he closed the door.

Stomach flip. Pursuit a definite possibility.

APRIL 14 · FRIDAY

Midnight

Skye is spending the night, and we're sitting here writing in our journals.

Mom made enchiladas for dinner. Yum! Afterwards, Dad suggested we play Blackjack for jellybeans. It was the most fun I can ever remember having with my family. Mom said it was the start of a perfect spring break.

Maddie went to Alexis's house after we finished playing. It seems like she is always leaving. Or maybe I'm somewhere else? Or maybe I'm not paying attention. We get along so much better now, I've almost forgotten about her. Not something I'd write in a greeting card.

Skye and I hung out in my room and listened to music.

"Your family is so normal," Skye said.

"Trust me, you just caught them on a good night."

"Well, our best night doesn't even come close."

I thought of Dr. S and gratitude.

"How are things with James?" I asked.

"Good. But sometimes, I swear he talks to Noah more than he talks to me."

My heart skipped a beat at the sound of Noah's name.

She narrowed her eyes at me. "So you still like him?"

"What are you talking about?" I said.

"Your face is the color of a tomato."

"No, it was just a passing phase. I think maybe I like Arman."

She raised her eyebrows. "Interesting."

"Interesting, why?"

"I swear I heard him say your name the other day in class."

"What'd he say?"

"I couldn't really hear, but he was talking to Kenya and Jose."

"The Marvel superfans? What could those three be talking about that has anything to do with me?"

"Maybe you remind them of Black Widow."

"Yeah, right. Can you imagine this body in her outfit?" I flared my hands for effect.

"Actually yes, I could. You're pretty harsh on yourself, Mack. You have a great body."

"Totally."

"Stop it. You need to learn to take a compliment. Just say, 'Thank you.'"

"Fine. Thank you." Sounds like something Dr. S would tell

me.

Is Skye being honest or just sweet? Guess it doesn't matter.

"Is Noah home this weekend?" The words came out of my mouth before I could stop them.

"Yes, but why do you care?"

"I don't, I was just wondering."

"He's leaving Monday for Mexico."

"What's he doing in Mexico?" Storm clouds gathered over my head.

"I imagine whatever all college kids do on spring break."

More evidence Noah is too old for me. I'm not even eighteen, and he's going to Mexico. I'm a child, he's a man.

"Don't be sad. He'll be here for our egg hunt Sunday."

"You're still doing it this year?" We've hunted for Easter eggs at Skye's every year since kindergarten.

"Yep. My mom is on a mission to make life as normal as possible, and that includes an Easter with lots of eggs. She seems happy, but I feel like she's supposed to be sad."

I didn't say anything.

"The worst part is I'm happy too, and I feel guilty. Last Easter sucked, and this will be a peaceful, controlled holiday. Breakfast with just the three of us, a visit with Jiji and Baba, and an egg hunt with my friends. You'll be there, right?"

"Of course. Right after I eat a chocolate bunny for breakfast with Maddie."

"Do you think I have to tell London and Rachel about my dad? I feel like it'll be weird if he's not there and I don't say anything."

"There will be so much distraction, you won't need to bring it up, unless you want to."

She nodded to herself.

I love sitting here writing in my journal with someone else. Skye keeps hers on the computer too.

APRIL 15 · SATURDAY

Noon

Skye went home about an hour ago, and no one is home. I feel pretty good. Almost perfect, just as I am.

Correction: Perfect just as I am.

Just got a text.

London: Come over
Me: U OK?

No response.

...

8:00 p.m.

Tonight was the worst night of my life.

London never tells me to come over—I drove straight to her house the second I got her text. I called her from the car. No answer. I texted. No response. When I got there, I rang the bell. No answer. Front door: locked. I went around the back. Patio door: locked. Kitchen window: cracked. I squeezed through.

"London?" Silence. No evidence of any activity in the

kitchen.

I walked towards her bedroom. My heart was about to explode out of my chest.

"London?" I heard a clink in the hall bathroom. The door was cracked open.

I pushed the door open and expected to see her cat slink out. Instead, I saw London sprawled on the floor. I knelt down next to her and put my ear to her chest. Thank God, her heart was beating. Then I saw the blood. I grabbed a hand towel and tied it around the cut on her wrist. I texted Skye and Rachel.

Me: Emergency. Come to London's right now.

I didn't know if I should call 9-1-1. She only cut one wrist. I know it sounds ridiculous, but it didn't seem life-threatening, and I was thinking how embarrassed she would be. How could I be so stupid?

I touched her cheek. "London, wake up." Her skin was cold, and she had a large bump on the side of her forehead.

"Mack?" London croaked, eyes closed.

"I'm here."

She turned her head to the side. Tears began to slide down her face.

I stroked her hair.

She shook her head back and forth.

I held her head still. "Stop. It's okay. You're okay." No blood had soaked through the towel yet. There was just a little blood on her shirt. I've seen my mom give blood, and they take a lot more than that. This is what I told myself, and the reason I didn't call 9-1-1.

About five minutes later, the doorbell rang.

I squeezed London's hand. "I'll be right back."

I sprinted to open the door. Rachel. We ran down the hall.

"Oh my God." Rachel knelt down. "London, it's Rachel. Open your eyes." She patted her cheeks. "Come on, open your eyes."

Rachel pulled up London's eyelids. "Her pupils are huge. Did you call 9-1-1?"

"No." The second I answered, I knew what a huge mistake I had made.

"Well, call NOW!" she screamed. I started crying as I fumbled for my phone.

"London, what did you take?" Rachel smoothed London's hair and rubbed her shoulders. "Wake up, London. Talk to me."

"Rachel?" London rasped.

"Hey, girl, it's me. You're going to be okay. Can you tell me what you took?"

"My room." Her eyes rolled up into her head.

"Mack, go look."

I ran to London's room and found a prescription bottle on the dresser. I grabbed it, ran back, and handed it to Rachel.

She read the label. "Oxycodone. It's her Mom's. God, I hope it wasn't full."

My head spun—I was having a complete out-of-body experience, further amplified by Rachel taking charge.

Just then, Skye ran in, followed by two paramedics wheeling a gurney.

One of the paramedics wrapped a blood pressure cuff around London's arm and pointed to the other arm. "What's this towel?"

"She cut her wrist," I said.

She gently untied it and blood started seeping from the wound. "That was smart thinking."

"Real smart," Rachel said.

The medic listened to a stethoscope and took off the cuff. "We need to get her to the hospital immediately."

The three of us watched in shock as the medics lifted London onto the gurney. As they rolled London out, I expected to see Rachel's face. My brain told me this scene was supposed to happen to Rachel, not to London.

Rachel patted my shoulder. "Come on. Let's go."

We followed the ambulance in Rachel's car.

"We need to call Jessica," Skye said. Tears streamed down her cheeks.

I couldn't think straight. What if London died? How were Rachel and Skye being so rational?

My hands shook as I left a message for Jessica: "Hi Jessica, this is Mack. London had an accident and we're taking her to the hospital... I'm not sure which hospital..."

"Probably Coast Community," Skye and Rachel said at the same time.

I continued, "Probably Coast Community. I'll text as soon as we get there." I knew I sounded hysterical, but I couldn't stop crying.

In a minute, I saw the sign for CCH. "How'd you know where we were going?"

"Seemed like the logical choice," Rachel said. She was crying, but calm. I couldn't understand how she was holding it together.

"Been there a time or two," Skye said from the back. Rachel looked at her in the rearview mirror.

At the hospital, we checked in and sat down, frozen. If London died, it would be my fault. I sobbed.

Jessica arrived twenty minutes later, and we watched her wave her arms at the front desk person.

"They won't even let her own mother back there." Her hair was everywhere and tears streamed down her cheeks. She hugged each of us.

She went up to the front desk about every ten minutes, and finally after the third time, they let her go in.

She kissed each of us on the top of the head. "You girls go home. I'll keep you posted." Her eyes brimmed with tears. "Say your prayers."

Rachel drove us back to London's to get our cars. We cried silently the whole way.

When we pulled up to her house, I couldn't help thinking, "What if London never comes back here?"

Rachel leaned over and hugged me. "We're going to get through this. London is tough."

I thought, "You don't know that."

Mom was in the kitchen when I walked in the door. I threw my arms around her. I couldn't even talk. I just cried.

"Are you hurt?" she asked as she held me.

I shook my head.

She didn't let go. "Shh...it's ok now. You're okay. Everything's going to be all right."

I burst into fresh tears. "Mom, it might not be all right. London might die. And it's my fault."

We walked down to my room and I told her what happened. She rubbed my head and said it wasn't my fault. But I know it is.

I'm just going to sit here and stare at my phone until I get a text.

APRIL 16 · SUNDAY

This was the saddest Easter ever.

Maddie tapped on my door this morning.

"Come in." I had been awake all night.

She sat on the edge of my bed and handed me a chocolate bunny. I sat up and hugged her and started to cry. I don't know how I have any tears left.

I lay back down and scooted over and she joined me. We opened the bunnies and bit their heads off like we do every year. We smiled at each other through our tears. Maddie, my sister. Maddie, my friend.

Tonight Gram brought us dinner, and we picked at our food and stared at our phones, hoping for some news on London's condition. Mom likes to say, "No news is good news," but even she stayed quiet.

APRIL 17 · MONDAY

10:00 a.m.

London is still in critical condition.

I can't stop thinking about how stupid I am. Why didn't I call 9-1-1 immediately? Why did I assume she was fine?

I wonder if Dr. Skyler is wrong. Maybe my thoughts reflect my reality, more than they create it.

Thoughts or reality?

- London might die
- I'm more clueless than I realized

Dr. S would encourage me to transform these thoughts. But would that help? Would it change what happened? Would it heal London? It feels pointless.

...

7:00 p.m.

Tonight I ate FOUR pieces of pizza, plus dessert. I stormed down the hall to get the scale. I couldn't stand to be clueless about one more thing. I was about to step on. *This is what you get, Mack.* For some reason, those words stopped me. It was like

I was giving in to an enemy, and I felt a flash of self-protective strength. I picked up the scale, walked outside to the trash, and threw it in. I might now be headed for a two-hundred-pound life, but I feel lighter. At least I got rid of something that makes me feel bad. Also, I haven't thrown up.

Text just in from Rachel.

> Rachel: I'm not ok. Sleepover? Need my friends!
>
> Skye: Yes!
>
> Me: Yes!

I texted Skye and she's going to bring the present we made. I'm ready to forgive and forget.

APRIL 18 · TUESDAY

Noon

Still no news. Just got home from Rachel's.

Last night we sat on the floor in her room and ate Chinese food. I'm done worrying about what I eat—I just want London to be okay.

"Have you heard anything?" Rachel asked.

I checked my phone for the millionth time. "Nothing."

"Dax told me today that Diego broke up with her Friday night," Rachel said. "God I hope she didn't try to kill herself over a guy." She opened a soda and took a big drink. Skye and I exchanged a glance. Was she making room for vodka?

"Rachel, we have something for you." Skye said.

"For me? Why?"

"In memory of your mom," I said.

Rachel ran her hands through her hair. "London picked a shitty day to try to kill herself, huh? I swear, if I have to think about two dead people on April 15th, I'll never forgive her."

Skye handed her a wrapped box.

She turned the box around. "It's heavy."

She ripped it open and held up a brightly painted porcelain

skull. "Wow, it's beautiful. Where'd you get it?"

"We made it," Skye said.

"For your collection," I added.

Rachel walked around holding out the skull. "Where should I put it?"

She stopped next to her bed. "Right here, next to this one my mom made."

She sat down on her bed and put her head in her hands. I expected her to pop up any second, say something sarcastic, and make herself a drink, but she didn't move.

"Is she crying?" Skye mouthed the words.

I shrugged. We got up and sat on either side of her. She was trembling.

"I can't do this," she sobbed. "I can't lose someone else. I won't make it."

I put my arm around her shoulder. "Don't worry. It's going to be okay."

"YOU DON'T KNOW THAT!" She pulled her hair with both hands.

I held her shoulders. "You're absolutely right. I *don't* know, but I believe it. And when London survives, it will be because of you."

"I barely remember what happened."

"You were amazing," I said. "You checked her pupils and you knew she took something."

She got up and paced the room. "You know, my mom used to say that to me, 'Rachel, you're amazing.' Now, I only hear it when some guy's trying to get lucky, and it's complete bullshit."

She sat down on the floor. "I know you two think I'm totally fucked up."

Our jaws dropped.

"It's okay. I *am* fucked up. I'm one-hundred-percent completely fucked up...But this thing with London..." Her voice cracked. "London doesn't deserve this. We don't deserve this. We can't lose any more people."

Skye and I moved to the floor. Rachel reached out her arms and we held hands in a circle.

Rachel fixed us with her eyes. "Don't laugh." She bowed her head.

"Mom, it's Rachel. I know you're up there. I haven't felt you lately, but I'm sure you are. Can you tell someone it's not London's time? We need her here. I need her here." Tears streamed down her cheeks. "I miss you so much. I'm going to be better, Mom." She opened her eyes. "Skye and Mack are here and they're going to make sure of it. They're watchdogs— pitbulls." At that, she chuckled. "Anyway, Mom, I know you have pull up there. Put in a good word for London. I miss you every day. I'm going to be a better daughter. I love you."

We sat in silence for a minute. Rachel wiped her eyes. "After that I need a drink."

My stomach sank.

She winked. "Just messin' with ya, pitbull bitches." She took a swig of her soda. "I'm not saying I'm never going to drink again, but I'll think about what you said."

We watched the movie Frida in honor of Mrs. Dorian, and ate until we were stuffed. I have never felt better.

OMG!!! I JUST GOT A TEXT!

> Jessica: Out of ICU. No visitors allowed yet. I'll keep you posted. 🙏

Dear God and Mrs. Dorian,

Please protect London and let her stay with us. We need her more than you know. Amen.

APRIL 19 · WEDNESDAY

My phone woke me up this morning.

Jessica: London is awake. 🙏 Come visit. 🖤

I forwarded her message to Rachel and Skye and added:

Rachel, you were right—your mom has pull!

Rachel, Alexis, Skye, Maddie, and I stayed the entire day at the hospital. London opened her eyes a few times but wasn't alert enough to talk.

Maddie and I drove home together.

She asked, "Do you think London's going to be okay?"

"I overheard the doctor talking to Jessica and it sounded like she was getting better," I said.

Mentioning the doctor made me remember Dr. S.

"Oh no, I forgot my appointment," I groaned.

"What appointment?" Maddie asked.

Shit, should I tell her?

"My therapist." No more lies.

"You're seeing a therapist?"

"Yep."

"Why?"

I took a deep breath and told her the whole story. She

listened in silence.

"Wow, Mack. That explains a lot."

"Did you ever suspect?" I turned the car onto our street.

"No. I thought you were doing drugs. Are you okay now?"

"I don't throw up anymore, if that's what you mean."

I pulled into the garage. She reached over and touched my shoulder. "I can't believe you told me."

"Why?" I shut off the engine.

"If it were me, I don't think I would have told you."

"Why?"

"I would be afraid you'd hold it over me or start checking up on me."

"Is that your plan?" I narrowed my eyes.

"No way. Thanks for telling me, Mack."

We hugged each other tight.

It feels so good to have her support.

APRIL 20 · THURSDAY

I went to the hospital early this morning. Jessica had spent the night and was brushing her teeth when I knocked.

"Come on in, sweet girl." She patted my shoulder and returned to the bathroom.

I sat in the chair next to London's bed. Her hair was up in a braided bun—Jessica's work, no doubt.

Jessica stood beside me and gazed at London. "So much pain behind that angel face. She hasn't said much—she starts crying if I ask a question."

She leaned down and kissed the top of my head. "I have to go to work. I'm glad you're here, Mack. Maybe she'll talk to you."

She kissed London's forehead. "I'll be back tonight."

I walked around the room, wishing I had stopped for coffee on the way. I smelled the roses I knew Jessica had brought from their yard—roses her dad had planted. If only he were still here, everything would be fine.

"Mack?" London's voice rasped.

I turned around. She was struggling with her sheet.

"Let me help you. Are you cold?"

She shook her head.

"Hot?"

She nodded.

I folded the sheet down to her waist. "Better?"

She put her hand on top of mine. My eyes welled with tears. I put my other hand on top of hers. Her smile widened as she put her other hand on top of mine. I laughed and pulled my hand from the bottom of the pile and placed it on top. She leaned down and kissed it. We locked eyes and started crying.

The dam cracked. I sat in the chair, put my head on the side of her bed, and sobbed.

"I'm sorry," she whispered.

I held her hand. "You don't need to be sorry. I'm so glad you're okay." I burst into fresh tears. "I thought you were going to die."

"Guess it wasn't my time." She rubbed her forehead. "It's hard to talk."

"I'll stay here all day. You don't need to say a word."

She smiled and closed her eyes, and I felt the rare joy of having said the right thing.

A nurse came in. "Lookin' good this morning."

Not lookin' so bad yourself, Mr. Nurse.

He straightened London's sheet. "You ready for some breakfast?"

She nodded, and he used the remote to lift the head of her

bed until she was upright.

"Thanks," she whispered.

"Don't try to get all sexy on me. Let me hear your voice," he said.

She seemed to be considering.

"Come on. One word. You can do it. I'll give you an extra fruit cup."

"Thanks," she croaked.

"Nicely done." He patted her hand. "I'll be back in a flash with your meal."

"Does it hurt to talk?" I asked.

"Just don't feel like it," she whispered.

I understood. Being in the hospital makes you feel like a science experiment—everyone watching to see how you'll respond to a particular stimulus.

I rearranged her pillow behind her head. "Do you want me to go?"

She shook her head.

"Okay. We can just hang out."

She closed her eyes until the nurse returned. "Here you go, sunshine. Eat up. Let's get some meat on those bones."

I have to admit I wished he was talking to me, and my mind latched onto one hundred and twenty pounds—and counting.

I shook my head to return to the present moment. London is alive! I may be fat, but London is alive!

She poked at the eggs. "Can you get me some proper food?" Her voice had improved to a notch above gravel.

"For sure! Smoothie?"

She nodded. "Strawberry-banana."

I could be of service and get a coffee too! "I'm on it." I got my purse. "Do you want me to help you use the bathroom before I go?"

She pointed to a bag on the side of the bed. "Catheter."

I winced. "Well, it's convenient anyway. Do you want your toothbrush or anything?"

She shook her head. "Thanks, Mack."

As I was driving, it occurred to me I should call Diego. Even if this was his fault, he had a right to know. Plus, what if it wasn't about him?

He picked up on the first ring.

"Hey Diego, this is Mack."

"Yes, my phone shows the caller—amazing new technology."

"Ha. Ha."

"You never call. I thought it might be important."

"Really? Why?" Spider sense calling bullshit.

"I don't know." He coughed. "I mean, I assume you know

London and I broke up?"

"Yes, I know. So why would I be calling you?"

"I don't know. Maybe to say she can't live without me and wants me back?"

"What are you talking about? I thought you broke up with her."

"What? No way! Other way around. We haven't spoken since Friday. It's been a fucking awesome spring break."

"I'm calling because London is in the hospital and I thought you should know."

"The *hospital*? What happened? Is she okay?"

"She's going to be fine."

"Can I go see her?"

"Let me check with her first." My mind was racing. "I don't get it—why did she break up with you?"

"She said she was fast-forwarding to the inevitable."

"Sounds like something she would say."

"Tell me about it."

"Well, I'm headed back to the hospital pretty soon. I'll talk to her and then I'll let you know. Okay?"

"Do I have a choice?"

"Not really."

"Then I guess it's okay."

"Great."

"Thanks, Mack."

"No problem. Talk to you later." Why did London break up with Diego? Why would she try to kill herself? None of it made any sense.

I returned to find London sleeping upright. I moved her food tray to the dresser.

She stirred. "Thank you. That smell was about to make me barf." Her voice sounded a little clearer.

"I'm sorry, I should have moved it before I left." I handed her the juice.

She took a sip. "Mmm. Makes me think of summer."

I stared into the tiny hole in my coffee cup lid, trying to think of a way to bring up Diego. I took a sip and said a silent prayer.

Please help me figure this out. Help me listen.

I knew what I had to do—<u>nothing</u>. I could hear all of the times people had said to me, 'You never listen.' Today, I would listen and listen.

"Do you want to talk about what happened? I understand if you don't, but I'm here if you do." It took all my willpower not to say anything else. Listen. Listen. Listen.

I had resigned myself to failure and was about to suggest we turn on the TV, when London spoke.

"I wanted quiet." She wrung her sheet between her hands. "I just wanted the voices in my head to be silent."

I nodded.

She put her hands on her head. "What the hell? Did my mom put my hair in a bun?"

I laughed. "She spent the night."

"My mom can fix me up on the outside, but she can't help me on the inside."

I knew exactly how she felt.

She pulled at the bun. "What am I going to do?"

"Are you really asking me?"

"Yeah, I'm really asking."

I set my coffee on the side table. What did I know about wanting to die? When I phrased it that way, I realized I knew a lot. I remembered the day I couldn't stop eating the cookies. I was headed for my death—willfully straight for it.

"You have to get help."

"From where?"

"A therapist. Someone who knows what they're doing."

"Are you taking a psychology class or something?"

"Very funny. I know what it's like to think death is an easier option than life. I know the feeling of being suffocated, like you just want to escape." Tears stung my eyes.

"You do?"

"Yes, I do." A flash of anger. Deep breath. This isn't about me. Not about me. Not about me.

"My therapist has helped me a lot," I said.

"*You* see a therapist? Did I wake up in an alternate universe?"

"You're not being very nice."

"I'm sorry."

"Maybe you could talk to my therapist. You would like her," I said.

"I'm tired." She pulled her sheet up over her shoulders. "I'm sorry I underestimated you, Mack. I always thought you were Mary Poppins."

I didn't respond, and soon she was sleeping. I'm impressive now that I have issues? Mary Poppins? WTF?!

About twenty minutes later, there was a knock at the door and footsteps.

"Hello?" A familiar voice.

I bolted from my chair. "Diego! What are you doing here?" My whisper was fierce.

"You didn't call." He brushed me to the side and went straight to London.

He stroked her arm, stopping at the bandage around her wrist.

My heart was in my throat. Should I force him to leave? Should I wake her and try to explain? She didn't stir. A voice told me to go home. I listened.

APRIL 21 · FRIDAY

London came home last night. Skye picked me up this morning to go see her.

"I'm glad you visited her yesterday," Skye said as we inched forward in a massive drive-thru line. "I wanted to, but I couldn't go again."

"Why?"

"It's too much. The smell, the memories. My dad was in a car accident a couple of years ago when he fell asleep at the wheel. He was in there for two weeks. We thought he wasn't going to make it."

She had never mentioned it. How could she hide that from us?

We ordered our coffees.

"Plus, other times. A cut, a fall..."

"I'm so sorry." My image of Skye's home life morphed every time I talked to her. I had always pictured them sitting around the fireplace after a family dinner, reading and having intellectual conversations. Now, I saw her dad spilling his drink and hurling his book into the fire.

We pulled up to the pay window.

"This should cheer her up." Skye passed me an extra-large

confetti-surprise smoothie.

"I wonder if she'll actually drink it." I studied the rainbow contents. "It probably tastes good at first, then makes you totally sick."

"Yep, it's like wrapping paper. Makes you smile—a short-lived thing." Skye sipped her plain coffee.

She drove through the back streets and parked in front of London's.

"Is that Diego's car?" she said.

"Yup." My stomach knotted.

Jessica answered the door. "What a nice surprise. Come on in. Just in time for waffles." Something about her southern accent makes you feel important and welcome. Not the norm in So Cal.

London and Diego were seated at the kitchen table. Shit. How was I supposed to apologize to London about Diego arriving at the hospital with him sitting right there?

I sank down in the soft dining chair next to London. Skye handed her our gift-drink. "Salud."

"So fancy." London took a sip and grimaced. "Delicious." We laughed.

"How are you feeling?" I asked.

"Much better." She put her hand on Diego's shoulder.

She sipped her drink again, shuddered, and pushed it away. "That should be illegal."

Jessica sat down with a plate piled with waffles.

"Thank you," we said at the same time.

"Where's Rachel?" Jessica asked.

"She's shopping with Lauren today," Skye said.

"That's a first. So, what's new with everyone? Mack, how's your sister?" Jessica's great at making awkward situations comfortable.

"Maddie's fine." I wanted to help fill the silence but couldn't think of anything to say.

"How's your brother, Skye? How's college?" She set her hand on top of Skye's.

"Noah's fine. He's in Mexico right now—comes home tomorrow."

I realized my mind had been Noah-free all week, but now I was overtaken by an image of him exiting the plane, buff and shirtless. Then I pictured him tripping. Much better.

"These waffles are awesome," Diego said.

"Thank you. My grandmother's recipe." Jessica took a bite.

We finished eating and London cleared our plates and tossed them in the trash.

Diego stood up. "Think it's time for me to hit the road.

Thank you, Mrs. Wright. See you girls later." Oh, that smile.

London walked Diego to the door, and Skye and I helped Jessica clean the kitchen.

London came back in and kissed Jessica on the cheek. "Thanks, Mom."

We went out on the patio. Sunshine and ocean breeze, like a summer preview. I felt so grateful to be at London's house, WITH London.

"Mack, I can't believe you called Diego," London said.

Shit, I wanted to bring it up before she did. "I'm so sorry. I told him not to visit until I asked you if it was okay."

"Yeah, he told me, but I don't get why you called him in the first place."

"I didn't know what was going to happen. He loves you—I thought he should know."

London started crying. "There's no way he loves me. I'm a disaster."

"That's crazy-talk," Skye said.

London thrust out her bandaged wrist. "Well, I'm pretty fucking crazy."

I reached over and stroked her arm. "Girl, we're all crazy. Trust me."

"For sure." Skye lifted her sleeve to reveal a scar on her

forearm.

"You cut yourself?" London's eyes widened.

"No." Skye traced the line. "Last year, my dad threw a vase and a piece of it lodged in my arm."

"Why did he throw a vase?" London said.

"Who knows." She pulled down her sleeve. "He was drinking. I probably said the wrong thing. I can't remember."

Last year? Again, totally oblivious. Did I miss the clues or was Skye that good at hiding?

"I'm so sorry," London said.

"Can I bring you girls anything?" Jessica opened the kitchen window.

"No thanks, Mom," London said.

"Too bad Rachel's not here," I said. "Maybe tomorrow we can all get together."

"I can't tomorrow. Noah's coming home." Skye stuck out her lower lip.

Our serious talk had pushed Noah out of my mind, but whoosh...he was back.

"How about Sunday?" London said.

Skye sighed. "I'm going to yoga. Want to come?"

"*Yoga*?" London and I said at the same time.

"My mom keeps bugging me, and I told her I would go with

her. It would be so much better if you came with me."

"I guess I could try it." London raised her eyebrows at me.

"Why not?" I put my hands together at my chest and bowed.

APRIL 22 · SATURDAY

Last night I was plagued by negative thoughts, the first being I totally forgot to call Dr. S to apologize for missing my appointment. And she had left me a message too!

I was headed to the kitchen for a snack, when I heard Mom and Dad coming home from dinner. I stopped at the end of the hall and listened.

Mom: It was extravagant, considering our circumstances.

Dad: I thought you'd enjoy it.

Mom: I did, but we need to start facing reality.

Dad: We are—in the big picture.

Mom: The big picture scares me.

Dad: It's going to work out. You'll see, I can do this.

Mom: I know you can.

At that point they moved into the den, and I slinked back to my room.

I never thought money could be problem. Are we broke? I felt sick to my stomach—which, on the bright side, killed my desire to eat the leftover fried chicken in the refrigerator.

I can't find the energy to revise my thoughts. Maybe I should try writing to myself like Dr. S suggested. Maybe she won't get mad at me for missing our session if I've done a little homework.

I'm going to write this as I go. Like a court reporter in my brain. I need one of those for real.

Interview Transcript

Subject: Mackenzie Stewart

Q: What's troubling you?

A: Being fat and possibly going bankrupt

Q: Which troubles you most?

A: Being fat

Q: Why?

A: Because no one cares how much money I have, except me, plus I can hide being broke more easily than I can hide being fat

Q: How would you like to feel?

A: Thin, happy, in control

Q: How do you feel?

A: Fat

Q: Do you feel in control?

A: Sort of

Q: What are you in control of?

A: I don't throw up anymore

Q: Do you feel happy?

A: Sometimes

Q: What are you happy about?

A: London, Skye, Rachel, and Dr. S

Q: Anyone else?

A: Sort of Arman and Noah

Q: Are you feeling bad about anyone else?

A: I have an uneasy feeling about Maddie

Q: Why?

A: I have been ignoring her. I don't think she cares, but I feel like I should pay more attention.

Q: Anyone else?

A: My mom and dad

Q: Why?

A: I have been ignoring them, too. I don't know what's going on. Maybe we are broke. Maybe they are going to get a divorce and I'm missing the signs. I should talk to Maddie.

Q: Anyone else?

A: Myself

Q: Why?

A: I ignore myself, too. I don't pay attention to what I eat, or how much I exercise. I haven't been doing my positive thoughts. I get distracted by my friends and ignore myself.

Interesting. I knew I was worried about being fat and broke, but not the rest. Weird how it just came out. I think the big issue is, I haven't been paying attention. Not to my family or myself, and probably not to my friends, or Noah or Arman, either. Not in a way that matters. For example, I was paying attention to London, but I might have never noticed there was anything else wrong, and she probably would have died. My dad is another example. It never occurred to me he could have lost his job. And what could be going on with Maddie or Mom I don't know about? And myself...what's going on in there?

This reminds me of what Dr. S said about emotions: pay attention and listen. It sounds easy. I try to do it, and I think I am, then I realize I'm not. I'm totally clueless.

APRIL 23 · SUNDAY

I'm now having official self-conversations. Is this what happens when you interview yourself?

> Me: Good job, no fried chicken last night.
>
> Me2: Thank you.
>
> Me: Now you can have it for breakfast.
>
> Me2: Good idea.
>
> Me: Should you have it for breakfast?
>
> Me2: Shut up.

These were my thoughts as I zombied to the kitchen this morning, before my world completely turned upside down AGAIN.

Last week our English assignment was to write a play, and it seems like the perfect medium to relate the alternate universe that has become my life. Here goes...

MACK'S WORLD

Scene One

SETTING: MOM, DAD, and MADDIE are eating breakfast in the kitchen. MACK enters and joins them at the table.

DAD   Girls, Mom and I need to talk to you.

DAD runs his hands through his hair.

DAD   My break from work has been extended...indefi-
           nitely.

MOM   Dad's going to get another job, but in the mean-
           time, we need to make some changes.

MADDIE   What kind of changes?

DAD   We're transitioning to a simpler lifestyle. Downsiz-
           ing a bit.

MACK   Downsizing? As in our house?

           MACK chokes on her egg.

MOM   We're considering it.

           *MOM hands her water to MACK. MOM walks to
           end of table where DAD sits, and puts her hands
           on his shoulders.*

MOM   This change is going to be good for our family.
           Dad is pursuing a different career. In the mean-
           time, my salary will tide us over.

MACK (TO   Since when do our parents present a united front,
HERSELF)   like some couple out of a movie? Who are these
           people? Have my real parents been abducted?

MADDIE	We're moving?
DAD	Probably. It's a great time to sell.
MADDIE	Where are we going to live?
MOM	We might move in with Gram until we find the right house.
MACK	Gram's house only has three bedrooms.
MOM	You and Maddie would share a room.
MACK (TO HERSELF)	WTF? Move out of the house I have lived in all my life? Share a room?
MADDIE	I suppose this means we're not going to Hawaii.
DAD	Actually, that trip is already paid for, so we're still definitely going. We aren't destitute—we're being strategic. Gram has plenty of room for us, and it will give us time to save money and decide where we want to live.
MACK	Do we get to have any input?
MADDIE	Yeah, what about us?
DAD	Of course, you do. We'll work it out as a family.

MADDIE	This is too weird. Can I be excused?

MOM	Yes.

MACK	Can I too?

MOM nods. Offstage, MADDIE and MACK slam their bedroom doors.

END ACT ONE

...

ACT TWO

SETTING: MACK's room

MADDIE knocks on door.

MACK	Come in.

MADDIE	I can't believe this.

MADDIE flops on the bed next to MACK, and they stare at the ceiling.

MADDIE	Maybe we can get jobs so we don't have to move.

MACK	There's no way we can earn enough to make a difference.

MADDIE	Maybe we could sell things online?
MACK	Yeah, right.
MADDIE	You're such a downer. I read about a kid who sold old comic books and made $10,000 in one month.
MACK	Sorry, I'm sure you're right, but I don't think it matters how much we make. Mom and Dad have already made up their minds.

MADDIE AND MACK sit up on the bed and face each other. MADDIE claps her hands once and stretches one out to MACK, who returns the clap. They laugh.

MACK	But how are we going to share a room? I can't even imagine.
MADDIE	It wouldn't be *that* bad.
MACK	I know, but we'd never be alone.
MADDIE	What's so great about being alone?
MACK	I'll go crazy if I can't be by myself.
MADDIE	I'd rather have company.

MACK   Well, maybe you're used to it—you're always with Alexis.

MADDIE   Right. As if you would know.

MACK   What's that supposed to mean?

A tear falls down MADDIE'S cheek.

MACK   What's wrong?

MADDIE   I can't tell you.

MACK   Of course you can—I'm your big sister.

MADDIE   You acted like my big sister for a week, and then you went back to being you.

MACK   You're totally right.

MADDIE   I am?

MACK   One hundred percent. I'm sorry, Maddie.

MADDIE   Well, it's not all your fault. I haven't tried very hard either. I mean, you shared your problem with me, and I haven't even checked in with you—not that you care. But I'm wrapped up in my own troubles.

MACK   Is it about a boy? Or is it about Alexis?

MADDIE   Ha, not a boy.

MACK   So it's Alexis?

MADDIE   Well, sort of. Alexis is my soulmate.

MACK   Friend soulmate or romantic soulmate?

MADDIE   Romantic.

MACK   I'm confused. Alexis was seeing Tyler.

MADDIE   The feeling isn't mutual.

          *MADDIE signs the answer—puts her thumb
          to her chin and quickly moves it forward, then
          makes a hang-loose sign with both hands and
          rotates them in a circle.*

MACK   Does she know how you feel?

MADDIE   Yeah. She said she already knew.

MACK   Knew you liked her?

MADDIE   Knew I was gay. I didn't tell her I love her. I mean,
          she loves me too, just not the same way.

MACK   I'm so glad you told me.

MADDIE   How do you feel about it?

MACK   Fine. I mean, it's a surprise for sure. But, it's not a
          big deal. It seems like so many people are gay.

MADDIE   That's rude.

MACK   I'm sorry. I don't know why I said that. But, you
          are what you are, right? I think it sucks the girl
          you love doesn't feel the same way. Alexis is
          straight for sure?

MADDIE   Yes. Sad fact.

MACK   Too bad.

MADDIE   At least we have Hawaii.

          *MACK puts her arm around MADDIE. MADDIE
          rests her head on MACK's shoulder.*

MACK   Amen. Are you going to tell Mom and Dad?

MADDIE   I don't see any reason to, since I'm not going to
          be bringing a girlfriend home anytime soon.

MACK   I guess you're right. Why have the conversation?

MADDIE   I will eventually. I'm glad I told you. Thanks,
          Mack.

MACK   Thanks, Mads. I love you.

          END ACT TWO

It doesn't feel weird that Maddie is gay. What's weird is that I never had the slightest clue. Was she hiding it or did I just not pay attention? It's disturbing to realize how much I don't see. What else is there?!

Gotta go get ready for yoga. Skye is picking me up in an hour.

APRIL 24 · MONDAY

First day back from spring break. London's internship just ended, and we're all back together at lunchtime.

"So yoga was pretty cool," Rachel said.

"My mom thought you were very generous to join us," Skye said.

"I liked the teacher," London said.

"I liked how I didn't think of anything else for the entire class," I said.

"Come to think of it," Rachel said. "I didn't either. It was a nice break from my crazy mind."

"My favorite part was the end—dead man's pose," London added.

We froze.

She laughed. "I only liked it because you don't do anything."

"Hilarious," I said.

"It does make you think though...about being dead," London said. "Things kind of suck right now, but I'd still rather be alive." She looked at each of us. "You three mean the world to me. Thanks for saving my life."

Just then, Diego walked up and sat down next to London.

"Howdy girls." He put his arm around London's shoulder.

"How's it going?"

"Fine." She cleared her throat.

"So, did you hear about Eden's party this Saturday?"

We shook our heads.

"Huge blower." He couldn't sit still.

Rachel checked her phone. "Oh, here's the invite. She must have just sent it."

Diego turned to London. "Wanna go?"

"Maybe. That feels like forever from now."

The bell rang and we went our separate ways.

Isn't it a little too soon to be back to business as usual? Diego's acting like last week didn't even happen.

"Hey, Mack," a voice called from behind me. Arman.

He jogged to catch up. His black t-shirt sported a picture of a bone with the caption, *I found this humerus.*

"I like your shirt." Arman has been working out.

"Thanks." He brushed his hands over the words. "Did you hear about Eden's party?"

"Yep."

He held the classroom door open. "After you. I was thinking I might go. I mean, do you maybe want to go together?"

I was totally caught off-guard. "Sure...well, can I let you know later in the week?"

His faced turned red. "Yeah, sure, no problem."

"I do want to go with you. I just sort of have a lot going on at home right now." I wouldn't be surprised if my parents have already sold our house. Maybe we're moving to Mexico this weekend.

"It's fine, I understand."

"Thanks for asking." I kissed him on the cheek and went to my desk.

Seriously bold, Mack! A kiss in the classroom, in front of everyone? Very unlike me. Something about Arman makes me confident, like I'm in charge. I'm conflicted about that feeling— on one hand, it's empowering, but on the other, I kind of like it when my stomach flips.

APRIL 26 · WEDNESDAY

Dr. Skyler

As I drove to my appointment with Dr. S, I couldn't stop thinking about London.

When I took my seat, I launched straight in. "Can I ask you something?"

"Of course," said Dr. S.

"Would you be willing to see one of my friends?" I felt like Dorothy talking to the Wizard of Oz.

"Tell me about your friend."

"It's London—she tried to kill herself."

Dr. S frowned. "How long ago did this happen?"

"About a week and a half."

"How is she now?"

"She seems perfectly fine....but she seemed fine before it happened, too."

"How did you find out she tried to kill herself?"

"She texted me, and I found her passed out in the bathroom."

"It must have been traumatic for you."

My eyes welled.

"How are you coping?"

"Me?" We're talking about London here.

"You said London almost died, correct?"

"Yes, but she didn't." I tried to push away the image of her on the gurney.

"You were upset, yes?"

"Of course, but it's over. I mean, London's the one who needs to talk about it."

"I agree, London should seek counseling."

"Would you see her?"

"I can see you care about her."

"Why won't you answer me? She's like my sister. Will you talk to her?"

"I have limited openings right now, but I will see what I can do." She wrote something in her notebook.

"Thank you." At least it was something.

"With your permission, I would like to talk about how London's actions have affected you."

"Well, basically it showed me I'm clueless."

"How so?"

"I didn't know how upset she was. I didn't think to check for pills...And it's not just her. My dad lost his job, or quit—I don't know which—and now we have to move in with my grandma.

AND my sister just told me she's gay."

We were quiet for a minute.

"You see these situations as evidence you are clueless."

"Don't you? I should have had some idea. In hindsight, there were signs everywhere, but I didn't pay attention."

"Let's say you could have known all these things if you had paid better attention. What would you have done differently?"

"Well...I would have talked more to London and spent more time with her."

She nodded.

"Probably nothing with my parents, but at least I wouldn't have been totally blindsided. I could have mentally prepared or something...And with Maddie, maybe I would have been nicer. Also I wouldn't have felt so stupid when she told me."

"We can't go back, Mackenzie—we can only affect the current moment."

Not helpful, Dr. S.

"I would like to encourage you to examine what you have learned."

"Besides the fact that I don't know anything?"

"That's an important thing to learn—you *don't* know anything. No one does. Life is unknowable—it is something to be experienced and observed."

"I guess. But it doesn't mean you should be ignorant."

She waited. Come on, Dr. S, this is the part where you tell me I'm not ignorant.

Nope.

"So, I should examine what I have learned? I guess I've learned I should be nicer and pay more attention to the people I love."

"When you say *should*, who is giving the directive?"

"I am."

"I see. Would it be accurate to say, 'You *want* to pay more attention to the people you love?'"

"Yes."

"Do you feel the difference between should and want?"

I said the new sentence in my head, "I want to pay more attention to the people I love."

Dr. S said, "*Should* implies judgment, whereas *want* is an intention."

Another new concept to ponder.

"Did you bring your notebook?"

"No."

She held up a finger to signal, "just a minute," and walked over to her desk.

She took something from a drawer and returned to her seat.

"Would you like to use this?" She held out a small periwinkle blue notebook.

"You can keep it, if you want it."

"I should have remembered mine." There's that SHOULD again.

"Mackenzie, it's only a notebook. I would like you to have it."

"Thank you." I rubbed my hand over the soft cover. "I love this color."

"I thought it called to me." Dr. S winked.

She handed me a pen. "I would like you to write your intention."

Huh? What intention?

"Walk me through it again," she said. "If you had known about London, your parents, and Maddie, what would you have done differently?"

"I would have paid more attention to London and been nicer to Maddie...I don't know what I could have done about my dad and his job, but maybe I would have been nicer to him, too. I suppose I could ask him how he's doing, but that seems so weird."

"Good. Take those thoughts and turn them into intentional sentences. A good way to start is with, 'I want.'"

I wrote:

- I want to pay more attention to my friends.
- I want to be nicer to Maddie.
- I want to pay more attention to my parents.

"Finished?" Dr. S asked.

I nodded.

"Now, rewrite each sentence as a statement. For example, *I want to listen*, becomes *I listen*. The universe conspires to make your thoughts your reality, so the clearer they are, the easier it is to make them real. When you finish, read them aloud."

I rewrote my sentences and read them to Dr. S:

- I pay attention to my friends.
- I am nice to Maddie.
- I pay attention to my parents.

"How do they feel?"

"Good. I wish they were true."

"Change your thoughts, change your reality."

I know, I know!

She read her notebook. "Have you had the opportunity to interview yourself like we discussed last time?"

"Yes." At least I did one thing right.

"What did you experience?"

"I had some new realizations, but I also started talking to myself after I had finished."

"The more you do it, the less it will leave you feeling like you are two people."

It sounds unlikely, but Dr. S's predictions continually surprise me.

"Our time is almost finished," she said.

"What about London? Will you see her?" I asked. Please say yes. Please. Please. Please.

She handed me a business card. "Give this to her and tell her she is welcome to call me if she wants to. Let's start there."

I tucked the card in my jeans pocket. "Thank you so much."

We shook hands and said goodbye.

My phone vibrated.

Arman: Wanna hang out tonight? Maybe Cava?

Arman wants to hang out with me! But I don't think I'm up for a romantic encounter (is that what it would be?) after my session with Dr. S.

Me: How about tomorrow night?

Arman: Okay

Me: Thanks for asking!

Arman: Sure. See you tomorrow.

Me: See you tomorrow.

APRIL 27 · THURSDAY

THE MACKENZIE TIMES
Special Report: Arman Got Game

Arman said he'd pick me up at 7:00 and he texted me when he arrived at 7:15. When I opened the car door, he apologized and tossed a stack of papers from the passenger seat into the back. His car smelled like coconut.

He had on a red t-shirt with a picture of the universe and an arrow to Earth, with the words, "You are here."

"Another classic."

"You like it?"

"On you I do." Maybe I should add an arrow to the poster on my ceiling. It's kind of funny.

When we arrived at Cava, he said. "How about if you get a table, and I'll get our drinks? Latte?"

"How'd you know?"

"Just a guess." He grinned.

I chose the only open booth—coincidentally, the same spot where he had been sitting with Eden last week.

After a few minutes, Arman sat down and handed me my coffee.

"Thank you. Are you and Eden friends?" I heard the record-scratch sound in my head.

His smile vanished. "Uh, yeah. Sure."

"Just friends? I mean, it's none of my business, but I'm just wondering."

His smile returned. "Yep, just friends."

My face got hot and I looked down. My latte was topped with a mound of foam. "Wow, they're making fancy coffee tonight."

I was about touch the foam with my finger when I noticed the design.

I looked closer—the swirl said...

PROM?

I felt my cheeks redden. He reached his hands across the table and closed them over mine, around the cup.

"Will you go to Prom with me?"

"Are you asking me because neither of us has a date?"

"Well, actually I don't know if you already have a date. Do you?" He looked embarrassed. So cute.

"No I don't. I would love to go with you."

He leaned across the table, and I pushed my palms into the seat to lift myself up. We pressed our lips together, and pulled apart. I could hear the flame crackle. Magic.

"Mmm." Arman sat back and took a sip of his drink.

My thoughts exactly. Comfortable silence. Happy. Happy. Happy.

"Is everything okay at home?" Arman asked.

"What? Where did that come from?"

"Uh, sorry. You said yesterday there's stuff going on at home."

"Oh right, I forgot I told you. Things are fine. Thanks for asking." Nice recall! Mom and Dad only served up pasta last night. Miracle.

The door opened and in walked Eden, Melissa, and Diego. REALLY? Does Eden LIVE at Cava? Go away!

Arman waved and she came over to our table. Melissa and Diego got in line.

"Hey, Arman. Hey, Mack." She smiled and gathered her hair over one shoulder.

Keep a neutral face, Mack. Hide your thoughts. Is Arman smiling too much at her? Why isn't Diego with London? Why does Eden show up everywhere?

"Can you guys come to my party? We got the *best* DJ."

Arman asked me for an answer with his eyebrows.

"We'll be there." I lifted my coffee in a toast.

She clapped her hands. "Yay! Gotta order. See ya

tomorrow."

Despite the fact Eden has a beautiful face and a perfect body, she doesn't seem fake. I think she's a nice person. A really annoying, perfect, nice person.

"Can I pick you up for the party?" Arman asked.

"Sure. Sounds great. But since when are you all into parties?"

"I'm not, but it's Eden's house, so maybe it'll be okay."

"What does that mean?" Did I sound jealous?

"I mean Eden's cool so maybe it won't be your typical party."

"Spoken like someone who doesn't go to many parties." Definitely jealous. Newsflash: Don't tell your date that another girl is cool.

"Yeah, I guess. Anyway, I'll be with you," he said.

Aww. Forgiven.

We hung out for about an hour and talked mostly about baseball. He's totally obsessed with making it to the championships. Not a single glance at Eden.

APRIL 28 · FRIDAY

LUNCH REPORT

Absent: Skye and Rachel (working on a video for Spanish)

Present: London and Mack

Discussion...

Me: How are you feeling?

London: Fine, I guess.

Me: How are things with Diego?

London: I don't think he's cut out for all this.

Something told me I shouldn't tell her I saw him at Cava.

London: But, we're going to Eden's party. Oh, and he asked me to Prom, too.

Me: You don't sound very excited.

London: Sometimes being around all those people makes me feel so alone.

Me: I know what you mean. But maybe if we go together it'll be better. Arman asked me to Prom last night.

London: Mack and Arman, together again. Groundhog Day.

Me: Very funny.

The bell rang.

Me: Do you want to hang out tonight?

London: Diego said he might come over.

Me: Well, if he doesn't, maybe we can do something. I'll text you later.

She stared into the distance.

Me: Hello? Okay?

London: Okay! You're relentless.

The second bell rang, and we headed off in different directions.

EVENING REPORT

London said Diego was on his way over, so I asked Maddie if she wanted to go to the movies.

"Is anyone else going?" Maddie asked.

"No. Do you want to invite anyone?"

"No. What happened, no one else could go?"

"I didn't ask anyone else. I know I'm not the greatest sister, but I want to hang out more."

She grinned.

We watched Vin Diesel's four-hundredth car movie. Plot was torture, but that body. Sigh. Definitely a bonding experience.

On a side note, we were at the same theater where I threw up last time, but the thought of doing it never crossed my mind, even though I drank an Icee. Seems like the happier I am about my actions, the less I worry about my weight.

APRIL 29 · SATURDAY

6:00 p.m.

Wait, did I say I'm not worried about my weight?!

This morning I tried on every single item of clothing I own, and everything looks HORRIBLE. I considered raiding Maddie's closet, but couldn't bring myself to do it. I did the unthinkable—I asked her for permission. And to my surprise, she said yes.

"How about this?" I held up a cute gray sweater.

"If you promise to take care of it."

"How much damage could I do?"

"Considering my other sweater has disappeared, probably a lot."

"I promise. Are you and Alexis going to Eden's?"

"No, we're not talking." Maddie stuffed her hands in her pockets.

"Why?"

"I got mad at her last night because I wanted to hang out and she said she had things to do."

I didn't say anything.

"What if she never wants to hang out again?"

"It's just going to take some time for things to get back to

344

normal. Don't worry. You've been friends forever. Why don't you come to the party with us?"

"You don't think it would be weird?"

"Not at all."

She flung her arms around me. "Thanks, Mack. You're the best!"

I hugged her back. "It'll be fun. Thanks so much for the sweater."

I texted Arman.

> Me: I'm bringing my sister to the party. Is it ok if I meet you there?
>
> Arman: Sure. See you soon.

I texted everyone.

> Me: Driving tonight with Maddie. Want to come with us?
>
> Skye: Yes
>
> London: For sure
>
> Rachel: I'll meet you there
>
> Skye: Sleepover my house after?
>
> Me: Definitely
>
> London: IN

Rachel: Yaaas

I'm more excited about Skye's sleepover than Eden's party. At least my wardrobe issue is solved.

APRIL 30 · SUNDAY

So much happened yesterday, I have to break it up into chapters! Short story was our latest English assignment, so I'm trying it out.

A Night To Remember
By Mackenzie Stewart

Chapter One: *The Party*
Chapter Two: *Skye and James*
Chapter Three: *Rachel*
Chapter Four: *Noah*

THE PARTY

Arman walked up at the same time we did. Eden's parents directed us to the bottom floor. I can't believe they trust us so much. I wonder if they have cameras.

Eden was at the foot of the stairs. As we walked down, Arman whispered in my ear, "You look pretty." It was so nice to hear.

"Yay, you made it!" Eden gave us each a hug. "Go get something to eat." She gestured to the table covered with platters of party food.

We filled our plates and headed out to the patio.

"Mack, over here!" Rachel waved from a table where she was sitting with Dax and James.

We all sat down.

Dax stood up. "Heading to the bar."

James went with him.

"There's alcohol?" I asked.

"Yeah right," Skye said. "Lawsuit waiting to happen. Just soda."

I started to eat and realized I wasn't stressed. I felt free. It was an amazing experience. I replayed Arman's words, "You look pretty." I could almost believe it.

Arman leaned over. "You have something...right...here." He pointed to his lip.

I wiped my mouth with a napkin. "Did I get it?"

"Almost, let me help you." He put his hand on my cheek and kissed me on the mouth.

Electricity to my toes! My brain short-circuited, and I forgot where we were. Lucky for me everyone was busy talking, and the lights were dim.

He pulled away and smiled. "Sorry, I couldn't help myself."

Dax and James returned with a bunch of cups and sodas.

"Who wants to get this party started?" Dax waved a flask.

Maddie held out a cup. I pretended not to care.

London held one out too. "Just a little."

Dax poured clear liquid (vodka, I assume) into their cups and they filled the rest with soda.

"Cheers!" London and Maddie clinked. All I could think about was that two weeks ago London almost died. I wondered if anyone else was thinking the same thing.

Dax poured some for Rachel. "You want it straight or shall I add a little soda?"

"Did I say I wanted a drink?"

"Did the Earth tell me it was round?" Dax laughed.

"Hilarious, but I'm good."

"Well, just in case." He set it down in front of her.

She hit the cup with the back of her hand, and it went flying off the table.

"What the hell is wrong with you, Dax? I said I didn't want anything." She stormed into the house.

"Shit, where'd that come from?" Dax poured himself a drink.

"I better go check." I gave Arman a quick kiss on the lips. "I'll catch up with you in a little bit, okay?"

I found Rachel by the stairs.

"Are you okay?" I asked.

"Yeah, I'm fine."

"Is there anything I can do?"

"Can we go home? I really don't want to stay here."

"Sure. Let me tell Maddie and Arman. I'll be right back."

As I walked to the patio, my phone buzzed:

> Skye: Ubering home. Come over when you're done.
>
> Me: U okay?
>
> Skye: Fine
>
> Me: Promise?
>
> Skye: Yes
>
> Me: See you soon

I found London and Maddie on the dance floor with a bunch of people. I caught their attention and they came over.

"Is Rachel okay?" London asked.

"Yeah, but she's ready to go."

"It's fine with me if we leave," London said.

Maddie said, "Now?! No way. This is so fun."

"You really want to stay without me?" I asked.

"Absolutely. I know lots of people here."

"Will you text me when you get home?"

"Sure, Mom, if I remember."

I found Arman talking to Eden by the stairs. Really?! Every. Time.

"There you are." Arman kissed me on the cheek.

"Were you trying to find me?" Could've fooled me.

"I was a minute ago."

"I just wanted to tell you we're leaving."

Eden said, "Don't go. It's early."

Arman put his arm around me. "Stay, Mack."

I wiggled out from under his arm. "Sorry, I gotta go. Great party, Eden. Thanks."

"Can I walk you out?" he asked.

"Sure." I texted Rachel and London to meet me out front.

He held my hand as we walked up the stairs. At the top, he pulled me to the side.

"How'd I get so lucky?" He pulled me close and kissed me. His warm, soft lips turned my insides to goo. He held the back of my head with his hand.

"Ahem," I heard behind me.

I pulled away. Rachel and London.

I turned back to Arman. "I'm sorry. I have to go."

"I'll probably leave too—I only came here for you."

He walked me out and kissed me again at my car door. I pressed into his body, and for a brief moment, I considered letting them leave without me. But then, my inner voice spoke up, "I pay attention to my friends."

"Goodnight," I said.

He opened my door and we drove away.

In the car, Rachel let out a whistle.

"Shut up." I laughed.

SKYE AND JAMES

When we got to Skye's, Mrs. Sato let us in.

"Hi girls, she's in her room. Go on up."

Skye was lying on the floor, surrounded by tissues.

We sat down next to her.

"Are you okay?" I said.

"No." A stream of tears.

"What's going on?" London said.

There was a knock on the door.

"Who is it?" Skye called.

"Me." N.O.A.H.

Skye got up and opened the door a crack. "What?"

"James is downstairs." Chills raced down my spine as I strained to hear. "He's here to talk to you."

"Well, I don't want to talk to him."

"Skye, come on. I don't think he deserves this."

"Of course, you don't. Guys always stick together."

"You know I would never take anyone's side over you."

Awesome brother.

"Tell him he can wait, and if I feel like it, I'll come down."
She closed the door in his face.

"Totally rude, Skye," Noah called through the door.

Skye flopped down. "James can wait all night."

"Why are you mad?" Rachel asked.

"Do you swear this doesn't leave this room?"

We nodded.

"Okay." She took a deep breath. "Mack, you know some of
this, but not all of it."

She winced. "My dad has a drinking problem."

Rachel and London looked as shocked as I had felt when
Skye told me.

"Right now he's in rehab, but just before he left, things were
really bad. One day I found a new bottle of vodka he had hidden
in the pantry. I dumped it and put the empty bottle back. It felt
great. I didn't even care what happened...But, when he found
it he accused Noah and started shoving him. It was so awful. I
screamed at him that I was the one who did it and was glad. He
glared at me and went to his room. We haven't spoken since."

We were silent.

"So, I suppose you're wondering what this has to do with

James, right?"

We waited.

"Well, last night we were hanging out and sharing a lot of personal stuff. I decided to tell him about my dad and that story. At that point, Mack was the only one who knew about my dad, and I kind of told her by accident."

"So James was really sympathetic and nice, but then he asked me why I poured out the bottle."

She started crying. "WHY I poured it out! I feel like he didn't listen to a thing I said."

Rachel leaned in and hugged her. "I totally get it. He probably just didn't know what to say. I know from experience, people say stupid things when they're uncomfortable. They end up making you feel worse instead of better."

Skye looked at us. "Why do *you* think I poured it out?"

London: You had enough.

Me: You couldn't take it anymore.

Rachel: It was like, fuck this.

Skye: I love you girls.

"I know he asked a stupid question, but I bet James knows why, too," I said.

"Think I should talk to him?" Skye asked.

We all nodded.

She stood up. "I'll be back in a minute."

Rachel turned to me. "You knew about her dad?"

"Yeah." I was proud to be the insider, even if it had been an accident.

"I can't believe it. I thought Skye's life was Utopia," London said.

"Guess we all have our shit," Rachel said.

"That's for sure," I said.

We were quiet for a few minutes and then Skye whooshed in the door. Her face was flushed, and she was grinning.

"All better?" London said.

"Yep. And he asked me to Prom."

"I assumed you were going already," I said.

"We probably were, but it's nice to be asked properly." She blushed.

"Is he still here?" Rachel asked.

"No, I told him it's girls' night."

"Hell yeah," London said.

RACHEL

Skye said, "Why did you get mad at Dax tonight, Rachel?"

"Didn't you see? I told him I didn't want a drink, and he

served me like I was a child."

Silence.

London said, "I don't mean to sound insensitive, but it's pretty weird for you to not want a drink."

Rachel hung her head. "Yeah, I know."

What was going on?

She said, "I just feel different. When I saw you on that gurney, London, all I could think was, 'That should be me. I'm the one who deserves to die—not London.' I knew it was my fault this was happening to you."

London said, "No way, Rachel. I'm the one who did it. It had nothing to do with you."

"But if I lost you, I would be losing another member of my family. And it would be my fault for ignoring everything my friends told me. I'm so grateful you're okay, London. I'm so grateful for all three of you. And I just feel different, you know?"

We all three wrapped our arms around Rachel. We were like one person, totally united. I want to remember that feeling forever.

After a minute, Rachel pulled back. "Okay, chicas, enough sentimentality for one night."

We all laughed and wiped our eyes.

"Want to watch a movie?" Skye asked.

We gathered pillows and blankets.

"I'm hungry," Skye said. "Let's make a sustenance pitstop."

NOAH

We followed Skye to the kitchen. She flipped on the light and there was Noah, in flannel pajama bottoms and no shirt, eating peanut butter from the jar with a spoon.

He held the jar out to us. "Anyone interested?" Pink cheeks.

My face got hot and I wished I could disappear to gather my wits and catch my breath.

"That's gross, Noah," Skye said.

He took another bite. "Actually, it's pretty tasty."

"You need to put your name on that jar so no one else eats out of it."

He held up the lid. N-O-A-H in black ink across the top. He was clearly proud of himself.

We sat at the island and Skye searched for food.

"How about nachos?" she called from the pantry.

"Great," Rachel said.

Noah put the lid back on his peanut butter and poured a glass of milk. He drank it in one long series of gulps.

"Noah, what's your opinion of James?" Rachel asked.

"He's a good guy. I let him date my sister, so that should tell you something."

"*Let* him date me?" Skye returned from the pantry with a bag of chips. "Like you have any say in the matter."

"Let's just say I could make it unpleasant for him if I didn't think he was good for you."

"That's really annoying, Noah. It's none of your business."

Rachel interrupted. "Hey, hey, let's not ruin a good night. Noah just cares about you."

"Well, girls, I'll get out of your hair." He met my eyes and smiled.

I tried to control my return-smile. He seemed totally unselfconscious, as if he weren't standing there like a god, baring his skin for all to see.

Skye said, "You can hang around for some nachos if you want." She must have read my mind.

He raised his eyebrows. "I'll take you up on that. Be back in a sec."

Skye piled chips and cheese on a cookie sheet and stuck it in the oven. Then she started chopping tomatoes.

"Impressive," London said.

"Thanks! I should have let James stay—he would have loved this."

"Maybe you should text him to come back," Rachel said.

She stopped chopping for a second and considered. "No, this is a girls' night—I don't want to drag boy energy into it."

"Amen," London said.

"What about Noah?" I said.

Skye said, "Noah doesn't count."

Just then he walked back in. "What's that supposed to mean?" He had put on a plain black t-shirt. I was grateful and disappointed at the same time.

"You don't count as a boy tonight," Skye said.

"Too bad." Maybe it was wishful thinking, but I swear he looked straight at me when he said, it. "Who *would* count as a boy?"

Rachel held out her index finger. "James would count..." She pointed to London and held up another finger. "And Diego..." Another finger. "And Dax, if I were talking to him. And..." She leered at me and held up her fourth finger. "Arman would most definitely count."

Noah said, "Who's Arman?"

I wanted to DIE.

"Just a guy from class," I said.

"Yeah, a guy from class who's taking you to Prom," Rachel said.

FACE ON FIRE.

"So, you and Arman are going to Prom?" Noah asked.

"Well I've known him for a long time. I mean, we're just friends." Shut up, Mack!

"Right." Rachel laughed. "You guys sure looked like friends at the party."

I shot her daggers.

"Here we go..." Skye set a giant platter of nachos in front of us, complete with a bowl of fresh salsa.

"Wow, this is amazing." I reached in for a chip and prayed this whole conversation was a figment of my imagination.

Noah filled a plate. "I'll let you girls be boy-free. Thanks for the grub." He grabbed a paper towel and left the kitchen.

Nooooo, don't go! Could he possibly care that I'm going to Prom with Arman? What if I just blew my chance with him?

I channeled my stress straight into the nachos. Should I eat just a few? As many as I want? Am I getting fat? I know I am. Can other people tell? I think I've transitioned to mental barfing, which is not as gross, but nearly as exhausting.

This morning, we were back in the kitchen munching on bagels Mrs. Sato bought for us. Nachos, bagels. I'm going to blow up, but I love being able to eat without worrying about throwing up. But really, Body, when is enough enough?

No sign of Noah. Guess he slept in.

MAY 1 · MONDAY

London and I hung out at her house today after school. Jessica was home.

"Is there anything to eat?" London asked Jessica.

"As a matter of fact, I just made pasta with marinara sauce."

"Anything that won't make me weigh a thousand pounds?"

"Well, I also made a salad with the leftover tomatoes."

"That sounds good," London said.

"Go on outside, and I'll bring it to you."

We leaned against the deck railing. London is so lucky to live so close to the ocean.

"Why isn't Jessica at work?" I asked.

"Oh, she's always home after school, *now*."

"Do you like it?"

"Sort of. I mean, where was she before? She asked me if he-who-shall-not-be-named could join us for dinner sometime. Ugh! I don't want some stranger sitting at our table, eating with us like he's part of our family."

Jessica opened the patio door. "I'll just leave this over here." She set a tray on the table.

"Thank you so much," I said.

"You got it." She blew me a kiss.

"Seems like your mom is really trying."

"I guess. She's been a ghost for five years, but now that I'm *suicidal*, she's Mom of the Year."

"Have you talked to her?"

"I told her about Dr. Skyler, and she was like, 'Yes, I think that is an excellent idea.' And I wanted to say, 'Then why the hell didn't you think of it?' Anyway, I made an appointment."

"That's gre..." Screech. "I'm glad you did." Finally listening. Everything is not necessarily great.

I took a bowl of salad and an orange Italian soda (in a glass, over ice). "I wish my mom cooked like yours. This is so good."

I gobbled. London picked.

"I think you'll really like Dr. Skyler."

"I'm sure I will. Can we drop it for now?"

"Sure." Face slap.

"I really appreciate you trying to help. I'm not going to do it again—I was just...confused."

"Can I ask what happened?"

"Well, I was really sad about breaking up with Diego. But it wasn't just that, it was everything. I miss my dad and my mom is never here...*Was* never here. And the idea of her dating someone else..."

She twisted the ring on her middle finger. "I just wanted it all to go away."

"So you took the pills?"

She nodded. "I didn't plan it. I had a headache and I was searching for Advil in my mom's bathroom. When I saw the Oxy, I thought, "This could all go away, forever.""

I kept quiet.

"But when my hands started to go numb, it was so scary. I texted you then I started to cut myself so I could feel something. That's all I remember until I woke up in the hospital."

"London, I'm so sorry."

She rubbed the scar on her wrist.

"What's it like to cut yourself?" Ugh. It came out before I considered.

She squinted into the distance. "Calming, I guess."

"But, doesn't it hurt?"

"Of course it does. That's why it helps—it blocks out everything else. And when I'm done, I don't feel anything for awhile. It's nice."

It reminded me of how I felt after I threw up. I wondered if I should tell her my secret.

"I get what you're saying about not feeling anything afterwards."

She shrugged.

"I want to share something with you."

"What is it?"

"I wasn't in the hospital just because I had a concussion. It was also because my electrolytes were all messed up."

"From energy drinks?"

"No, from throwing up." I was so embarrassed, my eyes watered.

"You mean that night?"

"No, I mean all the time. That's how I used to stay skinny."

"No way. I can't believe it. Perfect Mack?"

My tears spilled over. "That's really mean, London."

She touched my arm. "I'm sorry, Mack. It just seems like everything is so good for you. It's hard to believe you have a problem."

"That's why I'm seeing Dr. Skyler. She's helped me so much. You were right about me being self-absorbed. I totally was but I couldn't see it. I still am sometimes, but I'm trying. I'm sorry I wasn't a better friend."

"You're the best friend in the world, Mack. Thanks for telling me."

She leaned over and gave me a hug.

"I love you, London."

"I love you too, Mack."

MAY 2 · TUESDAY

Discussion with myself this morning:

> Me: I am perfect.
>
> Brain: But you would be so much better if…
>
> Body: If nothing.
>
> Me: I am perfect.
>
> Brain: BUT…
>
> Me: SHUT UP!

Why is my brain getting loud again? Because my clothes don't fit? Because I'm eating nachos? Help!

Rachel wasn't at school today, and Skye and London were still working on their Spanish project, so I was solo at lunch. I found Maddie reading by herself.

"Hey."

She looked up. "Hey. Slumming?"

"Funny. Can I sit?"

"Sure."

"Still not talking to Alexis?"

She pressed her forehead into her bent knees and nodded.

"I'm so sorry, Mads."

"I wish Mom and Dad would move somewhere else."

"No way. That would totally suck."

"Only for you. You have friends."

"I know you and Alexis will work it out."

"Doubt it."

"I think you should tell Mom what's going on."

"What good would that do? It's just one more thing for her to worry about."

"You'll have someone else to talk to. Mom won't worry—she'll just be happy you told her."

"You think so?"

"Yep." I suddenly felt happy. I leaned over and gave Maddie a quick hug, then stood up.

And there—across the quad—stood Arman and (YEP) Eden.

They were laughing.

Maddie went back to her book. "Thanks, Mack."

"See you tonight, Mads." I stomped towards class away from the happy couple. Just friends. Hmmph. EMOJI (middle finger)

...

10:00 p.m.

I knocked on Maddie's door after dinner.

"Come in." She was doing a backbend in the middle of her

floor.

"Impressive." I flopped on her bed.

"Thanks. Alexis and I are doing a six-week yoga challenge. Well, we *were* anyway."

How can I live with someone and have no idea what she does with her time?

"I did a yoga class a couple of weeks ago at Skye's," I said.

"It's pretty cool, huh?"

"Yeah, but we had a teacher. How do you know what to do?"

She held up her phone. "Video series."

"Is it free?"

"Yep."

"Want me to do it with you until you and Alexis patch things up?"

"That would be great! Want to finish this class with me? It's almost over."

"I'm not very good, but okay."

We followed the teacher through a forward fold and some twists. My body is so tight, but I love feeling places I have never felt before. We ended by lying on our backs.

I turned my head to face Maddie. "Do you think Mom and Dad were acting weird at dinner?"

"No weirder than usual," she said.

"Do you think we should go ask Mom what's going on with moving?"

"I guess we could."

"Come on, let's go." Sister adventure.

From the kitchen we could hear Mom and Dad talking in the den.

Mom: It's not negotiable.

Dad: But it would give us a little more time to decide.

Mom: I'm not adding to our debt when we have a perfectly good solution.

Dad: I'm not sure stuffing us into your mom's house is a perfectly good solution.

Mom: Financially, it is. You're the one who got us into this.

Dad: And I'm going to get us out of it. You just have to give me a little more time. Please, just six months.

Mom: I don't know.

Couch springs. Shit! No time to hide.

Mom walked out of the den. We stood there frozen.

She narrowed her eyes. "How long have you been standing here?"

"Just got here," I said

"So, what do you girls think? Do I give your dad six months?"

"What do you mean? Are you getting a divorce?" Maddie's voice was high. Exactly what I was thinking.

"No, we're definitely not getting a divorce." Dad walked out and put his arm around Mom.

Mom said, "Should we wait six months until we decide whether or not to move in with Gram?"

"Yes!" Maddie and I answered together.

"Well, I guess that settles it." She walked towards the hall.

Maddie and I threw our arms around Dad. It reminded me of a picture we have of us hanging on his leg when we were little.

"Dad, you're the best," Maddie said. "Are we still going to Hawaii?"

I love how she gets straight to the point.

"Yep. June 15th."

Maddie raised a triumphant fist. "Yes!"

I clapped. "The day after school gets out!"

"Anyone want to join me for some ice cream?"

We followed Dad to the kitchen. "Rocky road or vanilla?"

"Vanilla. Do we have sauce?" Maddie asked.

Dad opened the refrigerator. "Voilà!" He held up the chocolate syrup.

Mom walked in. She had changed into her sweats. "I'll have the same."

Dad winked at her. "Mack?" He wiggled the chocolate.

"Sure."

Mom rubbed her temples.

"Are you okay?" I asked.

"Yep. Just thinking about a work problem."

"Personnel drama?" Maddie asked.

"No, a real problem—technical."

"You know, dramatic problems can be real too." Maddie folded her arms on the counter.

"True," Mom said.

"Here you go." Dad brought the sundaes to the island.

A familiar dark voice in my head said, "Prom is close. How much do you weigh?"

"So how are things going at school?" Mom asked.

"Pretty good." I pictured the ice cream congealing into fat around my stomach. Stop!

"Where has Alexis been lately, Maddie?" Mom asked.

"I don't know."

"Is everything okay?"

"Yeah."

"You sure? Did you have an argument?"

"Sort of." Long pause... "I need to tell you guys something," she said.

Total attention.

"I'm...well, it's..." Her eyes welled up with tears.

She searched my face. I nodded.

"I'm gay."

Confusion flashed across Mom and Dad's faces, then understanding.

Mom immediately hugged her. "Oh honey, I'm so glad you told us."

Dad put his arms around both of them and they stayed like that for a long time.

Mom turned to me. "Did you already know?"

I nodded.

"I'm glad."

"We should celebrate," Dad said.

Weird expressions from everyone.

"I mean, we should celebrate that you shared with us."

"Let's add it to the fact we're not moving, and we're still going to Hawaii," Maddie said.

Dad drummed his fingers on his forehead. "How about a little Rudolph?"

When we were little, Rudolph the Red Nosed Reindeer DVD signaled the official beginning of the holidays. As we got older, Dad would break it out to mark a special occasion. When I got my driver's license last summer, we all sat down to a glass of lemonade and a little Christmas.

"What do you think?" Mom asked Maddie.

"Sounds good."

Dad put our bowls in the sink. "I'm changing into sweats." He hugged Maddie. "I'm proud of you."

Once Mom and Dad were out of the kitchen, I said, "I know it sounds dumb, but I'm proud of you too. Are you glad you told them?"

"I think so. I'm still kind of freaking out. Thanks, Mack."

"Aww, I didn't do anything. It was all you."

"You know what I mean."

We hugged. A serious hug.

For the next hour we watched our favorite narrating snowman glide across the screen. It was a night straight out of a TV show, and yet...

A familiar anxiety is creeping in. I think my accumulating fat is taking over my thoughts. Today I tried to tell myself I was perfect again, and I couldn't hear over the shouting of my brain. I thought I was getting better. What is happening?

MAY 3 · WEDNESDAY

3:00 p.m.

I'm staring at my homework and thinking about going to my appointment. I feel like I'm back where I was when I considered not telling Dr. Skyler I threw up. I know she said healing doesn't happen in a straight line, but what if I'm never going to get any better? I don't feel like I'm going to throw up again, but I also feel like I'm never going to be happy with myself. I guess I'll see how it goes today and decide if I want to keep going.

...

7:00 p.m.

Dr. Skyler

We took our seats as usual, but Dr. S didn't ask me how I was feeling. It was like she knew I just wanted the opportunity to rant about how this wasn't going to work. Instead she said, "What was the worst thing that happened this week?"

I thought for a minute. "Probably when I tried on all of my clothes and none of them fit." Please don't give me a gratitude speech.

"I can see how that would be hard," she said. "What was the

374

best thing that happened this week?"

I thought. "Arman asked me to Prom. Oh, and we aren't moving in with my grandma."

"You look pleased."

"Yes, actually those are two really big things. I have been so upset about how I look I actually hadn't taken time to think about them."

"This exercise is a great addition to your toolbox."

"My toolbox?"

"In each of our sessions we have explored tools you can use to navigate your world. The best/worst tool we just tried is one of my favorites because it gives me perspective, and I usually remember something good I had forgotten."

I nodded.

"Would you like take a minute right now to start the list of tools you have discovered so far?"

"I'm sure I can't remember all of them," I said.

"I'll help you get started."

"Okay." I wrote TOOLBOX at the top of the page.

"Do you remember what we discussed in our first session?" she asked.

"I remember you said listen to my body, and take ten minutes at a time if I was having trouble."

"Were those tools useful?"

"Definitely." I added them to my list.

"Do you remember discussing the relationship between your mind and body?"

"Yes. More than once."

She smiled. "Another tool is to remind yourself that your mind and body both support you."

I nodded.

"Have you been journaling about our sessions?" she asked.

"Yes, on my computer."

"Your assignment is to go through your entries and add the rest of your tools to the list."

"Okay. I like the idea of having a list of things to choose from. At least it makes me feel like there's something I can do," I said.

"In time, you will discover additional tools of your own. There is no single tool that works for every person or every situation. The trick is to find what works for you."

"Can I tell you something?" I closed my notebook.

"Of course."

"I was considering not coming anymore because I'm not improving."

I thought she might look upset when I said this, but she just nodded, face neutral.

She said, "There's a saying that goes, 'Nothing happens and nothing happens, and then everything happens.' If you keep this in mind, it will help you through the times when you feel like you are making zero progress. If you use your tools, and work on your thoughts, your reality will change. But it requires patience and the understanding that it doesn't happen in a straight line or in an obvious continuous fashion."

"So do you think maybe I'm stuck in the nothing phase?" I asked.

She smiled. "I think you have made tremendous progress and should be very proud of yourself."

I don't know why, but my eyes stung with tears." I guess I'm willing to give it a little more time."

"I'm glad." She smiled.

Even if I'm stuck where I am, I'm a lot better than I was.

MAY 5 · FRIDAY

RUNNING LOG

May 4	May 5	May 6	May 7	May 8
30 min	30 min			
May 9	May 10	May 11	May 12	PROM

5:00 p.m.

I haven't made my Toolbox list yet, but I doubt the Running Log is on it. However, there are only nine days until Prom, and I must be practical. To judge its effectiveness, I will rely on how my clothes fit because the scale is gone for good.

Today in chemistry class, Arman and I were lab partners.

He asked me what color my Prom dress is, and I told him I didn't know yet.

"I kind of wanted to match you." So sweet.

"Maybe I could try to match *you* instead." I'm totally procrastinating. I'm afraid the store mirrors will send me into a full-blown breakdown.

"I have a black suit and a navy suit, and three different ties— black, red, and pink." He counted them on his fingers.

"Guys are so lucky. You get a few things and you can wear

them forever," I said.

"I guess, but I'd totally buy something new every time if I could afford it. How about if we go shopping together?"

"Yeah, right." Hard to imagine anything more uncomfortable.

"I'm a great shopper. Come on, it'll be fun." He kissed me on the cheek.

"Arman...Mackenzie..." Mrs. Deacon walked towards us. "How's your experiment going?"

Arman held up the worksheet. "Very well. Only one more test to finish."

"Good. Let's stay focused." She walked away.

"Let's go tonight. Maybe dinner first?" he said.

"I don't know. I have a ton of studying to do." Just great—let's eat before so I can be even fatter.

"You have to get a dress sooner or later. It's only nine days away."

"I guess you're right. Okay."

"Great!"

The bell rang. We turned in our paper and walked out together.

"Pick you up at six?"

"Okay."

He kissed me on the lips. Mmm…

We headed in opposite directions.

On the way to lunch I saw him talking to Eden by a classroom. I know I sound possessive, but STOP TALKING TO HER!

I cruised over. "Hey guys, what's up?"

"Hey, Mack." Eden smiled.

"Hey." Arman kissed my cheek.

Appears to be platonic. Am I being conned? Where there's smoke there's fire? Why does Arman spend lunch with her and not me? So confusing. And irritating.

"Going to eat. See ya." I pretended to concentrate on my phone as I walked away. Were they watching? Why do I think everyone cares what I'm doing?

At lunch Diego said, "So, who's driving to Prom?" It reminded me of when he wanted to drive with Tyler to Formal. A million years ago.

"I can drive," James said.

"We can't all fit in your car. I wish we could all go together," Skye said.

"Let's get a party bus!" Rachel said.

"Right," Diego said. "I'll just charge it to my Visa."

Rachel said, "I bet I could get my dad to pay for it. I'll ask him tonight."

We spent the rest of lunch talking about how much fun it would be.

Dax and I have fifth period together. I filled him in on the party bus idea.

"That's cool."

"You don't seem very excited."

"I don't get it."

"Get what?"

"Rachel. One minute she hates me, the next she's making Prom plans."

"Rachel's complicated."

"I guess. A party bus? But I suppose we won't be allowed to party, right? I'll have to be sober? Or is she over that already?"

"Is that all you care about?"

"Of course not. She's the one that made such a big deal out of it."

"Maybe because it's a big deal to her."

"If she doesn't drink, does that mean I can't?"

"I think you can do whatever you want. Have you guys talked at all?"

"No."

"Do you love Rachel?"

"Love her? Where did that come from?"

I was asking myself the same question. "I don't know, I just think maybe you should talk to her. But only if you really care. I mean, don't go digging if it doesn't really matter to you."

Silence.

Clean-up crew on aisle four!!! "I mean, it doesn't make you a bad person if you don't want to have a serious relationship. I think that's totally fine...but...if you do care about her, you should talk to her." Shut up, Mack!

He looked at me from the side of his eye and smiled.

The bell rang. I think his smile meant he cares about her, but who knows.

…
Midnight

Back from shopping.

Mom gave me fifty dollars. Thank you, God, for not letting us be broke. Yet.

Arman took me to a ramen restaurant.

> Body: Sooo delicious.
> Mind: Soooo fattening.
> Me: Shut up.

Arman: I'm so glad you like to eat.

Me: Is it that obvious?

Arman: It's a good thing. It's so annoying when a girl picks at her food.

Me: Might not be so good when I'm trying on dresses.

Arman: What are you talking about? You're perfect.

I almost choked on my noodles.

Me: Nice line.

Arman: It's not a line, it's true.

Me: Well, thanks.

LIAR.

Perfect? Who says things like that (other than Dr. S)?! Maybe he's full of shit, but it made me feel so much better.

First store: Short royal blue dress with spaghetti straps. I actually turned around in front of him. He gave it a thumbs up. Next: short red dress. Solemn shake of the head. Long black dress. Nope.

Second, third, and fourth stores: Nada. Mirrors are not my friends, but Arman made me feel good, no matter what they said.

"Want to get some ice cream?" Arman asked.

"Okay." Just what my body needs. "Are you getting tired of this yet?

"A little."

"Oh." I was expecting him to say no.

"But, it's fine. I like watching you."

He put his arm around my waist. Could he feel my fat? I turned my head and we kissed as we walked.

As I ate my ice cream, I tried to recall the sparkly energy pancake feeling.

> Brain: Help me out, Body.
>
> Body: You're doing great. Thanks for the treat.

Arman interrupted my personal conversation. "Hey, there's Diego and Tyler."

They were walking down the opposite side of the mall.

"Do you want to go talk to them?" I asked.

"Nah. Looks like they're in a hurry."

No argument from me. Diego and Tyler at the mall together? So weird.

We went back to the first store and I bought the blue dress. Bonus—10% off! Always buy the first dress that works—I should know this by now.

"I'll need a new tie," Arman said.

"Do you want to shop now?" I felt like I could go all night.

"Nah, I'm tired."

Pout.

Maybe I was the only one having fun. It occurred to me that I had been so caught up, I wasn't really paying attention. That's my problem. Either I'm obsessed with what other people think, or I completely forget about them. I wish I could chill and still pay attention.

When Arman dropped me off, we kissed for about five minutes straight. I didn't want to stop, but he pulled away. I wished I had pulled away first.

"I had a great time tonight, Mack."

"I had a great time, too. Thanks for dinner." I took my bag from the backseat and blew him a kiss.

Maddie was in the family room when I walked in. I took my dress from the bag and held it up. "What do you think?"

"Cute. I'd have to see it on though."

"I'll be right back." Whaat? Trying on a dress for Maddie?

I changed and returned.

"Girl, you're hot."

"Really?"

"Yep. You're glowing. Are you in love?"

"No, I've just never liked a guy who was also a friend. It's kind of cool."

MAY 6 · SATURDAY

RUNNING LOG

May 4	May 5	May 6	May 7	May 8
30 min	30 min	. 30 min		
May 9	May 10	May 11	May 12	PROM

I feel a lot better this morning about my body, but I'm still on the running mission. Only seven days to go.

At breakfast Maddie asked if Alexis could spend the night.

"Sure," Mom said.

"I take it you patched things up?" Dad asked.

"Yeah. We had a big talk yesterday. And in case you're wondering, we're not a couple. We're just friends."

"Honey, you could tell us if you were a couple. Dad and I support you."

"I would, I promise."

"Would that affect a sleepover?" Mom said to herself.

"It might be kinda like if Arman spent the night," Maddie said.

"Speaking of Arman..." Dad was constructing a tower from pancake pieces he had cut into perfect squares. "Mom said you went shopping for a dress last night?"

"Yep. I found one, it's super cute. And Rachel's dad might pay for a party bus so we can all go together." I was surprised at my sudden offering of information.

"Party bus?" Mom said.

Shit. Why did I say anything? I remembered one of Rachel's quotes, "Less is more."

Mom said, "Sounds fun." I could tell that's not exactly what she was thinking.

I checked my phone and texted Skye, London, and Rachel.

Me: Sleepover here tonight?

(If Alexis is coming over, I'm having people over too!)

Skye: Can't. Dad coming home.

Shit. Shit. Shit. I knew her dad was coming home from rehab today, and I forgot to say anything.

London: Plans with Diego. Sorry.

Rachel: I'm in.

I'm glad I'll get to be with Rachel one-on-one. She hasn't spent the night here since the beach party, and that doesn't exactly count.

Heading out for my run.

MAY 7 · SUNDAY

RUNNING LOG

May 4	May 5	May 6	May 7	May 8
30 min	30 min	30 min	0 min	
May 9	May 10	May 11	May 12	PROM

10:00 p.m.

Rachel and I stayed up super late and I was too tired to run today. Plus my legs are killing me!

Last night Rachel said, "So, how about Maddie?"

"Maddie?" I didn't want to assume what she meant.

"You know she's gay, right? Why are you acting like you don't know what I'm talking about?" Rachel said.

"I wasn't sure if Alexis told you."

"She didn't. Maddie did."

"Oh." I thought I would be the one who told Rachel. Sometimes I feel like the whole world is going on around me, and I think I know what's happening, only to find out I'm missing half of it. I make all these assumptions and I'm totally wrong.

"Why are you sad?' Rachel asked. "It's not like she's sick or something."

"I'm not sad. I just feel stupid that I didn't know," I said.

"Did you ever suspect?" Rachel asked.

"No. Did you?"

"Never."

"That makes me feel better. I'd feel even more clueless if you had."

"I'm the winner in the clueless department. How about Alexis and Tyler every day at my house? We can't know everything, Mack."

I wanted to tell her my secret. I wanted everything to be out in the open.

"Rach, can I tell you something?"

"Sure."

"I used to be bulimic." It's getting easier to say.

"Really? When?"

"Pretty recently. I still struggle with it, but I don't throw up anymore."

"Is that why you were in the hospital for so long?"

"Yeah. Did you know something was wrong?"

"I didn't *know*, but I thought you looked skinny, like way too skinny. I thought maybe something was up."

"Why didn't you say anything?"

"I don't know. It's pretty hard to talk about without offending someone, don't you think? Plus, who am I to talk about consumption issues?"

"I feel so much better now that I can talk about it. I told Skye and London, too."

"I'm so glad. I can't imagine you doing that to yourself."

We were quiet.

"I bet you've thought the same thing about me doing things to myself, huh?" Rachel said.

"I don't know."

"It's okay, you don't have to pretend. I don't treat my body very well. I get what it's like."

"I'm glad we can talk about it. Maybe we can help each other," I said.

"It's a deal." Rachel smiled.

This morning Rachel woke me up. "Necesito café." She tapped her phone.

> Rachel: Cava??
> London: Yep
> Skye: Sure

We arrived thirty minutes later. One glance around and no surprise...Arman and Eden.

I pretended I didn't see him. "I'll get the drinks, you get a table."

"Hey, Mack." A hand on my shoulder.

"Oh, hey, Arman. What are you doing here?"

"I came here to meet Eden."

I closed my eyes. Should I start screaming?

"She wants to ask a guy from Marina to Prom, and she's asking my advice."

"Why does she need your advice?"

"I don't know. Just because I'm a guy, and she's nervous about it."

Was he telling the truth? Eden is so pretty—he has to be attracted to her. I noticed his t-shirt—Darth Vader with the subtitle, "Warning: Choking Hazard." I had reached the front of the line. I ordered slowly. I was happy to make Arman wait, and consider how I wanted to act.

When the drinks were ready, I took the tray to where Eden sat.

"Hey, Eden."

"Hey, Mack. How's it going?"

"Pretty good."

I thought about asking them to join us. Nah.

"Well, I just wanted to say hi." I turned to face Arman, who was standing behind me. "I'll see you later."

He leaned in and kissed me on the lips. I felt possessive, like, "Ha ha—see? He's all mine."

"Do you want to sit with us?" The words flew out of my mouth before I could stop them. I guess I wanted Eden to witness the two of us together.

"Sure, of course." Eden scooted out of the booth.

We walked over to the table where Skye, London, and Rachel were sitting.

"Is it okay if Arman and Eden join us?" Their expressions confirmed the stupidity of my decision. Why would I want to sit with Eden?

"Of course," Skye said. "Perfect number of seats."

I set the tray on the table.

"So, what's new, Eden?" Rachel asked. "Have you recovered from your party?"

"Yeah, what a shit show."

"What happened?" I asked.

"Tyler and Dax got in a fight on the dance floor and totally demolished the DJ's equipment. Plus a bunch of people got hurt when they were slamming around."

"How did we not hear about it? I never saw any pics."

"I told them if they posted anything, my parents would

sue them for bringing alcohol to the party, and destruction of property. Plus, some other stuff I won't mention."

So glad we left early. Maddie must have left before it happened, too.

"Actually, a couple of people did post something, but I told them I would never invite them again if they didn't take it down. So that fixed that."

It must be awesome to be that powerful and popular.

Arman put his arm around me. "Good thing you got me to leave early."

"Why did you invite Tyler anyway?" London asked.

"I didn't. I think Diego told him about it. Dax was trying to get him to leave."

"Tyler's a nightmare," Rachel said.

"He's just troubled, that's all," Eden said. I hope she still likes him. Anyone other than Arman.

I was busy having this conversation with myself, when I heard a familiar voice say, "Hey guys."

My heart leaped, then stopped.

There stood Noah, all six-plus feet of him.

Maybe it was my imagination, but I think Arman pulled me closer.

"Just saw James at the carwash," Noah said to Skye. "He

told me you were here."

"Hi," Skye said. "Noah, this is Arman and Eden."

Arman took his arm off my shoulder and held his hand out. Noah shook it then turned to Eden.

He held his hand out to her.

"Nice to meet you, Noah," Eden said.

Don't say his name. 😡 I had intended to pull Eden away from Arman, not for *Noah* to pull her away. Nightmare.

He pulled a chair over from another table and sat across from me, between Skye and Eden.

"So, where do you go to school?" Eden asked.

"UCLA."

"Oh." Eden's eyes widened. "I assumed you were in high school—not that you look like you are in high school."

Noah shrugged and looked at me. I panicked and looked away. Why was he looking at me?

Just then James came in. Skye got up and waited in line with him.

"Well, this has turned into quite the party," London said. "Too bad Diego's not here."

"Speaking of...Mack and I saw him with Tyler the other night at the mall," Arman said.

"What were you doing at the mall?" London asked.

"Shopping." Arman winked at me.

I'm sure my face reached a previously unseen level of red.

"You should text him," Rachel said.

"Nah. I'm pretty sure he's working today."

"One of you actually works?" Noah raised his eyebrows.

"What's that supposed to mean?" Rachel said.

"Nothing." He held his hands up. "I didn't mean it like that. It just seems like all you guys do is drink coffee and party."

"What?" Skye walked up to the table.

He looked up at her. "Am I wrong?"

"Yesss, you're wrong. We study, play sports, volunteer..."

"Shop, text, dance..." James dragged another chair over.

"Very funny." Skye glared at him.

"I work," Arman said.

"You do?" Eden and I said at the same time. Guess they're not THAT close!

"Yeah. I fix computers out of my house."

"Cool," Noah said.

"So, where does Diego work?" James asked.

"Towers Collision," London said.

"Does he fix cars?" James asked.

"I think he does the paperwork. His family owns it."

"Since almost all of us are here, maybe we should talk about

Prom." Arman put his arm around me.

"Well, the party bus is all set." Rachel beamed. "Should we go to dinner first?"

"Maybe we should get burgers so we can eat in the bus," James said.

"Don't think so, Romeo," Skye said.

Everyone laughed.

Noah stood. "Think I'll leave you all to it."

"Hey, you don't have to go." Eden touched his arm. "I'm not going on the bus, and I'm still hanging out." I'm warning you, Eden, back OFF!

"I think I have officially passed the Prom-planning stage of life." He looked directly at me, then around at the table. "Have a good one."

And out the door he went.

Assessment:

1. He rebuffed Eden (mooahahaha), but

2. He was clearly saying, "I'm too mature for you kids."

"Hello?" Arman squeezed my shoulder.

"Sorry?"

"What do you think of Cheesecake Factory?"

"Sounds good." I studied his profile, and thought, *Arman is a good catch. I'm lucky.*

I leaned into his body slightly and smiled at Eden. A tiny evil smile. 😏

MAY 8 · MONDAY

RUNNING LOG

May 4	May 5	May 6	May 7	May 8
30 min	30 min	30 min	0 min	45 min
May 9	May 10	May 11	May 12	PROM

I woke up super early and went on a long run before school. Torture. Has running always been this hard?

Lunch convo:

"How was your dad's homecoming?" I asked Skye. Better late than never.

"Not bad. We're speaking now. Everything's all fresh and new—just how Mom likes it."

"I'm happy for you," London said. "I'd give anything to have my dad home."

"I'm sorry if I sound ungrateful," Skye said.

"It's okay, I understand.," London said. "I wonder if it's better to have a bad dad or no dad...Not that your dad is bad... just not perfect. You know what I mean, right? I'm not judging your dad."

Skye leaned her head into London's shoulder. "I know what

you mean. I'm glad he's home. And it brought Noah back for the weekend."

"Is he still here?" I asked. Not that I care. Much.

"He went back for finals week."

London groaned. "I can't believe we still have another month of school left."

"He'll be home next weekend, but he's leaving in a few weeks for an internship in San Francisco."

Whaaaaaat?! SAN FRANCISCO!?

MAY 10 · WEDNESDAY

Dr. Skyler

Dr. S wanted to start with a visualization today, but I couldn't even keep my eyes closed.

"I have an idea. Let's take a walk," she said.

Some sort of mental walk?

She got up and held the door open for me.

Guess not.

We exited the waiting room and entered the courtyard. She sat down on a bench, and I sat beside her.

"I come out here when my thoughts get too loud," she said. "Isn't this tree magnificent?"

"Yes."

"It's an oak."

"Oh."

"Probably more than a hundred years ago, it was an acorn. It bore no resemblance whatsoever to the tree it would become."

I might have rolled my eyes if we had been sitting in her office, but something about being so close to the massive tree made me listen. This humungous thing was once an acorn. Pretty cool.

"Close your eyes and feel your feet on the ground. Take a deep breath."

I breathed in. Calm.

"Beneath your feet are the roots of this tree. Somewhere, possibly as far as one hundred miles away, someone else is standing above the same root system. That person is also breathing the same oxygen produced by this tree."

Silence.

"Mackenzie, we're surrounded by miracles. Being alive is a miracle. The odds of being born are at least four-hundred-trillion to one. Compare that to a one-in-ten-thousand chance of becoming an oak. We see the miracle of acorn to tree, and yet we take our lives for granted."

"I never thought about it like that."

"Would you like to give the visualization another try?"

"Okay."

"Close your eyes and imagine you are holding a tiny baby chick. Cup your hands and feel the warmth of its fragile body."

I closed my eyes. I could feel the soft chick in my hands.

"Now imagine someone is trying to hurt the baby chick and take it from you."

I instinctively pulled my hands towards my chest to protect it.

"That's good. The chick is safe. You are keeping it safe."

I took a deep breath.

"Now, slowly see the chick change into you. Perhaps you are a tiny baby, or maybe a small version of yourself today. You are vulnerable and innocent."

Somehow the unexpected change of perspective worked. I could imagine I was holding myself.

"Send your small-self love and reassurance. Tell yourself you are there for protection."

I did.

"Now send that same love to your big-self."

I did. I could actually feel my love. So weird. Definitely comforting.

"Take another deep breath. Open your eyes when you are ready."

My head was quiet. I see why Dr. S goes to the courtyard.

"I liked that," I said.

"I'm glad it resonated with you. I'm continually impressed by your openness to new ideas."

She reached down and picked a small feather off the ground. She studied it. "Amazing. What are the odds a feather is sitting here right under our bench?"

She held it out to me. "Would you like it?"

I imagined the baby chick. I imagined my little self. I remembered the feeling of love.

"Thank you." I put the feather in my journal.

"I believe we have come to the end of our visit. Will I be seeing you next week?"

"Definitely."

"Keep up the good work."

"I will."

...

I can hear myself over my brain! Will it last? I'm inspired to write my Toolbox list. Here goes...

TOOLBOX

- Listen to my body
- Take ten minutes at a time
- Reminder: Mind and body both support me
- Reminder: The power to decide is mine
- Examine the intentions behind my actions
- Visualize visiting my body
- Ditch the scale
- My thoughts become my reality
- Rewrite thoughts until they make me feel good, then repeat
- List thoughts I want to nurture and repeat daily
- Replace negative thoughts with grateful thoughts
- Perfection requires no effort
- Acknowledge my pain

- Pay attention to my emotions
- Focus on my body to ground myself
- Interview myself
- Replace "should" with "want" and then turn into a statement
- Best thing/Worst thing exercise
- Nothing happens and nothing happens, then everything happens
- My life is a miracle
- Love and protect my little self and my big self
- Yoga

These are the tools I found going back through my journal. Yoga was my addition. Even though I've only done it twice, it definitely makes me feel better. Dr. S was right that I would find tools of my own.

And on a page of its own...

Our THOUGHTS become our BELIEFS

Our BELIEFS become our WORDS

Our WORDS become our ACTIONS

Our ACTIONS become our HABITS

Our HABITS become our REALITY

MAY 11 · THURSDAY

10:00 p.m.

I feel so much better after my session with Dr. Skyler. I have abandoned the running log for now. What can I change in three days anyway? Perfect as I am!

This morning Dad said he wanted to go out to dinner tonight, and I went into immediate panic. I still don't trust my parents. Any second, I expect to hear, "Well, actually, we were afraid to tell you, but..." I think I have PTSD.

We ate at a soup and salad buffet.

Maddie said, "So, what's up with this restaurant choice?"

"Getting in shape." Dad picked up a carrot and pointed it at her.

I narrowed my eyes at him. I wondered if he meant we should get in shape, or he's getting in shape.

He patted his stomach. "It's part of my personal makeover."

Is Dad crazy or is this good?

"You probably think I'm a little too old for a makeover."

Maddie and I laughed. Exactly.

"Someday you'll understand. Your body gets older, but inside you stay the same."

#midlifecrisis

"I can see your skepticism, but here's the plan. I'm starting my own architecture firm."

"But I thought that's what you did before," Maddie said.

"I worked as an architect at a firm—not the same thing." He set down his fork. "I need to share my vision, rather than simply re-creating someone else's. I know it might not make much sense to you, but I'm excited, and we are going to be more than fine, financially." He looked at Mom. "You'll see."

Mom's facial expression said, "We'll see…"

"Sounds good to me," I said.

"Me too," Maddie said.

I like this dad.

"How about the two of you? It's almost the end of the year. Any big plans?"

"Prom this weekend." I was annoyed he didn't remember.

"Ah, yes, Prom. Are you still going with Arman in the party bus?"

Points for Dad.

"Yep."

"Sounds fun. How about you, Miss Maddie?"

"Not much. Alexis and I might go to the movies."

"Very nice. And how about you, Mom? Any news you want

to share?" Dad grinned.

"I got a promotion." Mom's face lit up.

"Congratulations!" I said. "What kind of promotion?"

"The kind that comes with more money." She let out a puff. "Finally."

"Will you be doing the same thing?" Maddie asked.

"Basically, just at a higher level, and with bigger companies. I'll have to travel more."

"More? You don't travel at all," Maddie said.

"Yes, I'm aware of that, but now I will be."

"Will you be gone a lot?" Maybe this was the catch?

"I'll be traveling about one week per month. We'll have to figure a few things out, but I think you'll be able to handle it."

Mom gone. Dad home. Weird.

Maddie narrowed her eyes. "Are you telling us the truth?"

Exactly what I had been thinking.

"What do you mean? Did I really get a promotion?"

"Yeah. You guys aren't getting separated or something, and making up a story so we don't know, are you? I mean, we're old enough to handle the truth. Don't lie to us."

She burst out laughing, and Dad did too.

"No, your mother is not lying. She got a promotion because she's a huge asset to her company." Dad put his arm around her shoulder.

"And we are not getting separated," Mom said. "Life is bumpy, and marriage has to navigate the ups and downs. We're not splitting up just because things are stressful. No matter what, we stay together."

It's amazing how happy I feel when Mom and Dad are getting along—like all is right with the world.

MAY 12 · FRIDAY

3:30 p.m.

Just got home from school.

Conversation in chemistry class:

Arman: I bought a matching tie. Wanna see? (holds up his phone)

Me: Nice.

Arman: I bought some new shoes too to change it up.

Me: I think it's cool you think about clothes.

Arman: What do you want to do after the dance?

Me: I don't know. Eat?

Arman: Anything else?

Me: I'm not sure. What do you have in mind?

Arman: I think Eden might have a post-Prom party. Would you want to go?

Me: Silence.

Arman: It might be fun if we all went.

Me to myself: EDEN, AGAIN?! (head explodes)

Me: Yeah, maybe.

Arman: We don't have to, but her parties are always fun.

Me: Yeah, I know they're fun—I'm usually at them. Why do

you know about her party, but I haven't heard about it?

Arman: We have first period together, and she just told me she was thinking about it.

Me: What's going on with you and Eden?

Arman: Nothing, I swear. We're just friends."

Me: Let's talk later.

Maybe I'm just not mature enough to be with a guy who has such a good female friend.

...

7:00 p.m.

I just tried on my dress and IT'S TOO TIGHT. I feel like I'm literally going to die. Arman got a matching tie and I don't have anything else to wear. I look horrible! What was I doing— thinking I could just eat what I want and be happy with who I am? Bullshit. Bullshit. Bullshit. What does Dr. S know? I don't know what I'm going to do.

...

2:00 a.m.

I cried myself to sleep and woke up around midnight. I texted Rachel to see if she has something I can borrow. Haven't heard back—I'm sure she's asleep.

Even though I knew it wouldn't make the dress fit, I started doing situps. There was a tap at my door.

"Come in."

"What are you doing?" Maddie sat on the edge of my bed.

"Trying to make my fat go away."

"Mack, stop."

I kept going.

She threw a pillow at my head.

"Shit, Maddie. What do you want?"

"Actually, I came in to talk to you about something, but seeing you like this is really upsetting."

"Like what?"

"Exercising like a maniac in the middle of the night."

"What's so upsetting about it? Why do you care?"

"I honestly don't know. I thought you were doing so much better, and now it feels like it was all an act."

"Well, I don't know what to tell you. Sometimes I feel like life is good and I can control my destiny. And sometimes I feel like a fat, ugly, stupid, crazy person."

"How can you feel like that? You're perfect."

"Are you insane?" I pinched the fat on my stomach. "You call this perfect?"

She rolled her eyes. "I call it a normal stomach."

"Easy for you to say."

"To me, your life looks easy," she said. "You're totally mainstream. You get good grades, have a boyfriend, have friends. I can't understand how you don't see that."

"Well, to me, *your* life looks easy," I said. "You're tall, skinny, athletic, and you never care what anyone thinks."

"You think I don't care what anyone thinks?"

"It sure doesn't seem like it. I wish I could be like you in that way—really in lots of ways."

"Well, I do care. I wish I didn't, but I do. I don't want to be thought of as different. I don't want to be an outcast. I don't want people to watch how I act if I'm with a girl."

"You're not different. People might look at first, but only because it's new. After a while no one's going to care."

"You really think so?"

"I know so."

"Thanks, Mack. You always make me feel better."

"I do?" Grinch heart swelling!

"You make me feel like everything's going to be okay. I think that's why it's so upsetting to see you all upset. If your world isn't okay, then mine isn't."

No pressure there.

"Why are you so freaked out?" she asked.

"My Prom dress doesn't fit."

"Are you sure? It fit perfectly last week."

"I guess I gained weight."

"Let me see it on you. Maybe you're being too critical. It's supposed to be tight."

"I don't have the strength to see it again. I'm so fat and ugly."

"Oh, come on, it's just a stupid dress. If it doesn't look good, it's the dress, not you. Don't you know that?"

"No, I was not aware of that."

I squeezed myself into the dress and cringed as Maddie studied me.

"Well, I see what you mean. Was that dress cheap?"

"I got a good deal."

"I think that's the problem. It's not lined, and it pulls in strange places. It's the kind of dress that only looks good if it's a little bit big because it's not well-made. But, your body is great."

I flumped down and heard fabric rip. I started crying for real.

Maddie stifled a laugh. "See?"

"See what? It's totally not funny, Maddie."

"That dress is a piece of crap."

I shifted and heard the entire seam give way. "What am I going to do?" I felt like the Hulk.

"You still have time to shop tomorrow. Or maybe you can borrow one from Rachel."

"Yeah, I texted her earlier." I ripped the dress off—very satisfying—and put on my robe.

"What do you think of Arman?" I asked.

"I don't. Why?"

"I really like him, but I hate that he's such good friends with Eden. I'm not sure if he likes me."

"Of course he likes you."

"How do you know?"

"Who doesn't?"

"Lots of people. I liked Diego, and he didn't like me—for very long anyway. And then there's Noah."

"Noah?"

"Skye's brother. I can't get him out of my head. Every time I convince myself he's too old and doesn't like me, he shows up and I can't stop thinking about him."

"You're blushing!"

"No, I'm not. Let's go see what there is to eat." I feel huge, but I must be getting better since I still feel worthy of some food.

Maddie surveyed the fridge. "I could make French toast."

"Sounds awesome. Since my dress is destroyed, it doesn't really matter how fat I am at this point."

"Mack, I wish you wouldn't talk like that."

"I'm simply stating a fact."

"You know that's not true. You're prettier than I am, and when you act like you're ugly, it's like saying I'm ugly, too."

Dr. S's words about miracles ran through my head. Maddie and I were eating in the kitchen together. We were friends again.

"Mads, you're right about my words. I'm going to work on them."

She smiled. "That's good."

"Dr. Skyler says your thoughts create your reality. Do you think that's true?"

"I don't know. I couldn't change the reality of being gay by changing my thoughts."

"But maybe you could change how being gay affects your life. Maybe it could be the best thing in the world."

She pressed her lips together. "Yeah, maybe."

She dipped bread in egg, while I flipped through Mom's travel magazine and held up every single tropical picture. "Here we are in Hawaii."

We sat down at the table to eat.

Maddie said, "Maybe we can work on our thoughts

together—share with each other."

"I'd like that. I have one for you…"

"Go ahead."

"People love and accept me just the way I am."

She nodded.

"You have to repeat it." I was channeling Dr. S.

"Only if you say it with me," she said.

We laughed and said it together. It's easier to believe it about Maddie, but I'm going to work on it for myself.

"I just thought of a better one," I said. "I love and accept myself just as I am."

We said it together

I love and accept myself just as I am.

My cheeks flush when I say it, so I think I need more practice. Good thing Maddie and I can do it together. I feel like I'll be more likely to stick with it. That's a good one to add to my Toolbox: *Have a partner*. Dr. S. will be proud.

MAY 13 · SATURDAY

3:00 p.m.

Miracle morning...

> Rachel: Dropped off a bag of dresses on your front
> porch. LMK if something works.
>
> Me: Just woke up. Thank you!!!

Only one dress fit, but it fits perfectly. AND it's black with tiny blue crystals. That's some kind of voodoo, if you ask me. Or maybe one of Dr. S's miracles.

"Now that's a dress," Maddie said.

I wanted to cry. "It's ridiculous to feel this moved by clothing."

"Yes, it is," she said.

"You don't get it, but that's okay. I love and accept myself just as I am."

She laughed. "Me too."

> Me: One of them worked!
>
> Rachel: Awesome! Can I come by and pick up the
> extras?
>
> Me: Now?
>
> Rachel: Yes

Me: Sure.

I hung up the dress, packed the others, and brushed my teeth.

Ten minutes later, Rachel arrived.

She looked through the bag of dresses. "Think I'll do this one."

"You'll rock it." I wore it like a tight candy wrapper, but I reminded myself, It's the dress's fault, not mine. I love and accept myself just as I am.

I walked her to the front door.

"Did you see London's text?" she asked.

"No."

"We're getting ready at London's at 4:00. Pics at 5:30." She checked her phone. "Shit, it's late. I gotta get moving." She called over her shoulder, "The bus will pick you up at 3:30."

I had an hour and a half to get ready. I scrolled through my messages.

Arman: Hello?

I didn't return his text last night.

Me: Sorry! Been running around.

Arman: Everything ok?

Me: Yep U?

Arman: Yep. See you at six.

Me: Can't wait

Arman: Same

Heart eyes. Sometimes I think people use emojis when they are trying to imply more than they mean.

I drank a glass of water. A fleeting thought of why I used to drink water. Amazing, I'm actually taking care of myself.

As I waited for the shower to warm, I studied my naked body in the mirror. I tried to see what Maddie saw. I put my face close to the mirror. "I love you." I laughed. I would die if anyone saw me talking to myself. I washed my body and wondered if Arman would be touching me tonight. Somehow, I can't picture it, but those kisses were nice.

I'm waiting at my window for the party bus. And there it is! I can see Rachel hanging out the window. Here we go...

Me: I love and accept you just the way you are.

MAY 14 · SUNDAY

What a night. I want to write it all down while I still remember.

When the bus pulled up to the house, Mom, Dad, and Maddie met me at the front door.

Mom hugged me tight. "I'm very proud of you."

"So am I," Dad said.

"Thank you for trusting me." I hugged them both.

Maddie bounced on her toes. "I'm so jealous! Can I see?"

Rachel had come up to the front door. I set my things down and hugged her. We both squealed and jumped up and down. How can you help yourself?

Rachel, Maddie, and I got on the bus. You could stand up inside and seats and a bar lined the edge.

"This is amazing," Maddie said. "I wish I could go with you."

"I do, too. Thanks for talking me off the ledge last night. You saved my life."

"I'm not sure about that, but glad I helped." She bounded off the bus. "Have fun!"

We picked up Skye then London. We wanted to drive somewhere all together before we got ready.

Rachel poured sparkling water and handed us each a glass.

"To the best friends in the world."

We clinked our glasses together and drank.

"And to Mom." Rachel looked up. "Please watch over us."

We were all quiet for a minute. It felt like Mrs. Dorian was right there.

"Where should we go?" Skye wiped her eyes.

"Let's drive by Eden's and blast the music," I said.

I got three "Are you crazy?" looks.

"I thought you liked Eden now," Skye said.

"Yeah, I'm just kidding. She's fine."

"When she's not hanging out with Arman," Rachel said.

I snapped my head. "You see it, too?"

"I see your face when she's around. You do a pretty good job of being sweet, but I know your evil side, my friend."

"What evil side?" Shrek Puss in Boots eyes.

"There's nothing wrong with wanting to rub it in Miss Perfect's face now and then," London said.

"Have I told you lately that I love you, London?" I said.

"I got your back, sista."

"We all do," Rachel said.

"Damn straight," Skye said.

We clinked our glasses together again.

"To sticking together," I said.

"No matter what," London added.

"No matter what," we all echoed.

"So back to business—where should we really go?" Skye asked.

"How about Cava?" Rachel said.

"Maybe Noah will be there." London winked at me.

"Noah isn't even around," Skye said.

My heart sank. Not that I thought we'd see him, but I liked the idea of the possibility.

London scooted over next to Skye. "Is everything okay?"

"It's fine. I just wish he could have seen this."

"Let's just go back to London's," Rachel said.

"Yes." I held up my drink. "The only people who matter are right here."

Everyone raised their cups. I wonder if there's a world record for the most toasts in an evening.

By 5:45 we were all ready.

"Let me take one picture before everyone arrives," Jessica said. "Squeeze in close."

"Here Mom, you get in, too. Let's make it a selfie." London moved over to make room for her.

"No, no, just the girls," Jessica said.

"You're for sure one of the girls," Skye said.

London held out her phone and got us all in the picture.

London hugged Jessica. "I love you, Mom."

"I love you too, honey."

We all started crying and had to go back upstairs to fix our makeup.

The boys arrived and we took pictures with the parents. Everyone loaded onto the bus, and Rachel beamed as the boys expressed their appreciation for our sweet ride.

"Hang on a sec." Dax ran off the bus.

He shook Mr. Dorian's hand then bounded back on.

"What was that about?" Rachel asked.

"I was saying thank you."

"Nice, Dax," I said.

I rolled down the window, and we all yelled, "Thank you!"

The parents were so happy.

I looked over at Rachel. "What's wrong?"

"It feels too perfect."

"Good God, Rachel. Snap out of it." London pretended to slap her face, left and right. "This is going to be the best night ever."

She smiled. "I'm sure you're right."

The Prom theme was *A Night Under the Stars* and there were silver balloons and sparkle lights everywhere. Arman and

I took pictures and danced for a bit, then stopped to get some water. I noticed London sitting by herself.

"Do you mind if I go talk to London?" I said.

"Of course not. I'll go check out the food."

I walked over. "Where's Diego?"

"He left." Mascara was smeared under her eyes.

"What?! When?" I sat down.

"About ten minutes ago. Said he was sooo sorry but he had to do something for his brother."

Rachel came over. "What's wrong?"

"Diego left," I said.

I scanned the room and prayed for Diego to walk through the door.

And that's when I saw it.

Arman.

Eden.

Dancing.

"You've got to be kidding me."

London and Rachel followed my stare.

"Wow. That's lame," Rachel said.

"It is, right? I'm not overreacting?"

"Well, it's not like they're holding each other, but yeah, I'd be pissed," London said.

Rachel said, "This dance sucks. Let's bail. Dax said his parents are out of town."

Arman was having a blast. The old me would have watched and said nothing. The new me stood up. "I'll be right back."

As I approached, I couldn't even fake a smile. Eden nodded and walked away.

Arman put his arm around me. "I was hoping you'd come over."

I moved away from his embrace. "Can I talk to you for a minute?"

"Sure." He frowned.

We walked to the opposite side of the room and sat down at an empty table.

Arman said, "Is everything okay? What's going on with London?"

"Diego left. We're thinking of going to Dax's."

"Now?"

How could he act like nothing was wrong? You don't dance with another girl at Prom. Is this not common knowledge?

I decided to go for it. "You know, Arman, it's not cool that you were dancing with Eden." My heart was pounding out of my chest. Was I being jealous and petty?

"Mack, I told you we're just friends."

"I don't care if you're just friends. It think it's lame."

"Do you want me not to be friends with her?"

"Is that what I said?"

"No."

"Are you telling me it never occurred to you that it might bother me if you danced with another girl at Prom?" It was getting easier to talk.

He grinned. "That must mean you like me."

I glared at him. "That's even lamer."

"Sorry. Mack, I really like you. You're one of my favorite people to hang out with."

"Gee, thanks."

"I guess it wasn't very cool to dance with Eden. I was just killing time."

"Yeah, but you're always with Eden." My jealousy was glowing neon, but I didn't care. I was sick of pretending that it didn't matter to me.

"She's my friend."

"And what am I?"

"You're my friend, too."

"That's it? Just your friend?" Part of me already knew this was the truth, but I didn't want to believe it.

He leaned in and kissed me on the cheek. "No, not just my

friend."

Tears sprang to my eyes. It felt forced and fake. I stood up and walked to the back of the room where it was darker.

Arman followed. "Mack, wait." He turned me around to face him.

I let my tears fall. It was impossible to feel any more embarrassed than I already was. "I know you like Eden. You spend lunch with her. You go to coffee with her. You danced with her. Why don't you just admit you asked me to Prom because neither of us was going with anyone else?"

Even though I knew everything I said was true, I was still hoping for him to tell me I was wrong. I've been wrong before. Once or twice.

"Mack, you're such a great person." He didn't sound like someone about to pledge his undying love.

"But you're in love with Eden."

Silence. He looked miserable, a small consolation.

"So, am I right?" Tears filled my eyes.

"Mack, your friendship means the world to me, and I'm not willing to lose it for Eden."

Here I held the power to make Arman and Eden miserable for life! But that's not what I wanted. As I thought about it, I could imagine being pretty happy being just-friends with

Arman. The old me would have thought maybe he would like me more if I were skinnier or prettier, but the stronger new me knows it's not about that. I guess some people just fit together better than others.

I wiped my eyes. "I guess we'll be friends."

I leaned over and we hugged.

Always," he said.

I stood up. "I'm gonna get going."

"You sure you don't want to hang out?"

I saw Eden watching us. "Nah. I'll see you next week."

I walked back to London. Even though I just got dumped, I felt powerful for taking the situation into my own hands.

"Any word from Diego?" I sat down.

"Nope. You okay?" London frowned. "Were you crying?"

"Yeah, but I'm fine."

My phone vibrated.

> Rachel: Dax's house. Let's bounce.
>
> Me: IN!
>
> London: Nice
>
> Skye: 👍
>
> Rachel: Bus in 5

"Let's be each other's dates." I held my hand out to London

to help her up.

"No Arman?"

"Nope."

"You sure you're okay?" she asked.

"More than sure. Come on."

On the bus I told Rachel, "Arman and I are officially just friends. The way it should be."

Rachel turned down the music and announced, "Hey y'all, Mack is officially back on the singles market. It's time to celebrate!"

She turned to me. "Now as soon as we find Diego, this night will be perfect."

Dax sat down next to us. "Are we keeping this party intimate, or should I let the world know?"

"We can't have a party when we don't even know if Diego is okay," Rachel put her arm around London.

"I agree," I said. Selfishly, I had zero interest in running into Arman and Eden.

Skye kissed James. "I'm good with just us."

"Then I guess that settles it. I'm gonna order some pizza," Dax tapped his phone.

We blasted the music and danced until we got to Dax's.

We had been there for maybe ten minutes when the doorbell

rang.

"Wait, does anyone else know?" Dax walked to the door.

"I mentioned it to Arman, but I didn't invite him," I said. Maybe he changed his mind and wanted to patch things up. Did he go back to Eden, only to realize he is still in love with me?

We all watched from the kitchen.

Dax opened the door, and there stood Tyler. So totally random!

He was out of breath and his face was covered with scratches.

"Are you okay? What are you doing here?" Dax said.

"I'm sorry, man. Your house was the first place I thought of."

"It's cool. Come in the kitchen."

Dax handed Tyler some paper towels and he wiped his face.

"What happened?"

"Diego and I were at a party and we got jumped."

"Where's Diego?"

"I don't know. We both ran. He hasn't returned my texts."

Rachel, Skye, and I moved to the other room to talk.

"Diego was at a party?" London started crying. "I'm so pissed off, but what if something really bad happened to him."

The doorbell rang, and we all jumped.

James opened the door.

It was the pizza delivery guy.

He took the food and was just about to close the door, when a voice said, "James, hold up."

I thought I must be imagining it. Up the walk came Noah, holding Diego's arm over his shoulder.

Diego's face was totally beat up and he had blood on his shirt. London ran over. They kissed and Diego kept saying, "I'm so sorry. I'm so sorry."

James: What happened? Noah, what are you doing here?

Noah: I was at a party and a fight broke out. I was driving away when I saw three guys pummeling another guy. I grabbed my bat from my backseat and they took off, and there was Diego on the ground.

Diego: You saved my life. Those guys never would have stopped.

Noah: Nah. But three on one—that's just bullshit.

Diego: I won't forget it.

James: How'd you know to come here?

Noah: Skye. I can see her location on my phone.

Tyler whispered something to Diego, then headed to the front door. "I'm out. Thanks, Dax. I owe you."

"No prob."

Rachel turned to Diego. "I can't believe you ditched London

to go to a party."

"I didn't ditch her. I had to take care of some business for my brother."

He kissed London on the cheek and said, "I'm really sorry. I'll tell you all about it later."

My mind was spinning. It was all so random.

Noah said, "So Prom's already over?"

"We left early," Dax said.

Noah looked right at me. "Guess it wasn't that fun?"

"It was fine." Face on fire.

He looked around the room. Was he looking for Arman?

"Well, I'm gonna go. You guys have a good night."

"Hey, stay for a while," Dax said.

Please! Don't goooo...

"I appreciate it, but I have somewhere I need to be."

He tipped his head at me. "Mack." Then, poof! He was gone. In and out like Superman.

I keep replaying it in my head. Mack. Mack. Mack. It was a statement, but what did he mean by it? Mack, I like you? Mack, I know you like me, but I don't like you? Aaah!

We spent the next hour eating and talking. I filled everyone in on the drama of my breakup. Diego offered zero detail about his fiasco. And pretty soon, it was clear everyone was ready to break off into two's.

I called a ride, and Rachel, London, and Skye walked outside with me to wait.

"What a night," Rachel said.

"I still can't believe Noah saved Diego," London said.

"I think actually it was my mom," Rachel said. "She put him in the right place at the right time."

"I think you're right," Skye said.

We all hugged.

"You're the best friends anyone could ever have," Rachel said.

"Tell me it will always be like this," I said.

Skye: Always

London: Yep

Rachel: Amen

I don't have Arman and I don't have Noah, but I have the three best friends in the world. And I have myself which I'm starting to realize is a pretty good thing.

MAY 15 · MONDAY

5:00 p.m.

The thought that I'm just fine without anyone else (a boy, that is) has made me feel so much stronger. I even felt okay seeing Arman and Eden together at school today. She'll probably start wearing printed t-shirts any day now. Maybe I'll buy her the first one, "Perfect AF." Just kidding. Only good thoughts about Eden from now on.

I don't want to do my homework. Once Prom is over, it feels like school should be too. Think I'll go lose myself in Noah fantasies and pretend he's not leaving for his internship in San Francisco.

I can't find Rachel's earrings anywhere. Shit. Shit. Shit. Hopefully they will show up by the time I get her dress back from the drycleaners.

Doorbell just rang. Probably the bathing suit I ordered. Hawaii here I come!

...

8:00 p.m.

I'm back from answering the door...

"Mack, it's for you," Maddie called.

"Can't you just sign for me?" I yelled.

No answer.

I quickly pulled my hair up in a ponytail. "I love you," I said to my reflection.

I rushed out and swung open the cracked front door.

It took a few seconds to register the face in front of me.

"Hi." Noah grinned.

"What are you doing here?" I looked for a delivery truck. Maybe I was hallucinating.

"Skye gave me these to give to you. She said she found them at Dax's." He held his hand out. Rachel's earrings!

"Wow, thanks! Why didn't she just bring them to school?" I asked.

"She forgot, and I said I would deliver them. You know, in case you were worried." I'm pretty sure he blushed.

"I was actually super worried. Thank you so much. Do you want to come in?"

"I'd love to."

"Have a seat. I'll be right back."

I forced myself not to sprint down the hall. I gently closed my door. A few seconds later, there was a knock.

"Yes?" He wouldn't come down the hall, right?

"Can I come in?" Maddie said.

"Sure."

"That's Noah, isn't it?"

I flopped on the bed, screamed into my pillow, and kicked my legs.

"Oh my God, you've gone over the edge." Maddie laughed.

"He brought back my earrings."

"Had your earrings, huh?"

I laughed. "Not like that. I wish."

"Well, get back out there and find out what he really wants." Maddie wiggled her fingers in a goodbye as she closed my door.

What else would he want? I started to get excited about the possibilities, then I remembered he's leaving. Oh well, there's always next year.

I came back down the hall. The upside of my realization was my face returned to its normal color.

Noah pointed to the wall. "These drawings are cool."

"My dad did them a long time ago." Eiffel Tower. Empire State Building. Leaning Tower of Pisa.

"Neat."

Awkward silence.

"So, I didn't see your date at Dax's. Was he there?" Noah asked.

"No. I left him at the dance."

"Yeah? Why?"

"It's where he wanted to be."

"Are you still seeing him?"

"I see him all the time at school."

He pursed his lips, like, "You know what I mean."

"We're just friends."

He smiled. "Oh. That's good."

"It is?" I couldn't hold back my smile.

"Yeah."

"Mack?" Mom's voice called from the kitchen.

"I'll be right back."

Mom, Dad, and Maddie were sitting down to eat.

"Would you like to invite your friend to join us?" No up-and-down eyebrows or googly eyes. Good job, Dad.

"Sure." No big deal. Noah at our house for dinner. It's cool. Riiiiight!

I went back to the living room. "Are you hungry? We have pasta and salad." I hoped my cheeks weren't as red as they felt.

"I'm starving. Thank you."

Noah ate two plates of pasta. "This is delicious, Mrs. Stewart."

"Thank you, I will pass your compliments to Luigi's Deli."

438

It felt like Noah had sat in the kitchen with my family a million times before. And correction—he's not even close to being old enough to be my father.

He helped clear the table. I rinsed the plates and he loaded them in the dishwasher. Sigh...

"It was nice to meet you, Noah." My dad shook his hand.

"It was nice to meet you, sir."

Noah turned to my mom and shook her hand. "It was nice to meet you, Mrs. Stewart."

"Very nice to meet you, Noah." I swear Mom blushed.

"I'll walk you out," I said.

We stepped out on the porch and I closed the front door.

"Thanks for coming over." I put my hands in my pockets.

"Thanks for inviting me for dinner."

"Any time."

He rocked on his heels. "Can I call you sometime?"

"Sure."

"Talk to you soon." He waved as he went down the front walk to his truck.

I closed the front door and sank to the floor. This was definitely a new feeling. Bliss.

I took my phone out of my pocket.

Me: You'll never guess who just came over!

London: Noah?

Me: HOW DID YOU KNOW?!

London: Just a hunch. I'm your best friend, you know.

Me: Yes, you are!

Me: Call u later

I went to my room and flopped on the bed.

Text message from an 800-number: Your order has arrived. (My bathing suit!)

The doorbell rang. I love technology.

I opened the door.

There stood NOAH.

"Hi." Embarrassed smile.

"Hi. I thought you were my bathing suit."

"This?" He picked up a package from the doorstep.

"Yep."

He held the package out to me but didn't let go when I took it. He took a step forward and searched my face. I leaned forward and closed my eyes. His kiss was soft, electric, and delicious. Fireworks and images of things to come.

I pulled back. "So you leave soon, right?"

"Nope. I took another job, closer to home..."

"...and closer to you."

"Me?"

He leaned in and we kissed until I thought my legs would wobble out from under me.

"Is it still okay if I call you?"

"More than okay."

"Good night, Mackenzie."

"Good night, Noah."

He let go of my hands and walked to his truck. He waved before he got in.

I closed the door and floated back to my room.

I stared at my face in the mirror.

> Body: So, now that a boy likes you, the world is perfect?
>
> Mind: I said *I love you* before he came over.
>
> My reflection: I love you, too.

ACKNOWLEGEMENTS

I send my heartfelt gratitude to the following people who have been instrumental in helping me bring this book into the world:

My husband, David Nalchajian,
for your love, support, patience, and brilliant ideas.

My daughter, and trusted critic, Cali Nalchajian,
for your encouragement, influence, and insight.

My son, Cole Nalchajian, for your hugs and belief I would finish.

My editor, Deborah Halverson,
for your literary acumen and confidence.

My mom, Pat Lampe, for your unconditional love,
invaluable critiques, and constant cheering.

My dad, Del Lampe, for your strength and belief in mine.

My sister, Deni Lampe Mileski,
for your incredible artistic talent and never-ending optimism.

My sister, Julie Mays, for your precise suggestions and enthusiasm.

My mother-in-law, Jo Nalchajian, for your love and faith.

My father-in-law, Richard Nalchajian,
for your kindness and generosity.

My sisters-in-law, Christina Nalchajian-Whitley and Nicole Nalchajian,
for your engagement and constant support.

My cousin, Ella Swanberg,
for your multiple reads, spot-on suggestions, and excitement.

My aunt, Ruthie DeVoogd, for your early critique and loving support.

My friend, Delia Deocampo, for your many reads,
holding me accountable, and celebrating every milestone.

My fellow writers in Valley Writers Group:
Jeff Cates, Jennifer Dauer, Wayland Jackson, Celestial Lentz,
Ginger Morganstern, Jonni Pettit, and Lin Terrana
for your crucial feedback at the beginning of this project, and
Doug Hoagland for your multiple reads and character insight.

My coworker, Rebecca Sustaita,
for your insight and technical assistance.

Lin Oliver and the Society of Children's Book Writers and Illustrators
for your inspiration, guidance, and resources.

Chandler Bolt and Self-Publishing School
for your platform for connection, information, and support.

Contributors to Twemoji graphics. Long live open source!

My high school classmate, Angie Molinari, for asking me
at our ten-year reunion, "Did you write your book yet?"

My friends and family for listening, reading,
and providing endless encouragement over the years:
Alisha Anderson, Mickie Aragon, Julie Burke, Kim Castellano,
Sarah Eck, Kathleen Enge, Wendy Fairchild, Marcia Falk,
Stephanie Fry, Linda Hutcheson, Maylin Hsu, Tracy Kashian,
Nam McGrail, Kelly Mullen, Christen Otta, Christine Porter,
Jenna Riebe, Stacy Roque, Tina Schuh, Joan Schoettler,
Shuli Suman, Shannon Stubblefield, Sofia Whitley,
Sally Williams, and Kammi Wilson.

All of the readers and writers out there—you are my people.

Dear Reader,

I struggled with bulimia in high school. Initially, I was hesitant to write a book about an eating disorder because I thought I needed to have the answer to curing it. But every person holds their unique answer inside. Our journey to well-being is guided by discovery, acceptance, and love.

Wishing you the best,
Nikki

NIKKI LAMPE NALCHAJIAN

Nikki Lampe Nalchajian writes because it fills her soul. She strives to empower others and inspire conversations. Nikki earned a bachelor's degree in English from University of California, Los Angeles, and a master's degree in computer science from California State University, Fresno. She lives in California with her husband, son, daughter, and dog.

VISIT **nikkinal.com** FOR
RESOURCES, BLOG POSTS, SPECIAL OFFERS, AND MORE.

Made in the USA
Las Vegas, NV
13 December 2020